THE RIVERSEDGE LAW CLUB SERIES

IN HER DEFENSE

AMY IMPELLIZZERI

Wyatt-MacKenzie Publishing
DEADWOOD, OREGON

ALSO BY AMY IMPELLIZZERI

Lemongrass Hope
Lawyer Interrupted
Secrets of Worry Dolls
The Truth About Thea
Why We Lie
I Know How This Ends

In Her Defense
Amy Impellizzeri

ISBN: 978-1-954332-44-7
Library of Congress Control Number on file.

Wyatt-MacKenzie Publishing
DEADWOOD, OREGON

Wyatt-MacKenzie Publishing, Inc.
www.WyattMacKenzie.com
Contact us: info@wyattmackenzie.com

DEDICATION

To Aunt Sharon & Uncle Steve
who are always in my corner

CHAPTER 1
Broken Promises

"There's no i in dead."

Opal slams hard on her brakes. She's been distracted by her son's bleating in the back of the car and the thoughts swirling around in her own brain that she cannot seem to quiet. She doesn't see the car whizzing down the road until it's directly behind her as she backs out of the driveway. It's almost too late by the time she comes to a complete stop. Almost. Opal exhales loudly in relief as the driver passes her by without a collision. A close call. She'll take it.

"There's no i in dead, Mommy."

Opal closes her eyes, shaking off the near miss that has just occurred steps from their front door. Ever since the nearby bridge construction began a few weeks ago, the previously quiet street she lives on with her son, CJ, has been overrun by traffic. Her road wasn't supposed to be an official detour route. Would-be bridge goers are supposed to travel the long way around Wolff Pond and then past Hemingway Park, until they get to that hole-in-the-wall bakery, the one with the melt-like-but-ter-in-your-mouth croissants, and then they are supposed to make a hard right-hand turn that will lead them to a road that bypasses the bridge construction. But they don't, because no one ever does what they are supposed to do.

"There's no i in dead, Mommy. Why aren't you listening to me? We need to fix this poster. I can't take it to school like this, Mommy."

No one does what they are supposed to do. Not even me. Especially not me. Opal thinks as she shifts the car into park.

"Mommy—"

Opal leans hard on the horn in a delayed act of frustration, even though the car that had come out of nowhere is now, well, nowhere to be seen.

CJ sits quietly for a moment in response to the horn that has been meant for him.

Remorsefully, Opal turns around and looks at the forlorn poster in her son's lap. Photographs of a makeshift herb garden in various stages of growth and death are plastered in a crooked line and while they are upside down from her vantage point, Opal can still see them clearly, having looked at the photos every day over the last week or so. She can't unsee them now if she tries. The last photo in the line shows a particularly gruesome sight of a brown and rotting rosemary plant set in a kitchen windowsill pot and cared for with nothing but misguided optimism. Opal has never had a green thumb. She bought the rosemary because she read somewhere that "rosemary means remembrance" and things had turned a corner. Things in her life were so good, so positive, so different, that *finally,* she wanted to *remember.*

So she'd bought some rosemary at the local hardware store, planted it next to the basil and mint that was growing unchecked on her windowsill and crossed her fingers.

Of course, the tide has turned quickly. She no longer wants to remember—not the rosemary plant nor anything else that has come crashing down on her in the last twenty-four hours. But CJ has gone and made that dead rosemary plant the centerpiece of his damn science poster.

Opal has been so embarrassed by her son photographing her failings as a home gardener for his third-grade life cycle homework, she hasn't noticed the misspelling in the short but true caption that she sees now as her son flips the poster toward her. The final caption is upside down for him but right side up for her. He points to it ominously as Opal nods at its solemn wrongness.

This plant is diead.

Opal faces forward again, leans on the steering wheel, and tries to come up with a new game plan for the morning.

Why is he noticing it for the first time this morning? Why now?

In order to make it on time, they have to be at school in exactly – Opal leans over and checks the car clock to confirm the dire straits they are in—*21 minutes.*

She didn't think they'd run late today. After all, CJ finished the project days ago, and left it on the dining room table, where no one ever ate, and that served only as the holding ground for homework and bills and cookies they wanted to hide from company. Even though she's been mortified by the photos, Opal has been so proud of CJ for being on top of things. For getting his homework done. For doing it carefully and neatly (albeit embarrassingly calling out his mother's lack of a green thumb and reckless optimism). For all the times she's passed that poster with a mixture of pride and embarrassment over the last few days, she hasn't noticed the typo, but now that she has—now that *he* has—there simply is no time to fix it.

CJ *needs* to be at school on time this particular morning. Or rather, *Opal needs* CJ to be at school on time today: for a number of reasons, not the least of which is that Opal wants to be alone for the remainder of the day. A rare day off and she already knows she's going to need the stolen time.

After all, she doesn't want the police to show up in front of CJ to question her about a dead body.

On the other side of Hemingway Park, Ingrid DiLaurio and her son, Drake, are heading to Cosie's Bakery for a croissant on a cheat day from Ingrid's intermittent fasting. She wants something soothing and buttery today. Especially today. The wide openness of the day is unsettling, and Ingrid wants to be prepared.

She parks her car a block away from the bakery and shields her eyes from the early morning sun as she gets out, realizing too late that she's forgotten her sunglasses. Cosie's is always packed, but on Tuesdays the small storefront overflows, following a dark Monday: the only day all week that the bakery is closed. On their walk from the car, Ingrid and Drake encounter a sea of faces hurrying to and from the bakery. A hand or two goes up toward them in recognition. Ingrid exchanges one nod and two smiles. The rest of the faces overlook her and her son blankly. It always takes Ingrid by surprise how few people really know her; or at least how few *acknowledge* knowing her when she is out and about the town, despite having lived here for over a decade. Riversedge, New York is an impostor of a small town; with the posh setting, upscale mom and pop retail shopping, very few chain stores, not one McDonald's in its city limits, and an enormous brick-face library built after a year-long capital campaign, the town of Riversedge makes an elaborate pretense of *wanting* to be a small town. Riversedge has a charming tree-lined Main Street, and an annual Memorial Day parade and just one each of a firehouse, police station and post office, but still, it lacks the small town feel you'd expect in a place this size.

Just four express train stops from Manhattan, Riversedge is really a city impersonating a small town. It's a suburb of New York City, with a transient population, and though it's small enough for everyone to know each other's secrets, few actually do.

While Ingrid stands in line at the bakery, holding Drake's hand, she checks her phone for recent emails and then reviews her notes for a taping scheduled later that morning. Ingrid is the host of a popular national weekly podcast, called *Too Busy to Die*, focusing on streamlining the mess in all of our lives so that we are no longer too busy to die, but instead, less busy to live. Well, that's the soundbite at any rate, and the segment to be taped this morning will cover decluttering plans anyone can tackle in a weekend, especially with spring right around the corner. Ingrid types something into her phone that she just thought of but isn't sure she will say out loud on the taping. (*"Spring cleaning" is an unfortunate term. Most people really need to do a deep cleaning weekly, and not just annually, or seasonally, or when someone dies*).

As she and Drake move slowly toward the front of the line, Ingrid reviews notes furiously and mentally prepares for the podcast taping to try to keep a few lingering and confusing thoughts about her husband, Peter, from clouding her vision. She doesn't want to stop and think about him right now. She doesn't want to think about how he's hurt her or how he's humiliated her in the worst way possible. She wants to think about her podcast taping and preparing Drake's homeschooling lessons for the next week, and about this buttery croissant that she's allowing herself to enjoy, on this one day, that she is permitted all week long.

At the front of the line finally, she orders two croissants. Drake points out a jumbo cookie he'd like to add to the order, but Ingrid smiles and shakes her head. He knows he can't win this argument. He's hardly even putting up a fight. Ingrid winks at him, a silent reward for his obedience as she turns and says, "That will be everything, thank you." The bakery clerk gives her a polite smile without a hint of real recognition and for once, this anonymity comforts, instead of pains, Ingrid. She takes her greasy brown bag from the bakery clerk, and hurries away from the crowded bakery, down the block to her car with Drake in tow, and the pair heads home to face whatever it is that is coming next.

✧

In spite of herself, Opal stands at the dining room table, cutting and pasting a new caption for her son's poster. She knows this is all costing precious time they don't have right now. Not this morning.

CJ isn't helping. He's got a new line of questioning for Opal.

"Mommy, how many tickets will we need for the poster award ceremony?"

Opal shrugs and rocks the glue stick back and forth on the new caption. The one that no longer has an "i" in dead.

"But Mommy, I need to know, because Mrs. Bardo says everyone is only allowed 2 guest tickets."

"Ok," Opal says absent-mindedly. She would love to stop talking about this freaking poster. She bites her tongue so those particular words don't escape her. She knows CJ repeats everything she says at home to that damn high-and-mighty Mrs. Bardo. Opal bites harder. She doesn't want to say *high-and-mighty* out loud either. That's an unfortunate phrase her mother used to use and Opal hates it so of course, it jumps into her mind at the worst possible times.

"Mommy, how many will we need?"

"Hunh?" All this tongue-biting has made her forget what they are even talking about. She rubs a sore tongue alongside the inside of her teeth and tries not to think about Mrs. Bardo.

"Tickets. How many guest tickets will we need?"

"Oh. Just the one, CJ."

"Mommy, are you sure?"

Opal knows what he's thinking, of course, but she avoids his unasked question lingering in the air, until he actually asks it, making it impossible to avoid any longer without lying.

"Mommy, will Uncle Pete be there?"

"No." Opal knows her response is too quick. She backpedals just as quickly. "What I mean is ... oh, CJ ...."

Opal crouches down to CJ's level and holds up the fixed science poster as a barrier between them as she tells him the truth. "Listen, CJ, Uncle Pete's not going to be around anymore. I know you liked him and I know you hoped he'd be around for things more often. Things like the science poster award ceremony and your birthday party and other things. But he's not our family. And he's just not going to be around anymore. And it's ok."

Opal sees her son's crestfallen face as she stands up, distancing herself from his watery eyes, and in a panic, she blurts out: "Hey, what do you say after school, we go to the Main Street Ice Cream Shoppe?"

CJ's face lights up instantly.

Success.

At the Main Street Ice Cream Shoppe, they have bubblegum flavored ice cream with real gumballs littering the pink frothy dessert. They serve it with a small paper cup, so you can pick the gumballs out and save them for later. It's the only gum Opal allows CJ to eat, and the promise is a treat reserved for special occasions.

Well, Peter is gone, Opal thinks, fighting hard to keep her emotions in check in front of CJ. *I guess this qualifies as a special occasion.*

"Come on, CJ. We're late. I have to write you a note and get you to school now. When I pick you up, we'll go straight to Main Street. I promise."

Opal lays the poster back down on the table, grabs a notecard out of the dining room cabinet and starts scribbling an excuse as to why CJ is late for the first time ever this entire school year. She notices her hand shaking a bit, and worries at her penmanship and what that lofty Mrs. Bardo will think and say, but she keeps on writing nonetheless. She glances up to see CJ admiring his newly fixed poster. A thick tuft of his light brown hair shoots straight up over his head locked in place by two twisting fingers. Opal's heart aches with the realization that even with the fixed poster and the promise of ice cream and the clinical description of Peter's departure from their lives, CJ is still anxious.

CJ always twists his hair in his fingers when he's nervous. It's a tic he's inherited from his biological father. That and those damn almond-shaped eyes that melt her every single time she looks at her son. CJ is Christopher Junior, named for a father he never even met, and Christopher the First was a habitual hair twister, among other things. Of course, the fact that CJ has never known his father has made it all the more confusing for Opal when she sees CJ unwittingly mimic Christopher in these small ways over the years.

As she watches her son twist his hair and study his science poster, she wonders, not for the first time, if she should have given him some other name. She laments that she has given Christopher the honor of having this lovely, perfect boy named for him. She wonders if she shouldn't have given Christopher quite so much, her son's name included.

Opal holds the rehabilitated poster out to her son who takes it happily. "Come on, CJ, we gotta get to school now."

With a note explaining his late arrival in one hand, and CJ's hand in the other, Opal heads out of the house for an encore. She folds CJ and his now perfect science poster into the backseat, buckles herself into the driver's seat, and starts to back out of the driveway, only to be stopped yet a second time by a car coming out of nowhere behind her. Two cars actually. "Don't twist your hair, CJ," Opal says nervously, glancing at CJ in the rearview mirror, as both police cars pull up alongside her in her own driveway. As she gets out of the car, she tells CJ to "stay put."

A tall, lean man who fills out his police uniform quite nicely gets out of the first car, and Opal nods hello to him. She recognizes him as Officer Tim Connors, who shows up at the hospital now and then on official business, where Opal works as a nurse, a step up from the department store makeup counter, which was her first job when she arrived in this town, and a giant step up from the other jobs she's worked since then, too. Tim Connors has a warm smile. The kind that disarms you instantly. *He must be a very good cop*, Opal has thought on occasion when she's seen him at the hospital. *I bet he can smile a confession out of nearly anyone.* And indeed, it's that disarming smile that he greets Opal with. Which must be why she responds to him with a sentence she will later wish she hadn't said out loud. "Oh. I was sort of expecting you guys." After she says it, Opal looks down at the ground in surrender.

A few minutes later, Officer Tim reads Opal her rights and then arrests her for the murder of a man named Peter DiLaurio and takes Opal away in handcuffs with her little boy in the other squad car following them. At a red light, Opal looks over her shoulder and catches a glimpse of her son in the back seat of the car behind her, with pain and shame in his eyes – or is that her own mirrored back at her? He is twisting that tuft of hair furiously. Opal wonders where his science poster is. Did he remember to bring it with him? Can she somehow get it to school so all his hard work is not for nothing?

Opal knows CJ must realize that she has broken her promise about Main Street Ice Cream. But he can't realize yet that she's broken a great many other promises as well.

At home, the police are in Ingrid's driveway. She exhales loudly, and Drake grunts nervously.

"It's ok, Drake. Mommy's going to go talk to the police officers. You stay in the car and let Mommy talk to the police, ok?" Drake says nothing in return but this isn't unusual. Drake rarely talks.

Selective mutism.

The diagnosis came four years ago. Peter always bragged about what a pleasure it was to have a child who wasn't too precious. A child who wasn't always interrupting his parents when they were talking to grownups. A child who wasn't always chattering away when his father was trying to unwind after a long day of work. Ingrid thought Drake was, sort of, *unusually quiet*, but what did she know? He was her first, her only, child, and she had been an only child as well. When he was two and three, Ingrid wondered if perhaps Drake would talk more when he had other options. Instead of pining about the start of school like she knew she was supposed to, Ingrid actually looked forward to the day when Drake would head off to school and find some more suitable companions than the ones he was obviously bored with at home. But it wasn't long after he started preschool that Ingrid was summoned in to talk to the teacher after classes had ended for the day and the children had all gone home. All except Drake.

"Frankly, I'm surprised you haven't sought out a professional opinion earlier than this," Mrs. Lopez said as she detailed the red flags she'd seen already in her short time of teaching Drake. Ingrid felt chided and scolded in the cold empty classroom. She found herself looking past Mrs. Lopez's head at a bulletin board made of fish and cut out laminated bubbles with the letters of the alphabet.

We are hooked on letters! The bulletin board announced.

Ingrid's eyes focused on the bubbles as Mrs. Lopez talked. She wasn't sure what she had missed and when Mrs. Lopez interrupted her thoughts with a persistent, "Mrs. DiLaurio?" Ingrid made excuses and stuttered about Drake's perceived speech issues, all the while screaming at Peter in her head.

You did this.

You made me think this was all ok.

You were so happy to have a quiet, well-behaved child.

You lulled me into a false sense of complacency.

And now our son is being labeled within weeks of starting school.

With the anger exploding inside her, Ingrid managed to keep her face calm and contrite and bring her gaze back from the bubbles behind the patronizing teacher's head. "Thank you so much, Mrs. Lopez. I'm grateful for you identifying an issue that's been bothering me for some time now. I'll make that appointment right away."

It didn't take long to get the diagnosis after that awkward meeting with Mrs. Lopez.

"Mute? But he talks. Not a lot. But he does talk. I've counted his words and he reached all his language milestones. I've recorded them in his baby book for the pediatrician." Ingrid tapped a closed book in her lap for emphasis.

Dr. Vee explained that selective mutism is a form of anxiety disorder that manifests itself in an inability to talk in certain social situations. Dr. Vee then gave Ingrid some brochures and pamphlets and the card of a psychotherapist in New York City that she said specialized in selective mutism in children Drake's age.

"It's fine, Ingrid. Lots of kids are shy. He'll grow out of it. You worry too much." Peter did everything but pat her on the head when she brought him the diagnosis, brochures and the card of the expensive psychotherapist who was, predictably, out of their insurance network. But Ingrid was armed with rebuttal information for Peter's condescension, having done her research following the appointment with Dr. Vee. Drake was not shy. He was anxious. Left unattended, this disorder would impede his development and his ability to function in school and in life. And he wouldn't just "grow out of this." It would require hard work and attention. Work Ingrid was willing to put in.

"And what about you, Peter? Are you willing to do the hard work to make our son feel comfortable enough to start talking to you?"

"Of course, I am," Peter said. He must have seen the resolve in Ingrid's eyes. Something that made him realize he wasn't going to win this argument. "Take him to the New York City shrink if you think that's what he needs. I'll do whatever it takes to help him. I promise."

Yes, he promised. But, like so many of his promises, Peter broke this one, too. As a result, Drake has only ever said a handful of words to his father. He's started to open up more to Ingrid recently, but Peter? Well, he's missed out. Drake hasn't won any father lottery, unfortunately, and Ingrid feels terrible that she has that in common with her sweet son.

As Ingrid closes the car door behind her in the driveway, the officer who's been waiting for her, takes his hat off and addresses her, "Ma'am? Are you Mrs. Ingrid DiLaurio?"

She nods, wordlessly.

"Ma'am, I need to talk to you. Maybe we could go inside?"

Ingrid shakes her head. "No, whatever it is. Please go ahead and tell me. My son is in the car, and I just need to know."

"Ma'am, I'm very sorry to tell you but your husband, Peter DiLaurio, was found, well, deceased, late last night, outside a property on the corner of 35th and Russell."

Looking up at the officer, who does indeed look sorry to tell her this, Ingrid is suddenly overcome with grief that the opportunity for Peter to make good on any of his broken promises is now officially over. Especially to Drake. Her eyes fill up with tears. A million words fill her brain, but she can speak none of them.

Is this what it is like for Drake, then? Wanting to say words but not able to find the breath or the energy to utter them?

The words continue to ricochet in her head. Letters and syllables and sounds that can't quite find a way to come together, no matter how hard she wills them to.

"We have a suspect in custody," the officer says while Ingrid is still waiting for the words to travel from her brain to her mouth.

The effort of trying to talk ceases then. There is a black weightless stillness and Ingrid leans all the way into it.

And later when she comes to and learns that Opal Rowen is in custody for her husband's murder, Ingrid will be relieved, even glad. Not that her husband is dead, or that this particular woman is across town in custody for his murder, but that Ingrid collapsed before she had a chance to say the words that were finally, at long last, making their way to the tip of her tongue right before she passed out.

She will be glad she didn't ask the officer, "Am I under arrest?" Because if she had found those words and asked that question, she might now be a suspect in her husband's murder instead of Opal Rowen.

CHAPTER 2
Three for Three

At the Main Street police station, Opal is being very careful, because the police officers have only just stopped asking their questions. Officer Tim has disappeared and she has mixed feelings about his absence. She's disappointed, because yes, she misses that smile of his, but she's relieved also because that smile is just too good, and God only knows what she might blurt out if he comes back.

Opal has now "lawyered up" (*their phrase*) and she can tell it annoys the police officers, but she insists that she wants to talk to a lawyer and she knows they have to provide one for her. While they all wait together for a public defender to show up, the police occasionally fire a question at her anyway (*"So what? Were you and DiLaurio seeing each other or something?"*) and she's pretty sure they're not supposed to be doing that before a lawyer shows up, so that's how she knows she has to be very careful.

The only female police officer she's seen all afternoon is offering her son crayons across the room. He has his science poster with him. Turns out he remembered to bring it with him after all. The poster is propped up against his chair with the photos facing Opal across the room, and it takes every bit of Opal's remaining resolve to keep from screaming out: "I don't want to look at that dead rosemary plant any more, for God's sake!" She's trying to be oh-so-careful, not to do or say anything that will make everything worse. CJ has stopped twisting his hair, a fact that frightens Opal. It seems he can't even soothe himself with his usual trick. He's quiet and visibly afraid, and Opal keeps looking over at him with forced smiles and nods. *It will be ok,* she communicates with her eyes. *I don't believe you,* he replies back with those almond-shaped eyes he inherited from his father.

Christopher was Opal's first boyfriend, her first everything, including her first lover. They were science lab partners in 10th grade, but not exactly "partners" in the true sense of the word. Opal had helped Christopher, who was not quite as ambitious about science as he was about video games, pass 10th grade science, and he'd made her feel like a hero for doing so. He had always been possessive, but after they slept together, he clung to her and amped up his attention and need. From Christopher, Opal learned many things, including that she could easily sneak out of her house without her alcoholic parents or older brother, Dean, even noticing. She learned that she could pass science, and actually excel in science, without too much effort. And she learned that sex made her feel beautiful and most importantly, powerful.

Opal decided that she didn't want to waste that power clinging only to one overly possessive, not too incredibly motivated, boy. She broke up with Christopher a year after graduation when she found out she was pregnant and he still hadn't managed to line up a real job or any real-life aspirations. She didn't tell him she was pregnant, and he moved on quickly enough. So quickly in fact, that she didn't regret not telling him. He was dating that blonde bimbo, Sally Carruthers, within days of their breakup. Opal would be damned if Sally Carruthers was going to be her kid's stepmom. No, she wanted to do this all on her own. She took every penny she'd saved from babysitting and waitressing gigs in high school and the post-graduation year, and moved an hour away where she found an affordable apartment in a quiet New York City suburb and a starter job at a local department store makeup counter. Her parents didn't bother trying to talk her out of her plans. They seemed relieved to have her out of the house. She'd kept her pregnancy a secret from her parents as well as from Christopher, but they must have known. She was starting to show by the time she moved out. Dean tried to talk her out of moving, but he wasn't successful. He said he'd visit her often and he did. For a time.

Opal gave birth to her son in her own bathroom after coming home from work one night. By the time she figured out that she wasn't just having gas pains, there was no time to make it to the hospital. She was alone in her bathtub, laboring for less than an hour according to an alarm clock perched on the countertop. But it could have been days according to her own internal clock. Time essentially stood still during that time. Opal called 911, but she knew they wouldn't be there in time. As Opal gasped for breath, and cried out from the pain, she wasn't nervous. She was on fire.

With each shearing pain, she repeated a mantra.

I'll do this alone.

I don't need anyone.

No one.

She told herself her cries were warrior calls. And childbirth? Well, it was harrowing and beautiful and exhausting, and when it was over, she pulled her son up on her belly, cut the cord with the same bathroom scissors she used to cut her bangs biweekly, and with a long, sweet exhale, she realized that she was wrong about not needing anyone else. She simply needed this sweet baby in her arms. In a tender, reflective moment, she named him Christopher Junior, CJ for short, and she resolved that she would do absolutely anything for this sweet child.

Even kill if need be.

Opal takes a deep breath and forces another smile across the room at CJ while he colors.

What will happen to my son, now? That's the only question she wants answered.

"You don't have any family in the area who could take him for the time being?" "No, there's no one," Opal says sadly. "So what will happen to my son, now?" she repeats.

No one is saying, but they are hinting. She learns that a social worker has put some calls into a few temporary foster families. "Just in case," they tell Opal.

"You need to cooperate with us and then we can cooperate with you," the female police officer said earlier to Opal. Opal can't figure out if she's supposed to be the "good cop" or the "bad cop."

And then Officer Tim leaves the room, and they finally stop questioning her, and there is a moment where it gets a little easier to breathe, but that moment is short-lived. While she sits in silence waiting for an attorney to show up, Opal thinks about Peter lying dead at the bottom of the rock pit behind the Russell Street property and she shudders, trying to get that particular image out of her mind. Ever since she saw Peter lying there yesterday, head smothered in dark blood, the veins in his face blue and visible under unblinking eyes, she could see a few steps ahead and it has not been a reassuring vision.

Opal knows she needs to get in touch with someone who can help her. Someone other than the public defender who is supposedly on his way now. But who? The inconvenient truth is that she's always pushed everyone away.

And who could blame her? When she wasn't pushing people away, she was getting them killed.

Maybe it's the fracture in her heart caused by losing Peter that lets something else come through. A memory she hasn't let herself have in quite some time.

Dean.

Of course, Dean isn't here to call because I killed him too.

"How far along are you?" Opal calls out to the female cop across the room. The cop has leaned way back in her seat, and is caressing her protruding belly in small, fast circles. Opal wasn't sure she could ask before, but now, given the gesture, it would seem rude not to.

"Eight months."

Opal smiles at her. "Home stretch."

"Yep. You could say that."

"Well, you know what they say. Don't rush it. They're much easier when they're still on the inside." Opal winks and the cop gives her a kind smile, but turns back to coloring with CJ, a visible reminder that Opal is not in control of anything right now, no matter how much small talk she tries to make mother-to-mother with the cop. And she can read the cop's expression loud and clear as she looks away from Opal. It says:

You and I? We are not alike. Don't even bother to pretend we are.

After CJ was born, it was harder and harder to make ends meet with the makeup counter job. That fire Opal felt in her bathtub giving birth all alone didn't pay for diapers and formula and doctor's visits and the high-priced babysitter she had to hire to watch and feed CJ for an increasing number of shifts at the mall. She was barely getting by before CJ was born. But after he arrived, it seemed that money was going out as fast as she could make it. And eventually even faster. When Dean would visit, she tried to put on a good front, but he could tell she was struggling. He offered her money but Opal knew he was in no position to help her. He was still living in their parents' basement, after all. He had inherited their parents' addictions and he had gambling debts and bar tabs to pay off. She didn't want to sink him any further than he already was, so she refused his help.

When a new job opportunity showed up at her feet, she didn't hesitate and she didn't tell Dean at first. She didn't want to hear what he'd have to say about it. She had to make her own decisions, for CJ and herself. The new job had strictly nighttime hours, which meant she got to spend more time with CJ during the day. When she went to work at night, Mrs. Jones from down the hall slept on the couch in Opal's apartment to stay with CJ and charged Opal half of what she had been paying a daytime babysitter. If Mrs. Jones knew what Opal's new job was, she didn't say. She just folded the blanket she'd been sleeping under on the couch, and wished her well when Opal returned each morning and paid her in cash, mostly small bills.

Even though Mrs. Jones didn't levy anything that looked like judgment, Opal was embarrassed each time she paid her. Especially as the weeks went by and it became clear that Opal had been had.

Opal had believed Billy "The Mouse" Russo who showed up at the mall to buy perfume for his girlfriend and said he could "rescue" Opal from her minimum wage department store makeup-counter gig. He told her she should come work for him because he only hired models and ran a respectable, upscale establishment. None of those things turned out to be true. The Mouse lied a lot, but it took Opal some time to understand that. Dean always told her she had a habit of trusting certain people right away. "And by 'certain people' Opal," Dean said, "I mean liars."

The Mouse was nicknamed for the bizarre whiskers he grew out on his face, but the nickname didn't otherwise fit him. He was a fierce and mean man. He ran drugs out of the back of a strip club frequented by businessmen and drug dealers, and he pimped out girls who didn't make him enough money in the front of the club. Opal had followed The Mouse out of desperation. The money was good right from the start, and she could finally breathe easier knowing she could take care of her son properly. On her own. Of course, her newly rediscovered power wasn't just about money. Opal felt bold up there on that stage. In control of her destiny for the first time in a long time, she felt superior to those men who frequented the club. They didn't frighten her or intimidate her, and The Mouse told her she had a good head for the business. "Not to mention your ass," he laughed as he said it. Opal ignored his crassness. She wasn't afraid of him, either. But eventually she came to understand that she should be.

The Mouse had lured her to his club, DIVAS, with the claim that he ran a very "high end" establishment, and that she'd fit in well there. But eventually Opal learned that, in addition to drugs, The Mouse was running a trafficking ring disguised as a dance parlor with girls of questionable ages and consent being sold like they were commodities. Opal didn't work out of the back, because she did well up front, so she did her best to ignore what was going on there. But her brother didn't. Dean warned her to get out of her new career "before it's too late." But, by the time Dean and Opal were having that conversation, it was already too late.

Within a few months at the club, Opal was The Mouse's girl. She was making him plenty of money and when Mouse told her one day, "Opal, I think it's time I have you start training some of my younger girls." Opal knew what that meant. Her days of ignoring what Mouse was doing in the back were numbered. When she tried to talk to him about quitting the club, and maybe even pursuing nursing school, an idea that had been brewing since CJ's birth, The Mouse let her know exactly what he thought of that idea. He left her with a bruised face and told her she'd have to take a week off without pay because she was "too disgusting to look at right now."

Opal, never confuse wanting to belong with being someone's belonging. That's what Dean had said to her. The last thing he'd said to her, in fact. Dean came to see Opal the day after she talked to The Mouse about leaving and ended up black and blue and green. Opal told Dean she had fallen down the steps in the back of the dark club where she "served drinks," but Dean said he knew exactly how she'd been making her money, and that she'd been hit.

Was it Mouse?

Instead of answering him or questioning why Dean knew the name of her boss, Opal looked down at the ground ashamed. Dean stomped out of her apartment yelling that he was going to "go teach Billy Russo an overdue lesson."

Opal ran down the hall with CJ on her hip, and asked Mrs. Jones if she could watch him for a few hours and then she headed to the club to try to stop Dean from whatever he was planning.

At the club, she stood outside Mouse's office, paralyzed with fear, and she heard them fighting behind a closed door.

You leave my sister alone.

Or what?

Or I'll kill you.

I'm sure you'd love for me to just disappear. Wouldn't that be convenient?

What are you talking about, Billy?

Opal leaned her ear closer to the door and wondered the same thing. What *was* Mouse talking about?

Let's not pretend you're innocent here, Dean. I would never have even met your sister if you hadn't told me about her over a few too many scotch and sodas at a club you had no business being in. You sold your sister to me for a gambling debt. How would you like me to let her in on that little arrangement, hunh?

You son of a bitch.

Listen, Dean. I've kept my word. I've kept her up front, but if she gives me any more trouble—or if you give me any more trouble—

Mouse didn't finish his threat. Instead, there was a silence. A long, loud silence. And then a crashing sound. Opal jumped back away from the door just before Dean burst through it, alone, looking flushed and sweaty. An angry heat radiated off him and sent Opal stepping back even further.

"Dean, what's going on?" Opal asked, her voice thick with fear, foreign-sounding to her own ears.

Dean didn't answer but only stormed past Opal with that final warning and wild eyes. *Opal, never confuse wanting to belong with being someone's belonging.*

And after that, Dean was never heard from again. Opal was sure he'd been killed at the hands of or at the command of Mouse, but Mouse just kept saying, *mind your business.*

"Your brother was a drunk and a gambler and had a lot of enemies. Don't be naïve. Let's not speak of him again. And let's not talk about you leaving anymore. Got it?"

Opal was racked with guilt and grief after Dean disappeared. She knew she'd killed Dean just as sure as if she'd put a gun to his head. But the words she'd overheard in Billy's office gutted her and they lived in her memory right alongside the guilt.

Dean had sold her.

She had gotten Dean killed.

Later when Mouse ended up dead, Opal didn't feel nearly the same guilt as she did for Dean.

But Peter? His death hurt the worst. And now she knew for sure that the men she trusted would always end up betraying her. And also end up dead.

Three for three, Opal thought. *And unless you're playing baseball, those aren't good odds.*

"Ok, Miss Rowen. The public defender is here to see you." A grim-looking man with slick hair walks in behind Officer Tim and sits down across from Opal, startling her out of her self-pity and internal walk down memory lane. The public defender pats her hand and winks at her, a smile breaking through his serious expression. "Hey, I remember you, Sweetheart. Do you remember me? Why don't you fill me in on what's going on here?" Opal can't quite place him. The men that she danced for back in the day form a blur of faceless images. But she recognizes that familiar smirk of recognition covering the public defender's face. She sees it often in her daily life, even still, years after she has left that life. In grocery stores, at the library, at CJ's school. Plenty of men living and breathing in this town who had once paid Opal to dance for them. And more. If they are with their wives, they look away and pretend they don't know her at all. But if they aren't, they look at her like this. Ogling and practically licking their lips. Fantasizing about an encore performance.

Opal looks across the room and gives CJ another forced smile. She couldn't save Peter, but maybe she can still save her son and herself. If only she had someone in her life she could trust. Other than Peter, there was one person Opal had trusted her heart with in the last few years.

Maybe.

No.

But maybe.

What do I have to lose?

Suddenly, the fire in Opal's belly returns.

"You know something. I'm not going to need a public defender, after all." She pats the slick man's hand and winks right back at him, before standing up and summoning Officer Tim who has stepped across the room to give them some pretense of privacy. "Excuse me, Sir, I'm going to need to place a phone call. I want to call my own attorney."

The police officers huddle around and confer and then seem to understand they have no other choice, so they hand her a phone and she whispers into a voicemail from a landline in the middle of the precinct just out of earshot of the female officer coloring with her son.

And then she waits for Peter's wife to call her back.

CHAPTER 3
You Owe Me

Ingrid has a funeral to plan alone, and so she starts a list of things she will need to do tomorrow.

Reschedule TBTD podcast guests for a week out. Maybe more.

Prepare Drake's homeschool lessons and behavioral therapies for a week out. Maybe more.

Interview new babysitters.

Plan the next chapter of my life.

She actually writes the last one down and subsequently stares at her whole list intently.

Yes, she will need to plan a brand-new chapter of her life. But for now, she will just need to get through the night. She remembers making lists after her mother's funeral when she was 15. There was comfort in the order. Her father assured her that what she was doing was good and necessary.

"What would I do without you, Sweetheart?" Ingrid's father had scratched his head after all the mourners left the house and stared at Ingrid as she wrote down which casseroles were in the kitchen freezer and which ones were in the basement freezer. His expression was one of surprise, like he hadn't expected to see her there. Ingrid remembers thinking when he said, "What would I do without you?" that she was enough. That even with her mother gone, she was enough for him to keep on wanting to live.

Of course, I was dead wrong. Ingrid leaves her list sitting on the kitchen counter, and finds Drake in the living room, sitting on the floor, building something fairly intricate out of Legos.

"Come on, buddy. Let's get you into your pajamas. You can skip a bath tonight."

Drake nods. He's been completely wordless since the police left. She has to believe he has questions. Questions he wants to ask, but questions that he can't quite form. She will try to anticipate his words and answer them for him. Tomorrow. Or maybe she should just let him form the questions for himself. She will figure all of that out tomorrow. For now, she just wants to get through the night with as much normalcy as she can muster.

In his room, Ingrid lays out his favorite mismatched pajamas with dinosaurs on top and dragons on the bottom and she turns to the bookcase while he gets ready for bed. She pulls a few of his favorite books out from a messy pile on the second shelf (*oh, how her podcast guests would be horrified to see that she can't get Drake to keep his books in any sort of order!*), hoping only for comfort and familiarity on this night. Ingrid ushers him into bed and tucks the duvet blanket around him with her usual rhyme. "Tuck, tuck, don't try to duck. Tuck, tuck, don't try to duck." Drake smiles and it makes Ingrid relax a little. He'll talk when he's ready. He'll ask his questions when he's ready.

One of Drake's first behavioral therapists had told Ingrid to talk to Drake often in jokes and riddles and rhymes to help create a fun and comfortable environment.

Never pressure him to speak. Reward any nonverbal communication and reward any speech. Even a whisper. Encourage him gently, quietly. Create an environment in which he feels comfortable to speak and he will.

Peter had rebuffed most of these suggestions. He refused to speak in rhymes and he refused to reward nonverbal communication. Soon after Drake's diagnosis, Ingrid had been folding laundry down the hall and heard Peter scolding Drake in his room.

No, Drake. It's impolite to point. Tell me, with words, which story you want me to read, and I'll happily do so.

Ingrid had raced down the hall and snatched the books out of Peter's hand. "Go!" She'd yelled too loudly to Peter and he'd stomped away from Drake's bed to the doorway. Drake pointed to a book in Ingrid's hand with a pirate dressed as a rock star on the cover and whispered, "This one."

"Wonderful! This one it is," Ingrid opened the book with a flourish and looked to Peter triumphantly while Peter rolled his eyes. "Dear God, you both enable each other. I think maybe you need to find yourself your own New York City shrink, Ingrid."

Ingrid replays the memory angrily as she sits on the edge of the bed, holding up a few story options. On this night, Drake doesn't use any words at all, not even a whisper, but merely points to his perennial favorite, and Ingrid opens up *The Musical Pirate* to read aloud. As she reads, there is a thought that dances somewhere just beyond reach until she catches it.

Peter is gone and still Drake isn't speaking. It's only me here, now. Am I the root of Drake's anxiety after all?

Ingrid lets the thought go. She refuses to hold onto it.

Back in the kitchen, Ingrid focuses on the imminent funeral planning. She doesn't want Drake at the funeral. He's only eight, after all. But then again, it *is* the funeral for his father. Ingrid hated being dragged to her mother's funeral when she was 15. But she didn't think she had a choice. Maybe she should give Drake a choice.

Is that wrong?

She's not sure and she doesn't have anyone to ask. There is no family left for Peter or Ingrid. They are both only children with long-gone parents. It's the common thread that brought them together, Ingrid once thought. It formed a mark of independence that they each smelled on the other from their first meeting.

Whether or not to bring Drake to the funeral is something she might have bounced off Gabby until the week before, when she had to let her go as Drake's regular babysitter. Ingrid moves

"Interview new babysitters" up higher on the list.

Ingrid decides she will tell the funeral director and Peter's colleagues at the office that she wants things to be small and intimate. In reality, with no one really to invite, it will likely be empty and depressing. Perspective and reframing, as Ingrid has learned over the years, is everything.

After she makes some notes for the funeral director, Ingrid plans her son's homeschooling lessons for the next few days, the way she has done for several years now. With his anxiety, she has become used to sheltering him, and now she will need to protect him fiercely from what will come next. His father is dead. There is a murder investigation and a suspect in custody. And the troubling thing is that the suspect is a woman her son knows. A woman who used to be his mother's friend. The mother of a boy who used to be Drake's own friend, as a matter of fact. When he finally finds his words, he will most certainly have questions for Ingrid, and the truth is, Ingrid has plenty of her own. But those will have to wait. She resolves to be patient and try to manage Drake's anxiety so he doesn't have a major setback.

While she is homeschooling Drake to accommodate his anxieties, Ingrid is also doing it for *her.* The pressure of those school moms for the short *(or long! Depending on how you looked at it)* year that Drake was in traditional school, was exhausting, and Ingrid was happy to leave them all behind. She'd tried out organized sports a few years later, but that too had been short-lived. Actually, a brief stint in tee ball last year nearly killed them all, Ingrid recalls with a shudder as she adds *buy a funeral dress* to her list. She doesn't want to wear anything she already owns to the funeral. She wants to buy something suitable, wear it once, and throw it away.

Ingrid turns back to her list and optimistically adds *prepare invoices for next month's sponsors.* In spite of the chaos she now finds herself living in, she needs her podcast to stay afloat. When she is behind her microphone, she feels powerful. She's sought out nationally for her connections and her tips and she relishes the acknowledgement and acceptance. Ironically, the national acceptance she's come to enjoy hasn't exactly translated into local recognition. She's had her face on national magazines including *Woman's World* and *Inc.*, but she's still a relative unknown in her own little town as demonstrated by the anonymity she experienced just this morning in Cosie's Bakery.

While she's making lists and notes at the kitchen table, Ingrid ignores a missed call. It's not a number she recognizes and she doesn't answer unknown calls on the first ring. She gets a lot of cold calls relating to her podcast. She has no friends or family of her own calling to check in on her; just a continued stream of calls from strangers wanting to be part of *Too Busy To Die*.

Ingrid lets it go to voicemail, making a mental note to check it later. While she resents the intrusiveness of strangers on her grief-filled night, she can't abandon her business. *Too Busy to Die* is an award-winning and highly downloaded podcast of tips and tricks with guests who collaborate with Ingrid to help promote both Ingrid's podcast and their own respective businesses. There is robust advertising revenue and each guest pays to be on the show, and that pay-to-play revenue is what makes *Too Busy to Die* profitable. Ingrid started the business with zero capital when she left her career practicing law in New York City, and it's become incredibly successful especially in the last few years, allowing her to work profitably alongside raising and home-schooling her son.

Sure, she's had some help along the way, but Ingrid prefers to ring the bell of a "self-made entrepreneur." She's worked hard, taken advantage of certain opportunities, grown the business, and it's all worked out spectacularly in the last few years. She doesn't see why any of that has to change just because Peter's gone. He wasn't the least bit involved in the business when he was alive. He wasn't involved with any bit of Ingrid's life during recent months and years, in fact.

As she looks at the upcoming schedule of *Too Busy to Die*

guests, Ingrid allows herself a rare moment of pride. But she quickly deflates, realizing that she has been running the podcast and the business alongside her mothering with relative success, but also with a husband and co-parent. He hasn't always been the best at either role, but even a lackluster husband and co-parent has to be better than none, right?

Ingrid's mind races as she realizes she needs to figure out how to keep making her life work now that she's a single mother. She may in fact need her business even more now that she is a widow and on her own. After all, Peter didn't believe in life insurance. Ingrid has always known this. He believed he'd live forever, and so there was no reason for betting against himself. Ingrid's podcast is successful, but so were Peter's real estate ventures, and now that he's dead, Ingrid will have to fill the financial vacuum left behind.

With her son asleep upstairs, his lessons for the next few days complete, and a few productive notes about the podcast going forward, Ingrid resolves to continue to avoid her empty bed, the loneliness of night, and the grip of grief. She fills a goblet of wine and turns on the television, not thinking about the fact that it will be time for the news and that Peter is actually the big local news story of the day. As the television screen springs to life, Ingrid gasps as she realizes a commentator is talking about her husband who was found dead at a vacant building lot the night before. They show a recent picture of him pulled from his public LinkedIn profile and Ingrid flinches. She's not sure she wants to stare at his face right now and so she reaches for the remote. But then the screen flashes a picture of Opal Rowen instead of Peter, and Ingrid leaves the television on.

Ingrid stares at Opal's image, trying to recognize the woman she once knew. Because yes, Ingrid knows her. This woman who the television is saying killed her husband was Ingrid's friend once. Her best friend for a time. Her only real adult friend ever. The news reporter has a lot of information about her. They say

28

she is a former stripper with a seedy past who turned her life around and became a nurse in a small hospital in a neighboring town to Riversedge. Ingrid knows all this, of course, but can't imagine what this has to do with the murder charges against Opal. Surely, they are not going to argue that strippers are inherently violent people. Ingrid rolls her eyes at the useless field reporter.

"We've just learned that Opal Rowen has refused the public defender." The reporter has perfect hair and makeup and is standing in front of Opal's home: a small, well-tended clapboard structure not easily visible in the dark background except for bright yellow crime scene tape decorating the porch.

Why is the house being labeled a crime scene? Peter didn't die there. Ingrid leans in closer to the television mounted on the wall and mouths the words the way she's seen Drake do sometimes when he has words in his mouth but hasn't exactly mustered the comfort level to say them out loud.

"What does this mean, exactly, that Opal Rowen has refused the public defender?"

Ingrid nods along with the anchor.

Yes, what does that mean? I'd like to know that, too.

The field reporter answers them both. "Well, it means that Opal Rowen needs both a lawyer and a defense, if she wants to beat these charges. Because for now, this ex-stripper with a questionable past is facing a first-degree murder charge. Back to you, Joe."

Opal leans back into the couch, sips her wine, and watches the screen switch from Opal's front yard to an erectile dysfunction drug commercial.

This is the news story? Opal's seedy past as a stripper and the fact that she needs a lawyer?

As the warm buzz of alcohol takes over, Ingrid's thoughts become jumbled. Ingrid is a lawyer but not really. She left her New York City law gig years ago. Eight years ago, to be precise. Mere weeks before she gave birth to Drake, she turned the lights off in her Park Avenue law office and never looked back. She had no real plans other than to be Peter's wife and her new baby's mother. She wanted to dive fully and completely into those roles, and she hoped the same intensity with which she'd practiced law and lived her life before would just travel with her to motherhood. That she'd somehow transfer her tiger-like instincts from Park Avenue to the nursery.

In most respects, she has to admit, it's worked. She took to motherhood fiercely and hungrily. In fact, when Drake was born, Peter complained that he wasn't sure how he felt about playing a close second to Drake. Ingrid bit her tongue to keep from telling him he wasn't a close anything. She would have hoped Peter would understand without her saying so: she was determined to be the kind of devoted parent she'd craved for a long time. And indeed the role of parenthood came to define her in a way that lawyering never had.

But she's *still* technically a lawyer. She's paid her dues annually, and kept up her accreditations and her licenses. She worked hard for her law degree and legal training. She always thought maybe she'd need that tool in her back pocket for a rainy day. Has the rainy day come?

Could I help Opal?

More wine. More confusion. And then a stark return from the confusion.

No, of course I won't help Opal. Opal is accused of killing my husband. Opal was sleeping with my husband. Opal needs a lawyer but it has to be someone else.

Ingrid's brain settles for good this time.

I can't help Opal, now. That will have to be someone else's job. It's not my job to save Opal. It's never been my job.

The commercial break ends, and the news resumes with the story of Peter's death. This time Ingrid doesn't even bother reaching for the remote. She wants to hear. She wants to watch. If people are going to be whispering about her, she wants to know what they are saying.

But as Ingrid continues watching, she realizes no one is talking about her at all. Peter is referred to as a married real estate tycoon, and Opal as his ex-stripper mistress, but not a word is spoken about Ingrid or her podcast or her identity. She knows she should be relieved that she's been left out of this salacious news piece, but she can't quite muster the feeling of relief.

She thinks about her sweet but anxious son sleeping upstairs and dreaming about musical pirates in his mismatched pajamas. She thinks about his first friend, CJ Rowen, a little boy who was once so kind to Drake. She wonders where that little boy is sleeping tonight now that his mother is in jail, accused of killing Drake's father.

Ingrid looks down at her phone then and remembers the missed call. She hits play. Turns out, it's not a cold call or an influencer or a potential podcast guest. And it's not a stranger. It's a woman whose voice she recognizes instantly, even though the woman is whispering.

It's Opal Rowen on the other end. "Maybe you heard, I'm at the police station? So, it turns out it's like the movies, and I get one call. And you owe me, Ingrid. So, you know what, I'd like that favor now."

CHAPTER 4
What She Deserves

After a meeting with the funeral director the next day, Ingrid shows up for lunch at the Riversedge Law Club. The Law Club is a members-only restaurant and conference space for the best and the brightest legal minds in Riversedge, New York. While some towns may be known for their hospitals or their biotech communities, and others for their manufacturing or flagship stores, Riversedge is known for its lawyers. The idyllic setting is just close enough to Manhattan for culture, convenience, and high-profile cases, but its topography is perfect for hiking and fishing and paddle-boarding and all the things lawyers always claim they want to do on their days off, but never do.

Ingrid remembers traveling through Riversedge with her parents when she was a young child on weekend drives. They lived a few towns and a lot of tax brackets away from Riversedge. Her parents, Roy and Judy Barton, were always years, sometimes decades, older than the parents of her peers, and were seemingly intimidated by Ingrid's pleas for outdoor activities on her days off from school. Weekend drives in the roomy family Cadillac were meant to appease Ingrid, and she accepted them as best she could.

As she got older and came to understand the age difference between her parents and her classmates' parents, Ingrid also came to understand that her parents went through years of fertility problems and prayers before she arrived on the scene to parents already in their 40's at her birth. She was born on

Christmas Day, which her mother loved to talk about as if it was the very first Christmas itself. But Ingrid's mother didn't like to talk much about the time *before* Ingrid was born. The first time Ingrid ever heard about that painful time was when she was eight and left a long letter for Santa Claus detailing all the reasons that she would like a baby sister. Or brother. She was clear in the letter that she would accept either, although a baby sister would be just a little bit better. Sheila Robertsen had gotten a baby sister over the past summer, and it was all she could talk about. While Sheila wasn't the nicest girl in the class, she sat next to Ingrid in school, and Ingrid thought about how wonderful it would be to have something to talk to her about and strike up a kind of a friendship. Not to mention the built-in friend she'd have at home if she had a baby sister, too.

When Ingrid asked her mother to mail her hand-printed letter to Santa Claus, Judy asked to read it first, as was her annual custom at Christmastime, and Ingrid waited excitedly for her mother to read about the exciting gift that would be all of theirs to share. But her mother's face had changed dramatically as she read the letter. Indeed, she'd had to leave the room at one point. Years later, Ingrid would remember that moment with blazing shame. When she returned, her mother's eyes looked pinkish but she was otherwise composed as she told Ingrid, "Ingrid, I don't think Santa Claus can bring us a new baby. He saves them for much younger parents. We were very lucky even to get you after writing a letter just like this for many, many years because we were already much too old for a baby when you arrived in the sleigh that Christmas morning. How about if you ask for a bike or something else this Christmas?"

Ingrid had written a new letter then, but it wasn't nearly as well stated or impassioned as the baby sister (or brother!) letter, so she was shocked when there was a bike under the tree after all. She didn't bother trying to talk to Sheila Robertsen about the bike.

Her mother's measured response to the Christmas letter

that year didn't give her much to go on, but it gave her just enough to understand that she better learn to be happy with the family she had, because there wasn't anything else—or *anyone* else—coming her way.

The weekend drives through the country were a bit old-fashioned but Ingrid didn't mind, since they usually ended with a stop in Riversedge, sometimes at the charming Main Street Ice Cream Shoppe, or at Tully's Book & Record store around the corner from Main Street. "Such a quaint town," Ingrid's father would always say.

"Keep your eyes open," Judy Barton would often warn when they arrived in Riversedge, and Ingrid and her father would give each other a knowing look and comically rolled eyes, knowing that it was Ingrid's mother's fervent hope that they'd run into Ingrid Rossellini: daughter of *the* Ingrid Bergman, whom Ingrid was famously named for. Ingrid's mother had read a magazine article once with a photo of Ingrid Rossellini shopping on Main Street in Riversedge, and ever since, had been certain they would run into her if they just stopped there enough times.

In all those weekend drives, they never once caught a view of Ingrid Bergman's daughter, but they'd eaten plenty of ice cream and bought a number of used books and records. Later, when Ingrid was practicing law in New York City and was looking for an apartment of her own outside of the pricey Manhattan city limits, Riversedge felt like a perfect choice, even though her mother had died long before, and wouldn't be around to keep an eye out for famous daughters any longer. In a way, living in the place she'd spent so much time with her mother when she was alive, gave Ingrid some comfort.

"It's so hard to mother while motherless," Judy Barton had said those very words herself one time talking about a neighbor whose child, Reed, was always running wild on the street, stealing Ingrid's toys and standing too close whenever he was around. He'd thrown a rock at Ingrid's head when she was six, and the blood pouring from her head had convinced Ingrid she was dying.

"You'll be fine, darling. Head wounds bleed like the dickens," her mother had said, as she'd blotted Ingrid's forehead fiercely and bandaged her up, but not before explaining that they'd need to give Reed a little grace. Reed's mother was a single mom, without much support, not even living parents, as far as Ingrid and her parents could tell. Judy gave Reed (and his mother) lots of leeway.

It's so hard to mother while motherless. Ingrid often thinks about that line uttered casually by her mother as a long-ago unwitting premonition of her own daughter's future.

In stark contrast, Peter hadn't spent a single childhood weekend driving through the country. Peter was a city boy through and through. Born and raised in Manhattan by academic parents, who were also older first-time parents, he'd been renting a Manhattan loft when Ingrid and he started dating.

They had met at Ingrid's Park Avenue law office. Peter was a self-made, fairly wealthy real estate financier who had hired Ingrid's firm to represent him on a real estate deal that was going south before it even began. Ingrid took immediate charge of the initial client meeting, and Peter told her on their first date months later, that's when he knew.

"Knew what?"

"Just knew." He'd moved her hair off her neck and kissed her boldly

"If this gets serious, I won't be able to bring you home to my parents. They're both gone, unfortunately." Ingrid studied Peter as he said it. It was a strange thing to announce on a first date. It startled her. Enough so that she blurted out, "My parents are both gone, too."

"Well, we understand each other's pain then, I suppose," he said as he kissed her again.

She pulled away slightly. "How did your parents die, Peter?"

"In a car crash. Killed by a drunk driver about five years ago."

Ingrid nodded, but she thought to herself. *No, I'm not sure you understand my pain at all, then.*

Since he was renting, and Ingrid owned her own place, Peter agreed to give up his loft and move to Riversedge when they got married (very reluctantly at first), but eventually he became so acclimated in the town, it was hard to remember that it had been Ingrid's town first.

From the start of their relationship, their social life revolved almost exclusively around Peter's work-related dinners and events, and his colleagues' partners became Ingrid's "friends." Of course, none of the relationships formed with Peter's circle were substantive in any way. They were just small patches on Ingrid's otherwise fractured and lonely life. Later when Drake arrived, he made Ingrid feel whole for the first time since her mother had died. As Drake grew, and in turn, as his reliance on Ingrid grew, she became more and more settled into her new life. Peter and Riversedge had nothing to do with it. There were just supporting characters in a life that suddenly revolved around Drake.

As time went on, Ingrid forgave her late mother for the choices she had made, and even came to understand them. But her father? Ever since she found her father's "Goodbye" note, she committed to never forgiving him and she held firm to that commitment. Ingrid channeled her anger at her father into her parenting of Drake, hoping that he would never feel discarded the way Ingrid had once felt all those years ago. She knew her anger toward her father and her devotion to Drake separated her from Peter and from the rest of the town. Yet she found it hard to belong to anyone or anything but Drake.

But Peter? Peter always found a way to belong so easily. Ingrid thinks as she climbs the steps to Riversedge Law Club less than an hour after finalizing the details of Peter's funeral. She wonders if she should quickly check in with the sitter. She's left Drake with a brand-new sitter, hired online through a caregiver vetting site just this morning. Ingrid decides not to call. She doesn't want to delay her lunch date any longer. She just wants to get it over with.

With its marbled platforms and elaborately carved columns, the Law Club announces that it is a prestigious place even before one enters. If a comparison has to be made—-and indeed it is unique in so many ways—but still if a comparison absolutely has to be made, the Law Club could be seen as somewhat equivalent to other suburban country clubs but without the golf or tennis or pools. The activity inside the Law Club is networking and deal-making. Some of the highest profile cases are said to have been won and lost inside its enormous brick-faced facade.

Ingrid arrives inside the Law Club, and gives her name. The hostess makes an elaborate show of checking her computer screen before telling Ingrid, "Ah yes, your member host has already arrived. I'll be happy to show you to his table." Ingrid digs her fingernails into her palms angrily, but smiles stoically as she follows the aloof hostess into the dining room she wouldn't have been allowed access to, had she not been invited by Tobin Rue.

Ingrid had never been granted membership into the Law Club during the years she'd practiced law in and around New York City, a wound she wouldn't have believed was still raw if she hadn't felt it open anew as she followed the waitress inside to meet Tobin. She'd wanted that membership badge of honor badly when she was still practicing law. In fact, she had lobbied hard for a few of the senior partners, who were all residents and neighbors within Riversedge, to sponsor her membership. But there was always a reason for denying it. She hadn't logged enough hours. She hadn't logged enough cases. She hadn't worked for enough local companies, or she hadn't worked for enough national companies. The list went on and on and changed and evolved constantly every time the subject came up. Eventually, Ingrid stopped trying and later, gave up her lawyer gig entirely, shortly after she and Peter got married. Drake was already on the way by that point. Ingrid was six months pregnant at the City Hall wedding ceremony witnessed solely by Tobin and his girlfriend at the time. With no family, and no real friendships cultivated at the Park Avenue law firm, there was no one to invite to City Hall but Tobin and the girl-friend.

Sue Something.

As Tobin greets her inside the Law Club dining room by kissing her cheek chastely and solemnly, Ingrid thinks about asking Tobin: *What was Sue's last name? You know the one you brought to our wedding?* But it seems ridiculous to ask. Even more ridicu-lous than the fact that a woman she doesn't know and didn't know was the only other woman who was actually present at her shotgun wedding without any shotguns.

"Ingrid, how are you? I'm so, so sorry. God, I don't have any words. Sit down, sit down. Let's talk. Tell me everything. How are you doing? Did I ask that already? What a dumb question." For a man who doesn't have words, he is saying a lot of them. Ingrid waves him off and takes a seat. Tobin is a longtime friend of Peter's. He'd been his personal lawyer, too, but apparently he had been a friend first. The lawyer thing was just a byproduct of the friendship, since Peter needed someone he could trust for various business dealings. "I met Tobin before I met you. Otherwise, *you'd* be my *only* lawyer," Peter had joked after intro-ducing Ingrid to Tobin for the first time.

Ingrid and Tobin had worked together a few times, once to help create a tax shelter for Peter before he and Ingrid married. There was a patronizing moment when Tobin told Peter over drinks to celebrate the deal, how impressed he was with Ingrid. Ingrid shrugged. She'd always been good at creating diversions and appearances. She didn't need Tobin to tell her that.

Now, Tobin reaches over and pats Ingrid's hand. As she shiv-ers, she wonders if it's Tobin's hand or hers that feels so cold. "Seriously, how are you holding up?" Tobin asks but she knows it isn't a genuine question. They aren't close. He was Peter's friend, not Ingrid's. Still, she wasn't entirely surprised when he called this morning. Ingrid is expecting some obligatory contact right now in the early days, but she's not expecting any real friendship to develop in the vacuum Peter's death has created.

Ingrid takes a sip of her water and says, "Hanging in there. I have to just stay focused on what needs to be done." She hands Tobin a printout of bullet points from her meeting with the funeral home.

"You've jumped headfirst into handling mode," Tobin observes.

"Well, I guess it's the lawyer in me."

Tobin nods with understanding. "And Drake, how's he doing?"

"As well as can be expected. He's with a sitter right now. I'm trying to keep him as far away from everything as I can right now."

"Understood."

They talk about the case a bit. Ingrid sips more water but wishes someone had offered her a glass of wine instead, as she looks around the room and thinks about how odd it is to talk about her dead husband as a "case" now inside the Law Club. But then again, it's odder that her husband is dead.

They order chef's salad specials and they make small talk over the meals. A large grey-haired man who smells of cigar smoke and pine trees stops by the table and leans down into Tobin. He whispers, but Ingrid hears him say "Congratulations on the new case, Counselor. This should be quite a boon for your career." She sees Tobin shrug uncomfortably. "Judge, this is Ingrid DiLaurio, Peter DiLaurio's widow."

Ingrid startles visibly at the word "widow" but tries to smile bravely. She sees something odd on Tobin and the Judge's faces as they regard her. When the Judge walks away, Ingrid leans forward, "What was that all about?"

Tobin wipes his face, and takes a long sip of his water, and Ingrid feels nervous without understanding why, waiting for him to speak.

"Listen, Ingrid, I know you have a thousand things to do and worry about right now, and I didn't really want to bother you at this delicate time, but I also didn't want you to hear about this from someone else, or worse, from the news."

"Hear about what?"

"I'm taking on Opal Rowen's defense."

"You're representing Peter's accused murderer?" Ingrid is more confused than angry. But Tobin looks chastised nonetheless.

"It's not what you think. I'm not betraying Peter's memory or anything like that. Opal needs a lawyer. She refused the public defender and keeps claiming she's waiting for 'her attorney' to show up." Tobin uses air quotes, a practice of his that is common and that Ingrid loathes. "Anyway, I need some *pro bono* hours for my partner bid this year. And the firm wants me to take this one on, so, well there it is."

Ingrid stares at Tobin for a beat, trying to process his news. This isn't what she expected at all. She expected some formalities, some sympathies, some condolences. Some empty promises that he'll be there for Ingrid and that if she needs anything, he's only a call away. Not *this*.

"*Pro bono* hours, Tobin? Really? You can't just help a local arts group incorporate or take on a quick landlord-tenant case for the local women's shelter? This is a little extreme even for a partner bid, don't you think?"

Tobin looks uncomfortable and sneaks a glance over his shoulder before leaning into Ingrid. "Listen, I know it might feel a little off to you, but she needs a lawyer and my firm is really interested in being involved, so I raised my hand to make sure someone else doesn't just turn it into a media circus."

"Tobin, I really don't know what to say. Do you know something? She actually left a message for me last night and I think she was going to ask me to represent her. Maybe I'm the 'attorney' she is waiting for." Ingrid matches Tobin's air quotes with her own, thinking perhaps she needs to speak his language as much as it disgusts her.

He shakes his head, but Ingrid goes on. "Tobin, the thing is: I *know* her. Well, I knew her anyway. A long time ago. I was her friend long before everything else happened. Last night, I had this crazy, fleeting thought that maybe I should actually consider representing her. Oh, God. This is all a bit surreal." Ingrid leans back, her desire to debate with Tobin about this topic waning already.

Tobin shakes his head firmly. Aggressively. "No, Ingrid. Just focus on Drake and yourself, and let me handle things. This could get messy."

"Well, messy *is* my business, now." Ingrid forces a small smile, but Tobin doesn't return it. Instead, he wipes his face again with his napkin, signs a slip of paper that's been discreetly placed in front of him by their server, and stands up to leave, signaling an end to their lunch. As a non-member, Ingrid won't be welcome to stick around if Tobin is leaving. She stands and follows out behind him wondering if later, anyone will remember seeing Tobin and Ingrid have lunch together that day. Will anyone think it odd when it becomes public knowledge that Tobin is defending Ingrid's husband's accused murderer? Or will they chalk it up to just one of many odd pairings that the Law Club sees in its private rooms, day in and day out? The goodbye in the parking lot is stiff and cold and Ingrid is sure now it's Tobin's fault and not hers.

After lunch, Ingrid isn't quite ready to go back home to relieve Drake's new sitter. She stops at a gas station, tops off the tank, and picks up a copy of the local newspaper. She pages through to read what they are saying about Peter and Opal. She winces at the mention of her own name in the printed news piece. *Wealthy financier leaves behind a wife, former Park Avenue lawyer turned podcast host, Ingrid DiLaurio, and a young son.* People are starting to talk about Ingrid, and it doesn't feel any better than when she was ignored.

Ingrid keeps paging through the paper, trying to see if there are any other developments in the case. The police said they'd keep her updated as they left her house the day before, but the bombshell news that Tobin is taking on Opal's defense already has Ingrid feeling like she's on the outside looking in.

On page six of the paper, Ingrid glances at a mention of Ingrid Rossellini, now a published author, giving a talk at the local university. She feels a familiar pang of loss that she can't share the news with her mother. She keeps paging through the paper until something she wasn't expecting stops her in her tracks. For five minutes after the gas nozzle has shut off, Ingrid sits in her car and stares at the small news piece buried on page 23, about an incident only the day before, and feels an uncomfortable warmth creeping up her neck as she reads between the lines that aren't printed on the page. There is a truth that no one will know now except Ingrid.

Well, no one alive, anyway.

Gabby is dead. And that means the only other person who knows how Peter died ... is dead.

Ingrid is startled out of her reading and re-reading by a rap on the window. She looks out at an angry-looking heavyset man with a ruddy complexion way too close to her face but separated by the window pane between them.

"Hey lady, you mind moving your car already?" He yells out through the closed window. "This isn't a parking lot. You need to move. Your gas is done and you need to keep it moving." He points to the gas hose that is still connecting her car to the pumping station.

Ingrid nods through a shocked stupor, and the ruddy man stomps away from the car in a trail of exasperation. Ingrid folds up the paper, tosses it on the passenger seat, and jumps out to disconnect her gas hose.

As she drives away, she thinks about the pseudo and sparse obituary she just discovered that no one seems to be talking about. It makes her feel sad. Of course she feels sad. It's tragic and she's not a monster, after all. But she can't deny she feels something else hiding behind the grief and sadness and loneliness that she wouldn't have thought was possible right now. *She feels relief.*

Ingrid doesn't exactly plan the detour, but she soon finds herself on the highway out of Riversedge and at the dance club where Opal used to work. Ingrid had known this bit of Opal's history but had never really known or cared where the club had been. The news reporter, however, had given the exact location last night and it turns out it wouldn't have been hard to find if she had ever tried. Which she hadn't. Until now.

The dance club is on a highway dubbed "the bypass" that is often used as a shortcut on the way from Riversedge to Manhattan. Ingrid has rarely driven into the city, choosing to take the train instead. But commuters pass by the place twice daily. She can understand that the location must have made it popular with those same commuters in its heyday.

One look at the place tells Ingrid what she already knows, which is that its heyday is long over. Ingrid parks in the empty lot outside a decrepit boarded-up building and gets out and walks around the perimeter of the lot, looking, observing, but with no real plan. There's an old rusted sign out front with female silhouettes leaning and curling in and out of each other to spell out the word, DIVAS.

On the side of the building are several broken windows that have been boarded up and there's a township sign taped to the door with duct tape indicating "No Trespassing" in bold letters and numbered township ordinances in smaller lettering below.

As she turns the corner toward the back of the building, Ingrid spots an overflowing, neglected dumpster parked on the only patch of grass visible on the lot, whose sweet stench of decay overwhelms her. She leans over and retches the entire overpriced chef's salad special Tobin bought her at the Law Club onto the asphalt in front of her.

As she climbs back into her car and drives away from DIVAS, Ingrid replays Opal's voicemail message from the night before over the Bluetooth speaker in her car.

It's the loudest whisper Ingrid's ever heard.

You owe me, Ingrid.

Opal stares at the colorless wall in front of her. She's been sitting like this for hours. On the far side of a filthy mattress, feet planted firmly on the ground, breathing in and out and trying to calm the fireworks exploding in her skull. They've taken her son and sent him into a foster home.

CJ is gone.

"It's just temporary," the female police officer said. Opal is sure now that the officer is meant to be the "bad cop." How else could she have said such a thing with a straight face?

CJ is gone.

The thought of CJ sleeping in a house full of strangers has made Opal's entire body rigid. It's like she's dead already and rigor mortis is setting in. She thinks about Peter lying at the bottom of that rock pit, covered in blood and remorse, his eyes stuck open like he was staring at her even in death. He looked up at her as if stunned and saddened with the realization in his last moments that their love was nothing but a giant lie.

It wasn't a lie. Even though you're dead now, Peter. It wasn't a lie. I swear it wasn't a lie. Not for me anyway.

Opal thinks of the things she should have whispered to Peter, even as he lay there. In case he could have heard her. Perhaps there was some way she could have made his last moments less— well—less terrible.

This is what her mind is doing now. With CJ gone and the prison walls boxing her in, she has gone a little insane. She is thinking now that she should not have left Peter to die. Instead she should have crawled into that hole with him. She should have lay there, inhaling the metallic smell of him bleeding out, and waited to freeze to death overnight with him. The only reason she'd fled the scene was for CJ, but CJ would enter the system now and there was nothing Opal could do about it, and leaving Peter to die like that would end up being for nothing.

Officer Tim of the dimpled, disarming smile told her to try to get some sleep. "You will get a bail hearing and arraignment in the morning," he said as if that should provide some relief. But there's no way Opal can make bail. It's not like she's made some rich friends in the last day or so. The house she and CJ live in is an affordable rental. The car is a cheap lease she can barely afford as it is, and she doesn't own anything else of value that she can put up as collateral.

Opal sits rigidly on the side of the bed and tries to quiet the doom that's taken over her consciousness.

Peter is dead.

CJ is gone.

Quiet. Just think.

Opal breathes. In and out. In and out. Between the breaths that empty her, a thought creeps in.

There is one thing.

Opal owns just one thing of value.

That godforsaken place out on the highway. She owns that dance club she used to strip in. The one she swore she'd never set foot in again. But she owns it. It's a piece of real estate, after all. It's an asset. Maybe she could use *that* to make bail.

She relaxes. The fireworks settle themselves. Maybe she can save herself and CJ after all.

I'll put the lot up as collateral and I'll make bail. I'll get out of here. I'll get CJ. And we will make a run for it. Disappear into some quiet town where no one will care where we came from or who we are. Everything will be all right.

But, no. The moment passes. The fireworks resume. Her brain starts firing and exploding all over again.

Opal can't tell anyone about the dance club. She can't use it as collateral; she can't even admit that she owns it. That dance club will implicate her more than help her. Opal exhales loudly, trying to push the dirty, unwelcome thought away. But it stays, mired in all of her bad decisions, tragic memories, and guilt.

The only reason Opal even owns that property is *because* Peter's dead.

CHAPTER 5
Even Blood

"Anything at all?"

"Yes, indeed. Anything. Cooking oil. Tar. Bubblegum. Even blood."

"Oh. Great. Even blo—I'm sorry. I need another minute."

Ingrid pales and stops the recording. "I'm sorry. I know I said I was fine. But that just took me by—I don't know what happened. This isn't very professional of me at all. I'm going to edit that part out. We don't need to start over, let's just pick up at the start of the solvent segment."

Josie who goes by @Josie_Is_Clean_Now puts her hand over her mouth and chokes on her own apology. "I'm sorry. You're in a bad place right now. I really don't think this is a good idea. Maybe we should reschedule after all."

@Josie_Is_Clean_Now has recently grown her Instagram page to nearly 300,000 followers. She hawks feel-good stories and a custom line of organic cleaning products. Apparently when she got sober four years earlier, she found God, sobriety, and antibacterial solvent. It's that solvent and clean living they are promoting in a taped segment of *Too Busy To Die* that Ingrid hopes she will be able to stretch over two to three weeks while she regroups over the future of her podcast and her business.

Because Josie's solvent gets out anything.

Even blood.

The emotion takes Ingrid by surprise and she has to stop the recording for a moment. Yet again. Josie had emailed Ingrid late last night to confirm the taping time. She didn't mention a thing about Ingrid's dead husband, so Ingrid realized that she didn't know. Even though Josie lived in nearby New York City and might have heard about the dead financier and his ex-stripper lover, she clearly didn't put two and two together.

So, if Josie was still willing to go forward with the taping, Ingrid would accommodate. Josie was a big get, and she was going to drive a lot of traffic to Ingrid's podcast and website, not to mention a five-figure sponsorship fee. Ingrid wasn't willing to start cancelling guests who didn't know who her dead husband was.

That morning, after getting Drake's school day launched, Ingrid set up her podcast microphone and plugged in a light mounted over her laptop in a corner of the kitchen, while Drake sat quietly in the next room, working on a lesson. At the designated time, Josie's dewy freckled face outlined with a bold floral headband popped up on the split screen in front of Ingrid. After a few obligatory niceties, she walked Josie through the paces of what the interview would look like: what points each woman wanted to be sure to hit.

But then, not long into their session, Ingrid had to stop recording three separate times because her voice was shaky. She finally told Josie what had transpired over the last two days. "Sorry," Ingrid said, "I didn't really want to talk about it, but I guess I need to come clean."

Pardon the pun, she said then, hoping to lighten the mood that had suddenly gotten dark with the revelation that her husband was found dead less than 72 hours earlier.

"Oh my God," Josie looked stricken. "Are you sure you want to do this today? We can certainly reschedule."

"No, no. Thank you for your kindness. The arraignment is this afternoon. And honestly, I need this distraction."

But now, after stopping the interview for the fourth time, Ingrid is embarrassed *and* shaken with grief. She can't lose Josie as a sponsor. She has to salvage this relationship, and quickly.

"Josie, let me just get some water and we will dive right back in. I promise. I really want to introduce this amazing product to the world." Ingrid holds up a bottle of Josie's organic citrus-infused cleaning solvent. The one that can get out anything.

Even blood.

Ingrid walks away from the laptop and fills a glass of water from the kitchen sink. She stands stoically at the sink, looking out the window at her yard. A small raised garden bed sits starkly off center in the yard, waiting for spring plantings. At this point, it's just a heap of cold dirt. She's waiting for the nights to warm, for the final spring frost to occur. The last few days have seen beautiful weather, but the nights have still been freezing.

Ingrid's mind is wandering and her hands are shaky. She realizes she shouldn't have been so dismissive of Tobin the day before. The news that he plans to represent Opal Rowen took Ingrid by surprise, but she should have pulled herself together and asked him more questions to prepare for the arraignment today.

Ingrid wishes she had asked him if there were photographs of Peter's body when the police found him. She feels like it's something she should have forced herself to look at now. She had declined to identify his body. She told the police she couldn't see him like that, and they told her that would be unnecessary anyway. Peter had fingerprints on file: part of a background clearing process both he and Ingrid had gone through a few years back when Drake was still in a traditional school and school volunteer opportunities required background checks. The police were able to identify him quickly. Even before they notified Ingrid that he was found dead and that his accused murderer was in custody, they knew the deceased was definitely, without question, Peter DiLaurio.

Because Ingrid had declined to view his dead body, the police had arranged for Peter to be transported directly to the funeral home for cremation, and Ingrid was coming to terms with the fact that she wasn't going to see Peter ever again, except possibly in photographs that would certainly be admitted into evidence at his trial. Maybe even at the arraignment. Perhaps it was short-sighted not to prepare herself. Maybe there was still time to call Tobin before the arraignment. She didn't want to act like this at the arraignment later when the subject of blood came up.

Head wounds bleed like the dickens. Her mother's quaint old words arrived unbidden and unwelcome.

Pull yourself together, Ingrid.

Ingrid finishes her water at the kitchen sink, and decides she will not call Tobin. She will not ask to see pictures of her dead husband. But she *will* reschedule Josie's taping until she can talk about blood without acting like a lunatic. Peter's dead and she's not going to be able to avoid that fact with cleaning solvents and detailed lists. Time to accept all that. Looking out at the empty garden beds, Ingrid does the one thing that has yet to appear on any of her meticulously detailed lists.

She lets herself miss Peter and she explodes with deep, gulping sobs.

CHAPTER 6
Justice Is Blind

Ingrid walks up the steps to the courthouse and gets in the security line, where she promptly feels a sense of déjà vu she had long forgotten. In two days, she's visited two places she hasn't been in since Drake's birth: first the Law Club and now the County courthouse. Although most of Ingrid's legal practice took place in New York City, she always had a handful of local cases to round out her docket, and she spent plenty of mornings arguing motions in the very building where Opal is now going to be arraigned for Peter's murder.

No one pays much attention to Ingrid as she feeds her over-sized purse through the security conveyor, walks through the metal detector, or approaches the grey-haired security guard to ask which courtroom the criminal docket is being assigned today.

"Courtroom 27. Up the stairs two floors, or wait for the next elevator around the corner." The security guard points both to steps and an elevator bank in opposite directions. Ingrid hasn't been inside the courthouse for nearly a decade and the elevator was already ancient when she last set foot inside. She chooses the steps and walks slowly, in no hurry to see Opal or hear about her husband's death, or even to see Tobin. When she arrives at the courtroom, she pauses outside the door, trying to decide whether it's too late to turn around and run far, far away from this whole thing. With her hand on the ornate door handle she looks up at a painting that hangs outside Courtroom 27. A blindfolded lady liberty with a swirl of letters surrounding her: "justice" translated into a multitude of languages. Ingrid remembers looking them up once, while sitting outside the courtroom waiting for a hearing to start. She found several typos in some of the translations. She can't remember which ones now.

Courtroom 27 is full. A few heads turn when Ingrid walks in but their glances are all fleeting. No one seems to know or care who she is. They turn back to what they were doing after only a short pause. Although no one seems to recognize Ingrid, she herself recognizes some lawyers in the courtroom from her practicing days. They are likely waiting for a motion argument or arraignment of their own. Opal is not the only defendant with business scheduled for the afternoon. Indeed, Opal's hearing will not be long. It should take no more than a half hour or so. There will be plenty of other accused criminals parading in and out of the courtroom, but Opal is the main show of the day, and the majority of the courtroom seats are taken by lanyard-wearing members of the press. Presumably, they are there to see the ex-stripper-turned-do-gooder nurse accused of murdering her lover, Peter DiLaurio.

Tobin has had a fresh haircut since Ingrid saw him yesterday. He is standing at the counsel table with his profile toward Ingrid, and he is talking with a woman whom Ingrid can only see from the back. The woman is not Opal. Her hair is too blonde and brassy to be Opal, unless Opal has dyed her brunette locks and lost some of the warm beauty Ingrid remembers from the last time she saw her. Tobin's companion is wearing a typical navy-blue trial suit, albeit not nearly as beautifully tailored as Tobin's. By the way she's scribbling on a yellow legal pad in front of her, Ingrid guesses that she's a young associate or an intern that Tobin has tapped to assist him on this case. Ingrid studies the duo as Tobin whispers advice or orders or something else as the blonde keeps nodding and scribbling.

Ingrid checks the time on her phone, only to see that the Judge is running late. She uses the empty time to check on the comments pouring in from her latest podcast posting. She had rescheduled @Josie_Is_Clean_Now and queued up a previously taped segment instead with a popular home designer and blogger. She expected the segment to generate a large number of comments, but she's still surprised when she sees that more than 400 comments have been posted already in the short hour since she posted the link. While she waits for the arraignment to begin, she reads with horror a few of the most recent comments that seem to center mostly around Peter's murder and the arrest of his mistress.

@afl45 Looks like your happy, clean, uncluttered home had a little clutter after all, no?

@strawberryblondeshavemorefun Is this the woman whose husband was just killed by the stripper?

@timefortea56 @strawberryblondeshavemorefun yes, but she was a reformed stripper. Get your gossip and facts straight

Ingrid feels a sharp pain in her stomach as she scrolls through more of the same. It seems people are starting to connect the dots, and if she thought it was insulting to be ignored before, this is worse. This is so much worse.

She's interrupted from her scrolling by the sound of a court bailiff announcing the start of the afternoon session. Ingrid shuts her phone off in time to see a door open behind the empty Judge's bench. Out comes the same grey-haired, paunchy man who had come up to Tobin in the Law Club the day before to congratulate him for taking on this career-boosting case. Defending his dead best friend's accused murderer. The pine and cigar scented man is now in an oversized black robe, and the bailiff announces his entrance, and suddenly Ingrid jumps to her feet along with the rest of the room, glancing again at the Tobin-Intern show, but only out of the corner of her eye, feeling like she's been caught watching something illicit.

The Judge leans over to a young woman sitting near his bench, and Ingrid quickly realizes this is his law clerk. She will not be introduced to the group or acknowledged in any way. Ingrid notices that Tobin barely even registers her. She wishes she could get Tobin's attention and signal to him that ignoring the young woman is a mistake. In the legal world, the law clerk handles the lion's share of the grunt work on the case behind the scenes. She will be responsible for scheduling matters and in many cases, writing the orders deciding the various pre-trial motions. Some judges are more hands-on than others. As Ingrid watches the clerk jot down some notes and hand the Judge several pages which he ends up reading directly from, she realizes this Judge is definitely one of those who is *not* hands-on.

Next are some garbled announcements by the Judge and some similarly garbled responses by Tobin, and Ingrid remembers that the acoustics in Courtroom 27 have always been disastrous. She strains to hear exactly what's going on but the only thing she can make out is the Judge asking Tobin if he's ready to start. Suddenly all eyes are on a door to the side of the Judge's bench, and a tall, well-built police officer is escorting Opal—still very much brunette, still very much beautiful—to the counsel table where Tobin is standing. The entire scene reminds Ingrid, perversely, of a father giving away a young bride to a new husband. Opal walks with her handsome police escort toward Tobin with her eyes down, demurely, looking up only when she arrives directly next to him, and the two turn in unison to face the Judge.

The Judge reads a litany of charges and rights to Opal. Ingrid ignores the legalese and instead studies Opal from behind. Her shoulders are hunched and her long brown hair is secured in a thick ponytail that drags in the middle of her back. She's wearing a black pantsuit that looks a little big on her. Ingrid wonders fleetingly if it's really not her suit, or if she's actually lost a few pounds in just the few days she's been stuck in a jail cell.

Ingrid doesn't have much time to focus on Opal, however, as she quickly becomes distracted by Tobin. He's jumpy and clumsy. He starts to speak while the Judge is still speaking and has to be reprimanded to wait. Then, when it is his turn, he drops his own legal pad a few times, trying to flip through pages to find his notes. Ingrid watches him lean over Opal to grab the yellow pad from his intern, and he actually knocks Opal off balance. She reaches to right herself on the arm of the chair next to her and looks over her shoulder in the process, which is when she spots Ingrid. Ingrid wants to look away, but she can't, especially as Opal's eyes widen and she looks like she's trying to signal Ingrid in some way.

Ingrid inhales deeply, willing Opal to turn back around and face the Judge, but instead, Opal keeps her eyes locked on Ingrid while Tobin is bumbling and tripping over himself and everyone else at the table. Opal ducks her head in Tobin's direction and raises her eyebrows at Ingrid as if to say, "You really going to let this happen?" And then she finally, *finally*, turns back around.

The rest of the arraignment does not go much better. Tobin is either so completely disinterested or else incompetent, it's laughable.

Of course he doesn't know what he's doing, Ingrid thinks. Tobin is a corporate lawyer, who has never even set foot in a courtroom, and who has taken on the case *pro bono* because of its high profile and his partnership aspirations. He doesn't have the first idea what he's doing and he doesn't seem to care. He's clearly not put an ounce of research into the case and he doesn't even seem to understand the procedures.

In the *coup de grace*, Tobin argues animatedly for a $1 million dollar bail to be set, and when he receives it, he turns triumphantly to Opal who only shakes her head somberly and whispers something inaudible. Ingrid knows exactly what she's saying. Opal can't make a million-dollar bail. Even at 10%, she'd have to pay $100,000 to post bond. She's not going to be able to do that. She probably doesn't even have access to $10,000. Didn't

Tobin bother to talk to his client before showing up this afternoon?

Ingrid puts her head down and slinks out of the courtroom in the midst of some press hurrying out to make deadlines and post their latest on this sensational story.

As she sinks into a hard bench outside of Courtroom 27, Ingrid grows reflective. These courtroom benches, a staple in every courthouse Ingrid has ever set foot in, have always reminded her of church pews, which is ironic, since Ingrid hasn't seen the inside of a church in a long, long time. Not since her mother died, as a matter of a fact.

But during the time she practiced law, courtrooms *became* her churches. While she never grew completely comfortable in her law firm office, she felt at home in the courtroom, where she felt guided by a force bigger than herself: *justice*. She was a seasoned litigator. She could handle herself in front of judges and juries. She had never once bumbled her legal pad or made herself or a client look like a fool the way Tobin just did.

Ingrid looks up at the blind lady liberty surrounded by "Justice" and errors. Justice and the truth are complicated, comfortable notions for Ingrid. She sighs with realization. Opal needs a new lawyer. Opal needs a *real* lawyer.

Ingrid puts her head in her hands on the court bench and begins arguing with herself internally.

I could take this case on.

No. How could I possibly take on this case? It's a murder case, for heaven's sake. It's Peter's murder case.

But she is going to go down the river if Tobin stays on this case. He doesn't have a clue. He's not seeking justice. He doesn't know a damn thing about justice.

She needs help.

Stop. Stop feeling guilty about Opal. Again. It's over.

Ingrid sits up and leans her head back against the courtroom wall. A few reporters are in the hallway, whispering into phones, dictating updates to the story brewing inside.

Ex-stripper can't make bail. She's going back to jail to await further court proceedings in the DiLaurio case.

Wealthy financier's mistress is penniless. Can't even make bail. Her lawyer seems to be an idiot, too. Maybe he's just a past client of hers from her stripping days doing her a favor. Don't print that, though. Wait, maybe do print that.

Opal Rowen has pled not guilty. Says she didn't do it. But if she didn't, who did? Is there more to the scorned, jealous wife angle by any chance?

At the last overheard comment, Ingrid tastes bile in her mouth. She thinks about the thousands of commenters on her podcast link who are talking about nothing other than this story right now. And it's just going to be worse as time goes on. Tobin isn't even formulating a press conference or trying to get ahead of the bad press. No one has asked Ingrid to make a statement as the dead man's wife. As far as they're concerned, she might as well be another suspect in the case. If Tobin handles this case, things could get very out of control. And there's no telling what will happen if Ingrid loses control of the narrative here.

Of course, there is another thing that troubles Ingrid. When the trial starts, then Ingrid is certain to get dragged into this mess and the anonymity she and Drake enjoy in Riversedge—the same anonymity she's had a love/hate relationship with—will be over. There's no telling what that kind of stress will do to Drake, or how he will regress. Now that they've come so far.

Just this morning, Ingrid asked Drake what he thought about Mary, the co-ed she's hired on the fly to help her out until she can get a more permanent babysitter, and he smiled and nodded, and then offered: "I like her even better than Gabby." High praise indeed.

Drake is doing well. Drake is talking. Ingrid is raising him while motherless and now husbandless, but still, she is surviving and succeeding. She can't let this circus overrun their lives. Besides, Ingrid knows Opal didn't murder Peter. And no matter what Opal has done, she doesn't deserve this.

Ingrid's decision-making starts to turn the corner.

I can take this case on.

I should take this case on.

Ingrid is willing to admit that representing the woman accused of killing Ingrid's own husband will raise a host of new problems. But, sitting there, listening to the crescendo of gossip around her, Ingrid decides to face these problems head on. It occurs to her that when her mother died, no one, not even her father, protected her from the chaos that followed. Ingrid resolves to do better for Drake. Just then, she hears another reporter talking into his phone.

"Yes, Opal Rowen has a young son but no other family. My source says the son is in the care of social services at this time."

Ingrid pictures CJ, a small boy who was always so kind to her son. A boy who must be terrified right now wondering where his mother is.

Yes, decides Ingrid. *I will represent Opal. It's the right thing to do.*

But before Opal gets up from the courthouse bench, she first pushes aside all the other less altruistic reasons why she might have a vested interest in representing Opal in her current murder trial.

CHAPTER 7
You Have a Visitor

A few days later, Ingrid arrives at the jailhouse early to fill out the requisite paperwork needed to get a visit with Opal. A frowning woman with deep wrinkles, salt and pepper hair, and a too tight government-issued uniform tells Ingrid she'll have to wait.

"I don't mind. Thanks so much for your help," Ingrid smiles at the woman. She's trying in vain to make friends with this woman but the woman seems to have enough friends because she doesn't bother returning the smile.

"I didn't ask if you minded. I just told you you'd have to wait. Have a seat over there and please don't come up here every five minutes asking if I've forgotten about you. Got it?"

Ingrid tries the friendly smile again before retreating to a row of orange vinyl chairs, each one more cracked open than the next, to reveal yellowed and crusty stuffing from inside. She selects one opposite from a young man who was already waiting and focuses her attention on an end table covered haphazardly with magazines which she impulsively decides to arrange in a pleasing display. Ingrid is pretending that people who end up in this room might enjoy the aesthetics of gossip magazines in a decorative shape while they wait to see someone they know: a family member, a friend, or a loved one, who is currently incarcerated.

And who is Opal to me? Ingrid wonders as she manipulates magazines on the plywood end table. She fits none of those categories, not even a friend. Of course, Opal *used* to be a friend. She used to be a very good friend. Ingrid's best friend for a time. Never mind that she was her only friend, Ingrid knew that if there were others, Opal still would have been her best friend back then. Ingrid felt a warmth and connection with Opal that she hadn't known before or since.

And then Opal had gone and ruined everything.

In the waiting room, the young man walks over to the frowning woman and asks how much longer he'll have to wait. Ingrid sees the woman's expression turn irate and she is tempted to jump up and yank his arm and tell him to come back and sit down and not ask for trouble with this woman who is clearly overworked and overtired. She wonders if everyone who enters these walls suffers from this same level of frustration and finds herself for a small moment feeling sorry for the frowning woman, the impatient young man, and even for her former friend, Opal Rowen.

Ingrid picked out Opal at preschool orientation. The infamous Mrs. Lopez had summoned the new preschoolers and their parents for a bonding activity on a summer afternoon before school started. The students were ushered into a classroom where they could engage in various "enrichment and socialization activities before I and my aides will assign each student to their own classroom tribe." Mrs. Lopez's directions sounded a little bit bizarre to Ingrid's ears given that they were discussing 4-year-olds and not gorillas at the zoo, or contestants in a reality survival show. Ingrid held her face as stoically as she could, afraid of revealing anything that might cast doubt on her mothering fitness. She looked around the room, away from Mrs. Lopez, trying not to burst into childish giggles right there in front of her peers. That's when she saw a woman across the room in a green-belted sleeveless dress (that reminded Ingrid spontaneously of the mint chip ice cream at the Main Street Ice Cream Shoppe) do what Ingrid herself wanted to do so badly.

She rolled her eyes.

It was fleeting and it was subtle, but Ingrid was sure she'd seen it. Ingrid felt an instant connection to this woman across the room with a small boy who was sitting patiently on her lap, twisting his thick hair over his head. After the eye roll, the woman in the mint green dress whispered something to the boy, tousled his hair and he hopped up and headed over to a parade of children forming at the door. As the parents were left behind, the line of kids headed off with an eager millennial who had just been introduced by Mrs. Lopez as Miss Elizabeth, one of her aides for the year.

It wasn't just the well-timed eye roll that instantly warmed Ingrid to this stranger. The comfortable way she responded to her son and the mutual way he responded to her, in a moment when other children were stomping and crying, said much to Ingrid. Drake joined the children parade without tears, even though his own separation anxiety was evident on his face as his eyes darted back and forth among the crying children, Miss Elizabeth, and his mother who had a plastic smile forced on her face, trying desperately to be encouraging without being distant. It felt hard and exhausting, and as Ingrid watched the mint chip-clad woman do it effortlessly, she felt something that was not jealousy, but envy. A deep desire to be *like that woman. A desire to know that woman.* Ingrid watched as the woman's little boy walked right up to Drake and said, "Hello." Drake said "hello" back without missing a beat, and Ingrid felt tears sting her eyes, with the hope that she was right, and that preschool was going to help her son open up and talk and express himself. Maybe this little boy and his genuine mother would be the first ones to help him do so.

At the end of the orientation, the woman in the green dress made a quick exit with her own son. Ingrid grabbed Drake's hand and hurried to the parking lot. She saw the woman stop next to an unpretentious sedan in the school lot full of oversized SUV's. This fact endeared her even more. "Hello!" Ingrid called out after the woman, who turned abruptly and looked startled, afraid even, when she saw Ingrid waving after her.

Ingrid took note of the startled expression fleetingly, and while it confused her, she plowed on. If Drake was going to succeed in preschool, something that was still a fervent desire of hers at the time, then she was going to have to go all in.

"I'm sorry. Do we know each other?" The woman shielded her eyes and took Ingrid in, assessing her. Ingrid hoped she passed whatever test the woman was subjecting her to.

"No, it's just that ... God, this sounds stupid now, but I have to admit, you seemed like the only one in that room who wasn't putting on a show for the other mothers. I just had to meet you. And your son, he was so kind to mine. My Drake is shy (*at the time, Ingrid still thought Drake's silence was shyness*) and well, I just thought it would be nice if we could get the boys together again before school starts. Help with the transition and all."

Ingrid stood still, waiting for a response, for what seemed an unusually long time. She was starting to believe she'd made a grave mistake assessing this woman as kind and warm. Ingrid stood there foolishly, her invitation floating in the open air like an embarrassing gaffe, and Ingrid was just about to say "never mind" when the woman's face opened up in a wide smile.

"That sounds like a great idea. Nice to meet you. I'm Opal Rowen. And this is my son, CJ."

"You have a visitor."

Opal acknowledges the news benignly from her jail cell, which she is starting to realize is going to be her new home for some time now. Visiting hours are strict and short. Opal knows she should be grateful for visitors, no matter who they are, but when she sees the paperwork, with the scrawling signature from her distant past, she feels something quite the opposite of enthusiasm. She is tempted to say no, to refuse this visitor, but something else gets the better of her. Curiosity, perhaps.

Curiosity mixed with desperation and fear. A dangerous cocktail. It's the same one that arguably landed her in the Mouse's care all those years ago. The same one that got her out.

She agrees to see her unexpected visitor.

And shortly after he leaves, she agrees to stay at the plexiglass window and see Ingrid DiLaurio, who has arrived at the tail end of visiting hours, on the same day as well. Because unlike her earlier guest, Ingrid is the one Opal has been waiting for all along.

✧

"Mrs. DiLaurio. Follow me."

A security guard disrupts Ingrid's nostalgic daydreaming by calling out to her from behind a plexiglass screen across the room.

Ingrid approaches and then whispers, brazenly, to the guard, "It's Ingrid. Just Ingrid. No Mrs. anything right now."

The security guard's expression cracks a bit. "You're something else, lady. Come on. Let's go."

After a pat down and more security checkpoints, Ingrid heads to a room with a row of chairs and more plexiglass dividers. Opal sits behind the last one, and when she sees Ingrid, she does something that transports Ingrid instantly to their first meeting in Mrs. Lopez's classroom four years earlier.

She rolls her eyes.

"Ingrid."

"Opal."

"I'm not really sure how to start here."

"Same."

"I guess I should start by saying I'm sorry about Peter."

Ingrid flinches at the bizarre confession. Opal sees her gesture and shakes her head quickly. "No, I didn't mean it like that. I mean, I'm sorry he's dead. It's just an expression. I'm not apologizing. I'm giving you condolences. I mean, to the extent you need them. Or want them. Or whatever." Opal's head bows down.

Ingrid jumps in. "Yes, well. It's terrible. I'm devastated, obviously. And it's just as terrible that you're in here, because I don't really believe you had anything to do with it."

Opal's bowed head jerks up suddenly. "You don't?"

Ingrid shakes her head. "Of course, I don't. And I don't want you going down in flames just because Tobin Rue is trying to become the next million-dollar partner at his firm."

"The public defender, though. Ingrid, he was horrible. He was, well, he was even worse. Let's just leave it at that." Opal thinks about how the public defender put his hand on hers, about how he ogled her, and *why* he ogled her, but she doesn't want to bring up the dance club and her stripping past to Ingrid. This is a sore subject between them. It might distract Ingrid from why she's come. It might stop her from saying what Opal thinks she's about to say. What Opal *hopes* she's about to say. They used to have conversations back in the day about whether Ingrid would ever go back to practicing law. She was still putting all her eggs in that podcast business when Opal and she knew each other. It seemed a bit misguided, but Opal didn't want to say that. She'd supported Ingrid, in every way, thinking that would cement their friendship. It hadn't worked in the end, of course. It had backfired royally. But even as Opal supported the growing podcast business, she'd ask Ingrid occasionally if she missed practicing law. Ingrid would always say, "It would have to be the right case for me to consider going back. It would have to be the *exact right case*." Opal is hoping this is the moment they've both been waiting for.

"I'm not suggesting you go back to the public defender, Opal. I'm here to offer my own services. I want to take your case. I want to defend you."

Bingo.

"Ingrid! Really?" Opal feigns surprise. She knew Ingrid would come around eventually. She didn't believe it would be easy or quick, but she knew Ingrid wouldn't be able to help herself. Ingrid owes her, after all. Opal wants to be careful playing that card. *But Ingrid owes her.*

"Well, before you get too excited, let's not forget, it's been eight long years since I practiced law, and I wasn't even a criminal attorney. I was a litigator, yes, but corporate litigation is quite different in practice from criminal law and there will be a learning curve. It might be steep."

Opal knows Ingrid is still trying to talk herself out of this. She suffers through the self-deprecating statements by Ingrid. She ignores them. She remains quiet. Until Ingrid says "Do you really even want me to take this case on? In spite of our, you know, history?"

"Of course, I do." Opal holds Ingrid's gaze the way she did in the courtroom when Tobin was bumbling and crashing. "I want you to represent me *given* our history. Not *in spite of it.*"

Ingrid's shoulders relax. Opal hadn't realized just how nervous Ingrid was until she sees that subtle movement. So, Opal keeps on. "I want someone representing me who knows me. Not too many people in this town know the real me. You understand?"

Ingrid nods. She is picking at something on her shirt sleeve. Something that Opal can't see. Now, Ingrid seems fidgety and nervous for someone who is on that side of the plexiglass and not the other.

Opal thinks back to those days of friendship that they shared. A year, maybe more. A blip really, in the scheme of things, but still significant. Before it had all gone to hell, she had liked Ingrid. She had rooted for Ingrid. The Peter that Ingrid had described in their "girl talks" back then was a louse. A disinterested, unsupportive, emotionally unavailable jackass. She'd held Ingrid's hand while she'd talked for months about getting up the nerve to leave him.

"You were brave to make the decision to raise CJ on your own. Someday, I'll be as brave as you," Ingrid had said once. "I'll walk away. I won't worry that it will be hard on me or hard on Drake. I won't worry about what people will think or what it will mean to be completely on my own. I'll just leave and I won't look back. God knows this marriage is over."

Later, the Peter Opal would come to know was a different person than the one described by Ingrid all those years earlier. He was kind and compassionate. He loved hanging out with CJ and spoiled him with attention from the first day they met.

Well, the first day CJ *remembered* meeting him, anyway.

It turns out CJ didn't seem to make the connection that Peter was his old friend Drake's father. The first time Peter showed up to pick up Opal for a real date, CJ brushed past the babysitter and put his hand out and introduced himself as if it was the first time ever meeting the guy and Peter had gotten a real kick out of him. Neither he nor Opal ever reminded him that they'd met once before, sort of, under different circumstances.

The "Uncle Pete" moniker was Peter's idea. Opal didn't think it was a good idea. She thought they should take it slow. But Peter had insisted. "Someday, I hope to be in his life in a more permanent way. This is a good way to get used to the idea," Peter had reassured Opal as he held her face, just before he kissed her goodnight, the way he had to do too often, when he was expected at home, with Ingrid and Drake.

Once Opal got to know Peter the way she did, the guilt she felt was fleeting, at most. It lived in her brain like a long-ago memory she couldn't quite recall. After all, Opal knew that Ingrid didn't have a relationship with Peter. She didn't even love him. Their marriage had been over years earlier. She had told Opal so herself.

Now, behind scratched and scarred jailhouse plexiglass, Opal looks at Ingrid, and sees not a trace of grief on her face as she talks about Peter. Opal lets go for good of any residual guilt about falling in love with Peter. It wasn't anything she planned. No point in beating herself up about it. Ingrid certainly seems to have forgiven her. She's here offering to defend her in Peter's murder case, for heaven's sake.

But, wait.

Opal thinks about the several reasons Ingrid might want to take this case on. Some of them less noble than others. She might even want to make *sure* Opal gets convicted and locked away for good to punish her for falling in love with Peter. Opal needs to know, so she decides to ask about the elephant in the room.

"So, why you? I mean, don't get me wrong. I'm glad you're here and all. But tell me something. I know all about why Tobin was taking on my case. Law firm politics and all that. He couldn't stop talking about how this case was going to make him rich in the long run. But why are *you* interested in taking on my case?"

"I don't want people to believe you killed my husband."

Of course.

Opal feels a familiar disgust reclaiming her. "I'm not even good enough to kill your husband? Is that it? When you found out who I was before, I wasn't good enough to be your friend, and now I'm not even good enough to be your husband's murderer? You are too much, Ingrid. Maybe calling you was a bad idea after all."

The two women wait it out in silence for a few moments. Opal finally breaks it.

"Well, even still. You are probably my best defense right now. After all, you owe me, Ingrid."

Ingrid stands up and gathers her things. "I'll talk to Tobin and get the necessary substitution of counsel papers filed within the next few days."

As she walks out, Ingrid hears Opal ask from behind her, "I notice you're not asking me about that day. Why I was there when Peter died?" Her voice is lined with a sinister tone Ingrid doesn't ever remember hearing when they used to be friends.

Ingrid turns and looks at Opal. "None of that matters. What matters is that the prosecution can't prove you killed Peter. I don't need to know anything more than that." Ingrid hurries to the door, leaving Opal behind.

✧

Opal is led back to her jail cell where the quiet is deafening. She goes over everything in her mind. Despite the evidence that was mentioned at the arraignment, including that Opal was at the scene and that her bloody footprints have been found near the rock pit where Peter died, Ingrid seems ridiculously certain that Opal didn't kill Peter. She didn't question why Opal was there at the scene. All of which makes Opal suspicious.

Did Ingrid kill Peter?

Opal shudders to think that she was ever actually friends with that woman.

Of course, it was never her fault that the two of them had become fast friends. Ingrid had approached Opal first. Preschool orientation with CJ had been brutal. All those pretentious mothers with their expensive hair and manicures and husbands who had been regulars at DIVAS many times over. Before, during, and after their perfect little marriages. But Opal wasn't there for them. She was there for CJ. And she wasn't there to make friends.

When Ingrid had confronted her in the parking lot, she looked a little wild-eyed and for a moment Opal thought she was coming to confront her. Like she knew who she was. Who she had been.

But no.

Ingrid wanted to get the boys together. That sweet quiet shy boy was hers. And CJ seemed to like him, so why not? Opal never intended to make friends with Ingrid. She never intended to let her guard down, but those playdates became more and more frequent. And they involved regular coffee at Ingrid's kitchen table and something else that was quite unexpected: *friendship.*

Opal told Ingrid about how she'd always been good at science, and how after CJ was born, she went back to school and got her nursing degree. She told her how she'd worked on a commercial cleaning crew at night in the hospital while her toddler son slept in the onsite 24-hour hospital employee daycare. How she'd made connections at the hospital that panned out when she finally graduated with her nursing degree. At first, she left out the part about working as a stripper when CJ was first born. She left out the fact that she stockpiled the money she made stripping and used it later to help pay for nursing school. She left out how she escaped from that life.

But eventually, as Ingrid confided in Opal about her son, Drake, about his diagnosis of selective mutism, about how her marriage was struggling for many reasons, including the fact that his father wouldn't cooperate with his behavioral therapies, Opal felt like she had to give Ingrid more than she'd already given her.

One day she got her chance. The two women were sitting in Ingrid's living room, and the boys were on the floor putting together a puzzle.

"You can do one eye, and I'll do the other," CJ said to Drake.

"No, the monster's only got one eye. You can do it."

"Only one eye? Let me see."

Drake held up the puzzle box to CJ and the boys laughed and laughed.

"One eye!"

"Only one eye!"

"You do the eye!"

"No, you do the eye!"

Opal had looked over at Ingrid and seen tears rolling down her face. She understood. The casual and comfortable way that Drake was communicating was huge progress. She'd taken Ingrid's hand and said, "Come on. Let's go in the kitchen and let them play in here."

At the kitchen table, Ingrid wiped her eyes and launched

into a rambling show of gratitude. "I just can't thank you enough. CJ has been such a Godsend for Drake. He's so happy. So calm. Thank you, my friend. Thank you so much. I don't know what I would have done without you this last year. Between helping me get up the nerve to leave Peter—I mean, someday I will get that nerve up. You know what I mean. And with Drake, and with the business and the investors. I mean—you know. You've just done so much for me."

Opal took that as her cue. She took a deep breath and dove in.

"There's something I need to tell you. Something I don't usually share with people who didn't know me in the past, but honestly, Ingrid, you've become such a good friend to me. I *want* to share this with you."

Ingrid just smiled at Opal, open and ready. "What is it? You can tell me anything."

"Well, I just don't want you to look at me differently when you hear this. It's not an easy story."

"Opal, it's fine. Just tell me. I'm not going to think any differently of you. No matter what it is."

And so, she did. Opal told Ingrid about her days at the dance club working for a burly owner named Billy "The Mouse" Russo. About how her brother had apparently sold her to him for a gambling debt. About how Dean disappeared under questionable circumstances, never to be heard from again.

Opal told Ingrid that The Mouse had eventually been killed in the back of the dance club during a drug deal gone wrong. She described how all hell had broken loose then, and how she'd escaped the chaos out a back door of the club and literally ran five miles home in nothing but a bikini and ballet flats. She told Ingrid that when she'd arrived home to her apartment that night, sweating and gasping for breath, and barely dressed, she'd paid her nighttime babysitter who kindly asked no questions, not even that night, and how Opal promptly enrolled herself in nursing school and sent an online application for the hospital's nighttime cleaning crew.

The whole time, Ingrid looked at Opal with that same open expression, her eyes wide, nodding, inviting, and so Opal kept going.

"It's been a long road, but I finally feel safe. For the first time in a long time, I finally feel at peace in my life. I just wanted you to know my whole story."

Ingrid said it wouldn't change anything between them.

"Not a thing, Opal," she'd said again as she hugged her good-bye after the playdate was over.

But it turns out Ingrid was just another one of those people Dean had warned about. One of those people Opal had trusted too quickly. Ingrid never called Opal again after that kitchen table confession. She pulled her son out of school the next year and started homeschooling.

Over the next year, during the heavy ghosting silence from Ingrid, Opal often wondered whether Drake ever asked for CJ. She couldn't believe Ingrid wouldn't have given in and called Opal just to get the boys together, if nothing else. It was evident the friendship had been good for Drake. But Ingrid never called.

And then, a few years later, at the baseball park, they all saw each other in that encounter that turned out to be both pivotal and tragic. Incredibly, Drake didn't bother acknowledging CJ that day at the baseball park. Apparently, shallowness, like hair twisting and almond-shaped eyes, was hereditary.

Opal lays back down on her prison cot, thinking about her visitors of the day, and even though she's not sure she had many choices, she's starting to think that Ingrid might not have been her best choice for that one prison phone call after all.

Ingrid doesn't let her guard down until she's in her car, and driving through the security gate outside the jail. With the radio turned up loudly, headed southbound on the highway, she lets out a loud primal scream.

After the release she turns the radio off and drives in silence back home. This is going to be the hardest thing she has ever done. Harder than any case she's ever taken on. Harder than her marriage. Harder than grieving Peter. Harder than managing Drake's diagnosis and behavioral therapies.

Something has changed in Opal. Ingrid doesn't recognize her long ago friend. Is it possible that this last week in jail has hardened her so quickly? Or did something else change the woman Ingrid once knew? The truth is, even though Opal has been back in her life for some time now, carrying on with Peter behind her back, Ingrid hasn't actually seen Opal since that gruesome encounter on the baseball field last spring.

What a year it's been. Ingrid thinks.

It happened at the finale of Drake's one painful season of tee ball. He was terrible at every aspect of it and Peter was embarrassed at Drake's distracted performance on the field every time he came to a game. Ingrid could see Drake's raw anxiety that seemed to overflow every time a ball was coming near him. He ran away and not toward anything, but still, he jumped into the car excitedly whenever it was time for baseball practice or a game. Ingrid admired his optimism but it pained her, too. Peter stopped coming to the games altogether, and the result was a slightly less anxious Drake. Certainly, Ingrid felt more relaxed with Peter absent.

In a move that would later be regretted over and over again, Ingrid convinced Peter, begrudgingly, to come to the last tee ball of the season. There would be a parade and ice cream, and Drake was excited about it.

The last game.

Ingrid felt relief that the season was over. "Come," she pleaded with Peter. "It might be his last baseball game ever. It's a rite of passage. Come celebrate it with me. With *us.*"

"God, I *hope* it's the last one," Peter had said instead of *yes*. But he came nonetheless. In the car on the way over, Peter said,

"Come on, Drake. I want to see you play with focus today. No waving from the field. No daydreaming. Keep your eye on the ball. Got it?"

Drake had nodded earnestly and Ingrid refrained from slapping Peter the way she wanted to.

With Drake on the field one final time, close to the end of the game, Ingrid had seen Opal and CJ walking toward her as she stood near the fence at the third baseline.

"Hi," the women smiled at each other politely with a unison greeting.

Opal shielded her eyes. "Is that Drake out there? Look how tall he's gotten!" She waved furiously at him as did CJ, but Drake looked from Opal and CJ to his father standing nearby and then back at the batter as he'd been told. Ingrid apologized on his behalf. "He's just really trying to stay focused. Last game of the season and all that. CJ, do you play baseball?"

CJ shook his head. "I'm only here to watch a friend of mine from class. He's playing on that field over there. Mom, can I go over there and watch?" Opal nodded and CJ ran off to the nearby field. Ingrid stood uncomfortably, trying to think of some small talk to engage Opal, when she was startled by Peter standing next to her who gave out a loud: "WHAT THE HELL!"

"Peter!" Ingrid turned to him in shock. Peter was holding his arm and hopping in a circle. His face was flushed. His voice sounded strangled as he whispered: "Something stung me."

Opal turned to Peter and pulled his arm to her. "Are you allergic?" Opal guided Peter to sit down in the grass and everything that came next was sort of a blur with a bunch of questions being fired at Ingrid. She remembered Opal asking if Peter was on any other medications (*no*). Do you have your phone on you? (*yes*) Can you call 911 right now? (*stunned silence*).

No really, Ingrid, can you call 911 right now?

Opal reached in her bag and pulled out an epi-pen and stabbed Peter hard through his jeans. A local paramedic crew was already onsite, stationed at the baseball complex in case of emergencies and they arrived at the dirt roadway near where Opal and Peter were now sitting in the grass. Ingrid was mortified as they had all their lights and horns blaring and Drake's team stopped the game to allow the ambulance access near the field. Drake came running off the field to Ingrid, and she held him as he looked up at her questioning with his eyes only. "Daddy's fine, honey. He just got stung by a bee, and he has to go see the doctor. Don't worry."

By then a small crowd had gathered near the ambulance to gawk at Peter who was being cared for tenderly by the woman at his side who was not his wife. As Ingrid comforted Drake and the paramedics loaded Peter into the back of the ambulance, Opal gave all the instructions and details of what had happened. As Opal said "Goodbye" and "You're in good hands, now" to Peter just before the ambulance doors shut, Peter looked at Opal with an expression Ingrid was sure she'd never seen on Peter before, and Ingrid stood back with the other strangers, a voyeur to a moment of awakening between her husband and the woman who used to be her friend.

Just then CJ returned to his mother from the adjacent field to ask what all the commotion was. Ingrid and Drake ran to the car to follow behind the ambulance. She never even said goodbye to Opal and CJ. And when they all got home from the hospital that night, and after they put Drake to bed, Peter suggested they call that nice woman to thank her for saving his life.

Ingrid had launched an angry response at him. "You know what she is, don't you? She's a stripper. A whore. And you were looking at her like she was some kind of angel."

On the drive home from the jailhouse visit, Ingrid goes over the defense strategy in her mind. She's determined to fix this mess Peter has left for her.

As Ingrid makes the last turn into her neighborhood, she

thinks about Opal's ominous words earlier that afternoon. And about her initial phone call to Ingrid the night of her arrest.

You owe me, Ingrid.

Opal knows Ingrid's secrets. Well, some of them, at least. And if this goes south, Ingrid might be facing something much worse than humiliation caused by Peter's and Opal's actions.

Ingrid might have to face the music for what she herself has done as well.

CHAPTER 8
Everyone Has a Secret, Ingrid

A week later, Ingrid is climbing the steps of the Law Club, at Tobin Rue's invitation yet again. He's agreed reluctantly to sign off on the Motion to Substitute Counsel, even though Ingrid reminds him it's not really his decision to make.

"It's your client's decision," Ingrid points to the signature line and hands Tobin a pen so he can carry out the formality.

"I hope you know what you're doing, Ingrid. This seems to be a pretty locked-in case. If you're trying to resurrect your legal career, I'm not sure this is the way to do it."

Ingrid closes her eyes for a moment to keep her emotions in check in front of Tobin. She has never wanted to "resurrect" her legal career. She closed that chapter willingly, happy to take on a role of mother and later, entrepreneur, as she has worked hard to find balance in a life post-Park Avenue. The idea that she'd take on this case—*this* one of all cases—as a *career move* makes her feel violently hostile toward Tobin. She breathes deeply. She knows that this is not the time or the place to lose control. Not here at the Law Club, and certainly not in front of her late husband's best friend.

When her breathing is under control and she trusts herself to speak again, she says: "You know something, Tobin. They questioned me, too, that day."

"What do you mean?"

"They questioned me the day they found him dead. I passed out, and they revived me, and then they questioned me. They asked me questions about where I was on the day before, around the time Peter was likely killed."

"What's your point? That's pretty standard stuff, don't you think?"

"Well, I told them I was at Pilates, and they didn't even bother to ask me what the name of the Pilates studio was or who had seen me there. They asked if they could look around my house, without a warrant, and I let them. They walked around my house for about five minutes, found nothing incriminating, of course. They walked out empty handed from the whole encounter."

"I still don't understand your point."

"My point is that no one has really done their homework here, and it's a murder case without a weapon or a motive. So yeah, I think I know what I'm doing."

Tobin looks around and leans forward toward Ingrid.

"Ingrid. Don't be naïve."

"What is that supposed to mean?"

"It means, don't assume there aren't secrets at play here."

"What secrets are you talking about, Tobin?"

Tobin laughs like Ingrid has just said something ridiculous.

"Come on. Everyone has secrets, Ingrid. I'm just saying, don't assume there's been shoddy police work. Don't assume that the end isn't simply a foregone conclusion."

Tobin stands up, signaling an end to the lunch and Ingrid follows him, mulling over his words, and trying to discern the warning contained there. All around them sit lawyers and judges making quiet deals over shrimp cocktail and bourbon. She would be disgusted by all of it if she didn't still find a small bit of herself wanting in. She wonders if maybe Tobin is right. If maybe some part of her is hoping to breathe life into her legal career again. Maybe this case is bigger than Ingrid is giving it credit for.

Ingrid says goodbye to Tobin in the parking lot—a real good-bye—as she feels certain now that the obligatory condolence calls will wane and probably disappear entirely. "You doing ok?"

he asks as he hugs her goodbye.

"Yeah, how about you?"

"Well, you know, now that you've stolen my *pro bono* case away, I'll need to find some nonprofit to incorporate." He smiles and winks at her and Ingrid wonders anew if she should have just let Tobin represent Opal to a sure conviction.

"The preliminary hearing is set for six weeks from now," Tobin reminds Ingrid.

"If you need anything, feel free to call me."

"I know, I know. Don't worry. I've got this from here."

Tobin looks like he is going to say something. He opens his mouth to start and then shuts it again and sighs loudly. He reminds Ingrid a bit like a frustrated Drake in this posture, so she does what she is used to doing for Drake. She waits patiently.

And whether Tobin finally says the thing he always meant to, or whether he has decided instead to say something else entirely, Ingrid will never know. What she does know is that Tobin leans down and whispers in her ear before he leaves her in the Law Club parking lot: "Ingrid, just don't let this thing suck you in, ok? The ending is not under your control."

At home, Ingrid pays and says goodbye to Mary.

Mary has helped a lot to initiate a new routine in the last few days but Ingrid is still trying to find her stride, balancing both the podcast and her work on Opal's case. And if she's being honest, she's wary about leaving Drake alone with someone who is essentially a stranger. Especially now.

"Come on buddy, how about you help me make some dinner?" Drake nods enthusiastically and follows Ingrid into the kitchen.

"Macaroni and cheese?" More enthusiastic nodding. "Everything good with Mary?" Drake nods, and Ingrid watches him carefully to make sure he means it. As Ingrid starts assembling ingredients on the counter, she blocks out the thought that creeps in there unwittingly. The thought that this is the kind of meal Peter would have derided Ingrid for recently.

"How can you take a tray of fat and carbs and call it a dinner? There's not a single vegetable or healthy protein in there." He'd looked shocked the first time he'd come home and seen Ingrid and Drake spooning the gooey deliciousness into their mouths at dinnertime.

She let Drake grate the blocks of cheese while she prepared a roux and grated bread crumb topping. He was proud of their creation, and so was she. It was a recipe from her childhood, and yes, it looked nothing like the Keto-inspired creations she more often whipped up for Peter and herself, but she didn't understand why Peter was so dead set against letting Drake help make something a little less "healthy" every so often. Especially since Drake finished his whole meal for a change.

Ingrid had made that dish with her mother dozens of times over the years. Judy Barton was a devotee to home-cooked meals and starch. Making dinner was a way of connecting with her daughter when words or other means escaped her. Standing over the grater watching the cheese bits curl and fall one on top of another and then again and again, Judy would ask Ingrid how school was or if there were any boys at school she was interested in. Secrets were spilled over that cheese grater. Judy would share her own secrets, too. Ingrid grates cheese with Drake in silence and remembers one of her last dinners with her mother.

"Do anything wild today, Judy?" Teen Ingrid would use her mother's first name sparingly, and only on occasions like this when she was soliciting her mother's secrets.

"Just some light vigil work today. Hardly wild stuff."

"Can I go with you tomorrow?"

"Absolutely not. It's much too dangerous."

"But fine for you? That's hypocrisy, Mom."

"No, it's reasonable. When you're a grown-up, you can make your own decisions. But for now, I have to make them for you."

"How come Dad tries to make your decisions for you, still? You're a grownup, aren't you?"

Her mother's eyes got dark as they did each time they had this conversation, which was often at that point. Ingrid's mother had joined a small but vibrant activist group that lobbied hard for women's reproductive rights and the group had begun a week-long vigil at a newly opened women's clinic, helping young women get past the picketers.

Her father couldn't see the point. Ingrid heard his voice, soft and hurt, late at night when they thought she was asleep.

"Judy, after all we went through to have a baby, how can you help other women get rid of theirs?"

"I just can't stand the idea of these poor women having nowhere to go. They are not like us, Roy. The women that come to the clinic are alone and impoverished. They would have no access to medical care at all without that clinic. And the people who picket? They scream hateful, terrible things at these women who are on their own and terrified. I can't be on that side. I have to be on the side of those women."

"But Judy, look what you're helping them do! How can you feel good about the fact that many of these women are just coming to the clinic to kill a baby?"

"No, Roy. I hate that some of them are making that choice. Hate it. But it's not my choice to make. And it's not those hateful picketers' choice either. When I think back to that day when I found out I was pregnant with Ingrid, time stood still. I was so grateful and relieved and overjoyed. I look at these women facing the same news with such fear and I just feel so guilty to have had this much happiness in my life while others have had so little."

"Oh, Judy." Roy Barton had never really understood, and neither did Ingrid if she was being honest. It seemed her mother was getting all caught up fighting for strangers for reasons that were completely inaccessible. But still, when Ingrid heard Judy stand up for herself and her cause, it made Ingrid feel something that she recognized as pride. Unfortunately, Ingrid barely had a chance to enjoy that pride for Judy's activism work, because by the end of that vigil week, Judy was gone.

Drake asks Ingrid, "Can I try?"

Full of emotion as she thinks about Judy Barton's last week and hears Drake use his words carefully and tentatively, she nods and hands the grater over to him. He seems to remember that Peter hated this meal, as he turns to her and says, "We love this mac and cheese. You and me."

"Yes, we do, sweetie." Ingrid pushes hair out of Drake's eyes.

Ingrid had mentioned Peter's over-the-top reaction to the mac and cheese to Gabby. In hindsight, she has no idea *why* she'd mentioned it to Gabby but she had. Probably because there was no one else *to* mention it to. Gabby had clucked her gum, looked up from the toys she was helping Ingrid clean up in the playroom, and said, "Sounds like Peter is watching his figure. Better watch out or he'll come home with a red sports car next!" She winked as she said it, to lighten the mood, and Ingrid had forced a chuckle. But the seed was sown.

Ingrid's suspicions were up.

Peter might indeed be starting on a midlife crisis.

Peter might be contemplating having an affair.

Peter might already be having an affair.

That was about a month after the incident at the baseball field, when Opal had shown up like Florence Nightingale with her own never-used epi-pen and a glowing smile. Peter's warm response to Opal, and Ingrid's vicious response to Peter had of course already been on her mind. But after Gabby's offhand comment and wink, Ingrid started thinking about the event in a whole new way. She started watching Peter more carefully.

It was only much later that Ingrid realized *Gabby* was the one she should probably have been watching more carefully.

Later that night, after making a tray of homemade macaroni and cheese and eating it without any criticism from Peter, Ingrid lies in bed, and counts the number of words she's heard Drake say all day and the day before, and she worries about dropping a ball or two.

Before taking on Opal's case, Ingrid hadn't taken her focus off Drake in a long while. Indeed, Peter used to tell her she was much too obsessed with Drake and that it wasn't healthy. Ingrid found it easy to dismiss him when he said things like that.

Gabby had told Ingrid exactly the opposite.

"I wish I had a mom like you. The way you dote on Drake? It's amazing."

Ingrid basked in the glow of Gabby's approval. If she thought too hard about the pleasure she derived from her 25-year-old babysitter's approval, she'd feel a flush of embarrassment, so she tried not to think too hard about it.

Nevertheless, as Peter started spending less and less time at home, Ingrid started relying more and more on Gabby. They cooked together and folded laundry together. Gabby had a never-ending supply of energy and it was infectious. She insisted she didn't want to leave at the end of her shift. She was always offering to do one more thing to help Ingrid with Drake. Ingrid was so grateful if even just to hear another person talking in the house at the end of the day.

In between babbling about what an amazing mom Ingrid was and what a little genius Drake was, Gabby would drop little nuggets of information about the childhood she'd left behind.

Gabby had moved from Ohio to New York straight out of high school with a wallet full of babysitting money and a head full of dreams cultivated from four years in a row of being picked as the lead in her high school musical. But she lacked a real network of familial support.

"My mom's always been much more interested in her latest boyfriend than actually being a mom." Gabby told Ingrid one time over a sink full of dishes.

Ingrid felt her heart ache for this girl who was far from home, and seemingly motherless, much like herself. "Oh, Gabby, I'm sorry. I'm sure she loves you and is proud of you even if she has a hard time showing it."

Gabby had landed as Ingrid's babysitter after her dreams of Broadway fell through for good, and while Ingrid knew she should be encouraging her to pursue something a little more permanent, a little more grown-up, she couldn't deny that having Gabby around for both herself and Drake was a wonderful thing.

Until it wasn't.

CHAPTER 9
Slow Clap for You, Girlfriend

It's a few days before Ingrid is able to set up her podcast microphone in her kitchen again, dialing in @Josie_Is_Clean_Now for their rescheduled session. She's nervous about whether the taping will actually happen or not. A few scheduled guests have begun canceling on her. They've made up seemingly valid excuses about "schedule conflicts" and "diminished sponsorship budgets," but Ingrid wonders if there really *is* such a thing as bad publicity. It seems maybe people don't want to be associated with her given Peter's death and the increasingly high profile of the murder trial. She can't let everything she's worked for go down the drain. She has high hopes that her decision to represent Opal will help turn around the negative publicity.

"Ingrid, how wonderful to see you." Josie's kind eyes greet her as she arrives in high definition in front of Ingrid, and Ingrid sighs deeply in relief.

"Josie, thank you for agreeing to reschedule. I am so excited to talk to you today. Anything we need to get out of the way before I start the recording?"

"No problem. I'm excited about this as well. Oh, and Ingrid, before we start? I just have to say, I've read in the paper that you've taken on that woman's defense."

Ingrid nods and is about to quickly change the subject when Josie says, "God, I have to say. It's amazing. Truly inspiring. It does look from the outside like they're simply trying to make a case against this woman based on her bad choices of the past.

As a recovering mess myself, I felt for her. I did. When I saw her story, I thought, well, there but for the Grace of God, go I, you know? But, holy cow, what *you're* doing? To take on the defense of your husband's accused murderer? How easy it would be to simply look away and let whatever happens happen in your grief! But you're diving in. And taking action. And making sure justice is served. It's truly amazing. Slow clap for you, girlfriend."

Ingrid smiles, happy she didn't dismiss Josie before she got to lob all that praise her way.

This is working. This is already working, Ingrid thinks as she hits record.

Opal is trying hard to will sleep to come but it's useless. She always has a hard time sleeping whenever they serve carrots at dinner. You'd think it would be the mystery meat, or the glue-like oatmeal, or something, anything, else besides carrots. But, no, it's always the carrots.

She can't eat them. Even though she's mostly starving here and enters the dining hall ravenous each night, if they are serving carrots, she has to push them off her plate into a napkin before her gag reflex sets in. It's an old trigger from childhood. Her alcoholic mother would always, without fail, make carrots after a long bender. Something about being drunk for days on end, leaving Dean and Opal to fend for themselves, eating beans out of the can because they didn't know how to work the stove, or eating the remains left behind in the cereal boxes that filled the neighbors' recycling bins each week, always led to ... carrots.

It was Dean who had learned at some point that the neighbors' kids always dumped the cereal boxes into the recycling bins with the crumpled cereal bags still left inside. They were never completely empty. Just filled with some leftovers and the decadent sugary powder that the kids didn't bother finishing.

Dean and Opal would scour those recycling bins each week and hide the cereal dust in their rooms to enjoy when their parents predictably went missing as they did every few months or so.

And then her mother would reliably return with carrots as the peace offering. They must have been the cheapest, healthiest food she found in her haze. Opal couldn't stand the things. Cooked, raw, it didn't matter. But she'd choke them down, just to please her mother. To show her what a good girl Opal could be, if only her mother could stay sober and clean forever now.

She'd sit through the meal and the façade and the pretend promises and apologies, and later she'd vomit the carrots back up again in the bathroom, and go to bed hungrier than ever, with a belly ache worse than any night of hunger during her parents' drunken absences.

Carrots are bad.

The first time she'd shared that bit of her history with Peter, he'd held her in his arms and told her everything would be ok. That she'd never have to eat carrots again. He'd reminded her that she had survived that and so much more and that everything would be good from here on out.

But now, here she was, still having carrots forced on her. In jail. And Peter was gone. And CJ was gone. And it seemed pretty clear that she hadn't survived a single fucking thing.

CHAPTER 10
I Can Help You

On Tuesdays and Wednesdays Ingrid heads to a local coffee shop to work on the case. On these two days she has reserved Mary for a large chunk of time, and she takes advantage of the help to get a change of scenery, review the prosecution's discovery documents and brush up on her criminal procedure rules. She has a preliminary hearing to get ready for and the date is rapidly approaching. She is nervous enough about the imminent court appearance to have put all her podcast guests on hold for six weeks. She knows it's a risk, and as she queues up old episodes to replay, she stares at the file for Opal's case and wonders what she has taken on.

While she works, the pre-recorded podcast segment plays in her earphones. Listening to these interviews carefully curated and created over the years helps her keep her focus. The one she's listening to now is a particular landmark in her podcast career.

This guest was one of her first big gets. Ingrid had actually paid *her* to appear on the podcast, instead of the other way around. Ingrid had come up with a plan that if she could secure a few big gets, others would follow. She'd explained the business model to Opal *(who knows? Maybe Ingrid Rossellini will come on the podcast someday!)* and Opal had looked at her with naked skepticism, but still supported Ingrid's dreams with lip service, and even came up with the way of getting Ingrid the capital to pay her first (and as it turns out last) paid guest. Advertising revenue started streaming in shortly afterward. It all worked out as Ingrid planned.

Well, almost.

Ingrid takes a break from listening to the podcast replay to go onto her *Too Busy To Die* social media channels where she's shared several recent replay episodes. Thousands of likes, shares, and comments float under the posts, and she scrolls through quickly just to assure herself that people are still listening. People are. Yes, there are many, many comments that reference Peter's death and the trial, but mostly people are listening to what she has to say about living the kind of life you don't have to escape or hide from. Ingrid is about to close out from a recent thread, when one comment catches her eye.

I'm so proud of you.

She pauses only a moment before she hits "x" to close the screen. She feels a chill up her spine as if a ghost from the grave has reached out to her.

Ingrid turns back to the case file, but she's distracted by thoughts of Drake. It's been nearly three weeks since Peter's death, and after almost complete silence, Drake has been speaking a bit more to Ingrid over the last week. Mostly, logistical questions and sentences.

Can I skip math today?

Read this one.

I hate string beans.

He hasn't said a word about Peter. Not a word.

Ingrid sat with Drake in his room on the night of the funeral, while he was clad in his favorite mismatched pajamas, and explained to him that Peter was dead. That he'd gone to heaven, and that he wouldn't be coming home. She had read an article penned by a child psychologist that advised being very clear and emphasizing that death was final. There was nothing in there about the talk of heaven—she'd ad libbed that part—but Drake accepted her explanation and other than a few tears as she hugged him that night, he seemed to have moved on readily from the idea of Peter.

Much more easily than Ingrid has, in fact.

Ingrid is having trouble sleeping. Her mind has been racing day and night with thoughts that mostly center around the trial and things she still doesn't know or understand about the prosecution's case.

If they have truly produced everything they have—and by law they are required to do so at this point—then they really have not much at all.

The file contains transactional documents regarding the purchase of the Russell Street property by Peter's development company. There were plans to renovate the existing warehouse building on the site into luxury loft-style apartments with a courtyard and pool. Excavation for the pool had begun, and the rocks that had been pulled from the huge gaping pit in the courtyard had been arranged in small piles around the hole that would later become a resting place for bikini-clad singles with enough disposable income and good credit to lease the high-end units which were expected to be finished by the fall.

Photographs of Peter's body lying at the bottom of the excavated pit had gutted Ingrid when she first opened the file. She'd put them away and brought them out again after a few glasses of wine.

The file also contains photographs of the surrounding rock piles and shoe prints in Peter's blood that are believed to be Opal's, a coroner's report that assigned the cause of death to blunt force trauma of the head, and the time of death as between 12-5 pm. Also, the transcript of a 911 call that was placed anonymously at 8 pm that day has been produced.

Check the property behind 3511 Russell Street. You'll find Peter DiLaurio there. And he's not, I don't think he—well, I don't think he'll be alive when you find him. I can't say any more than that. Just. God. Please just don't leave him any longer than he's already been there.

The call, now a digital file produced in the case, was made from a blocked number but traced back to a cell phone registered in Opal Rowen's name. An expert witness report has been produced stating that the shoe prints on the scene also belonged to Opal Rowen, the same shoes she was actually wearing at the time of her arrest, and that the murder weapon was probably one of the rocks taken from the rock pile above the location where Peter's body was found, and that his head wounds were consistent with being struck with a rock both in the front and back of his head.

The file also contains pages upon pages of incident reports from seven years earlier pertaining to the DIVAS Dance Club on Route 92 and a mugshot of Opal from the same time period. Apparently, she was arrested once before for assaulting an unnamed patron during an incident at DIVAS that had resulted in the police being called to the scene. The incident report is skimpy, as is the outfit Opal is wearing in her mugshot. Her breasts are nearly completely exposed, and Ingrid is horrified that whoever took the mugshot that day used an uncharacteristically and inappropriately wider angle than usual. Opal had been brought in and processed, but the unnamed patron declined to press charges, and the case against Opal had been summarily dismissed.

There is also a stack of records relating to other real estate acquisitions by Peter's company. Ingrid hasn't gone through those documents thoroughly just yet; she plans to look through them this week, but she can't imagine they'll have any relevance to the case.

It seems the prosecution's whole case rests on the fact that Opal had been there at the scene either just before or just after Peter died, and that she'd phoned the police to let them know where to find him, albeit anonymously—or so she thought—and that she'd had a rather colorful past, including assaulting an unnamed male patron at a strip club where she worked, seven years earlier.

Ingrid didn't know much about criminal law, but she knew the case against Opal was tenuous at best. She was tempted to treat it as an "easy" case, but Tobin's words of admonition rang in her ears.

Come on. Everyone has secrets, Ingrid. I'm just saying, don't assume there's been shoddy police work. Don't assume that the end isn't simply a foregone conclusion.

As Ingrid pages again through the sparse file, and jots down notes and research regarding arguments she can use to have Opal's prior work and arrest history excluded from this case altogether, she keeps wondering what secrets Tobin was talking about. She wonders why the police and prosecution are so willing to pin Opal with Peter's murder.

And why, she wonders, when exhaustion gets the better of her, *am I standing in the way?*

While she's researching and reading in the coffee shop, Ingrid gets a call from a number she doesn't recognize. She lets it go to voicemail, and then retrieves the voicemail immediately.

It's a woman asking if Ingrid is taking on new clients for the consulting arm of *Too Busy to Die.* Ingrid would normally ignore such a call. In the early years of the business, she'd hire herself out as a consultant to clean out closets and declutter pantries: a sort of practice-what-you-preach exercise to complement the fledgling podcast. But she hasn't had to hire herself out for such gigs in years, not since the sponsorships and ad revenue began rolling in.

Yet, even though those consulting days are largely in the past, Ingrid can't bring herself to ignore this new voicemail from a woman named Jane Stewart. The name, though relatively common, is particularly familiar to Ingrid since Jane Stewart was a law partner at Ingrid's former Park Avenue firm. Ingrid wonders if it could possibly be the same person, and so she calls her right back.

Ingrid tells Jane she's sorry, that she's overextended, but that she simply wanted to call her back.

Just as a courtesy.

"I know you're busy. And I know you're back in the law game. Good for you. I'd like to chat—former colleague to former colleagues. You available?"

Ah, so it *is* her. It's the same Jane Stewart Ingrid used to work with a decade ago. The same woman who would never sponsor Ingrid for the Law Club, or help her rise in the ranks of the firm before she left. But now? Now she wants to chat: *former colleague to former colleague.*

Ingrid is annoyed but also curious, a familiarly dangerous combination.

Jane wants to meet for coffee in their mutual town of Riversedge, a place where they've been living a few blocks from each other all these years, but never once gotten together socially.

Riversedge is only impersonating a small town.

Ingrid feels like reminding Jane of this fact, but she doesn't. Instead, Ingrid tells Jane that she is at a downtown coffee shop right now, doing work, and happy to wait there for another half hour. Jane calls her bluff.

I'll be right there.

When Jane arrives, Ingrid notes that she has changed very little in the last decade. During the time Ingrid worked on Park Avenue, Jane was the only female law partner in Ingrid's department. She's wearing the same sleek grey bob and beautifully tailored pantsuit Ingrid remembers from the last time she saw her. Jane is in her late 60's; maybe older, it's hard to tell. She really has aged very little in the last decade. After she greets Ingrid with a firm handshake and takes a seat at her table, Ingrid says, "Wow. It's been a while, hasn't it?"

"Actually," Jane says, "not as long as you think. I saw you with Tobin Rue a few weeks ago at the Law Club. I was happy to see you, but I didn't get a chance to say hello before you left. I wanted to tell you that it's been wonderful to watch your post-law success. I wanted to mention, too, that I listen to you on my Friday morning commute."

"You listen to my podcast?" Ingrid asks, with a little pride commingled with surprise.

"Indeed, I do."

The two women sit in silence and for a moment, Ingrid wonders if Jane has simply come here to tell her these things and only these things. But then Jane continues on.

"I've scrolled around your website, and I see you take on consulting clients. I'd really like you to take me on."

"I'm so sorry. I really don't do that anymore. You know, organizing closets and such."

Jane looks down at the table, and then murmurs, "I need a good deal more than my closets organized."

When Jane looks up, Ingrid realizes that she's misjudged just how much Jane has actually aged in this last decade. It's like Jane's whole face has relaxed now, and a bone-tired expression has been revealed behind the mask.

"Not one day, Ingrid."

"Excuse me?"

"Stage four lung cancer and I've never smoked a day in my life. Not a one."

"Oh, I'm so sorry." Ingrid feels a pang of guilt for her anger at Jane never getting her into the Law Club. It seems like a silly thing to hold against someone, especially someone who is now dying.

"So am I. My doctor says I have about six months, maybe a year if I'm lucky. I got the whole 'get your affairs in order' talk. And believe me, a few months ago, if you'd have asked me, I'd have said, 'my affairs *are* in order.' But when you look at things, really look at them, you start to realize how truly wrong you are. About everything.

"Oh I—"

"I never got around to having children. I mean, I used to think I would get around to it. Possibly when I was in my 40s; even when I turned 50, I didn't rule it out. But I never did. So now, my niece and nephew are the sole heirs to my fairly sizable estate, and I want to go through my things before I just turn everything over to them."

"You never married?" Ingrid asks. She's trying to figure a way out of this. She's still getting through Peter's death. She's not sure she's ready to take on the death preparations of this woman she doesn't know so well anymore, and never really liked when she did.

"No, I never did. Although, to be honest, unlike having children, that was something I never *did* believe I'd get around to doing." She chuckles at her own joke. Ingrid tries to laugh, too, to make the moment less awkward, but it comes out more as a hiccup.

"I was always married to my career, and now, it turns out, my career isn't the least bit interested in helping me get my affairs in order, or sitting at my bedside as I die."

Ingrid flinches at her bluntness. Jane sees and apologizes. "Sorry, it's just that I don't really have time now for all the soft language people would like me to use about dying. My own partners have cut me loose. They gave me a nice package and exercised the termination clause on my equity agreement. Assholes."

Ingrid doesn't remember Jane ever cursing when they were practicing law together. She was very formal, very tight-laced and highly wound. Another person might have referred to her as a "bitch" but Ingrid resisted such characterizations of female peers. Jane was tough and aloof, though. No doubt about it. In fact, she never once hosted a single social event in her Riversedge apartment that apparently overlooked the actual river's edge that the town was named for. Rumors about the opulence that the single female partner of their department lived in were wide-spread but largely unconfirmed as Jane always held everyone at the office, including Ingrid, at arms' length.

Until now, that is.

"So. Can you take me on, Ingrid?"

Ingrid resists after making the customary apologies and sad

speeches about how sorry she is to hear this news. She isn't going to take on a new consulting client. Not at this time, anyway. She waves her hands over the papers and open computer screen in front of her. She fans the pages of the yellow legal pad in front of her containing pages upon pages of notes.

"Yes," Jane says. "I know all about how you've taken on the defense of the woman accused of murdering your husband. I have to admit. It's curious."

Ingrid is annoyed that Jane has used the word "curious" instead of "heroic" or "amazing." She shakes it off quickly. "Yes, well, so you see, the timing is just terrible."

"Well, maybe the timing is actually quite perfect," Jane says.

"Perfect? How so?"

"I can help you. You were a brilliant, talented legal mind. I always admired your creativity."

"Did you? Thank you."

"You were bull-headed, though, too. I can remember several examples of your stubborn perseverance. No, I see in your face, you think I may be insulting you. But I'm not. I think stubbornness is a necessary and endearing quality in lawyers, especially female lawyers. And now, I see on your face that you think I'm being sexist. No, I'm not. I'm being factual. Anyway, I'm not entirely surprised you've taken something like this on, but the truth is, you never really worked on a criminal docket before, did you?"

Ingrid shakes her head sheepishly. Jane seems to be able to read her every thought through her face so she tries to hold her face more stoically.

Jane nods enthusiastically. "I can help you. I handled my fair share of white-collar crime back in the day. Much better pay than your typical murder clients, I guarantee you that. But, still. The same rules apply. I can mentor you. On the side. A barter of sorts. No one needs to know. You help me get my affairs in order. I'll pay you your customary consulting fees, and also, I can help you."

I can help you. These words: they are intoxicating for Ingrid at a time when she is so desperately alone. They are like an oasis in the desert. She's not sure she can trust them at all. She wants to grab them but she's afraid all she'll be left with is hot, dry sand.

If Jane is serious about paying Ingrid to consult for the next few weeks, she can put her podcast on the backburner, albeit temporarily. She can continue replaying old taped segments, and take a little time off from hustling for advertising revenue and guests, focusing only on the trial looming over her. She can direct all her attention strictly on representing Opal, and getting her own life with Drake back on track, and then, she hopes, things with the business will sort themselves out later on.

While she's debating and thinking, Ingrid's phone rings, and while she knows it's rude, she takes it anyway, putting a finger up to Jane. She needs a moment to decompress from Jane's words and proposal, even if it is just another potential consulting client she needs to turn down.

It isn't. It's Opal's social worker.

"Ingrid. I'm so glad you picked up. The temporary foster family that Opal's son, CJ, was placed with the night of the arrest, cannot keep him any longer. He's going to move homes again."

Ingrid rubs her eyebrows. This is sad news, but she's not sure why she's the one getting a call about it. And then comes the punchline. "Opal wants you to take him. She asked me to call you."

"Me? Of course not. I have a perfectly full plate. A much-too-full plate, as a matter of fact. I have a case to try. *Opal's murder case.* And a dead husband. And a son to raise alone. And," Ingrid looks over at Jane, "a new consulting client."

Jane looks radiant. Her face looks young again. "So, you're taking me on after all?" she stage whispers from across the table.

Ingrid nods her head and shakes right hands with Jane while still holding the social worker's call in the other.

"Bottom line. I can't take Opal's son in."

The social worker sighs with defeat on the other end. "Well, can you at least do me a favor? The relocation was so sudden. Opal says he needs his favorite teddy bear to help with the transition. She says no one bothered to get it before the first placement and she really wants me to get it along with a few other things from the house and take it to him. The police still have the place cordoned off. Can you meet me there in an hour? I might need a good lawyer to help me out."

It takes Ingrid a moment to realize that when the social worker says she needs a "good lawyer" she's talking about *her*.

"Yes." Ingrid says to both Jane and to the social worker. And as soon as she says the word, she already knows she's agreed to way too much.

CHAPTER 11
Some Kind of a Superhero

At Opal's house, there are several members of the press standing on the lawn and a handful of trucks with various news logos on their flanks. Ingrid is incredulous as she pulls up to the curb, thinking for a moment that they've been camped here around the clock for weeks ever since Opal's initial arrest. But as she gets out of the car, and they swarm her with questions, she realizes they are here for a new reason. A development that they seem to have heard about before Ingrid. She's embarrassed to be behind the curve, but she holds her face still and tries not to let her embarrassment show as they barrage her with questions. Her meeting with Jane earlier that day reminded her how much of her emotions she wears openly on her face when she's not careful.

Mrs. DiLaurio, what do you know about the new body that's been found?

Do you think the police's finding of a new body at the old DIVAS lot helps your client's case or hurts her?

What can you tell us about the newly found remains?

Ingrid waves them off angrily and stomps her way to the front door, annoyed that she's been so busy reading the sparse file the prosecutor produced and talking with Jane and taking care of Drake that she failed to read a single piece of news in the last two days. Whose body was found? What are they talking about? She'll be damned before she'll let them know she has no idea what they mean. She is almost to the door where a woman in an ill-fitting grey dress is standing with a beige tote bag under her arm decorated with the insignia for the county's child services department.

One female reporter, who introduces herself as Angela from Channel 62 as she shoves a microphone in Ingrid's face, stops Ingrid on her trek from the car to the social worker. Ingrid recognizes her as the field reporter she saw on the television screen that first night after the police showed up to tell Ingrid that Peter had been found dead. Apparently, Angela has been covering this story from day one.

Mrs. DiLaurio, are you really defending your husband's murderer?
Was she his mistress?
Did he know she had a sordid past as a stripper?
Why are you coming back here to her home?

Ingrid stops and faces Angela and her microphone. She realizes too late that this is a mistake. "Leave me alone please. I'm just here getting some of my client's son's belongings. Have a little decency."

"Are you taking him in?"

"Of course not. How do you know so much, anyway?"

"How do you know so little, Ingrid?"

Ingrid ignores her stinging words.

"I've heard from my sources that the son needs a new place to stay. Are you going to let your husband's mistress's son stay in foster care?"

"Stop calling her my husband's mistress. There's no proof of that."

"Right, no proof. You're such a lawyer. So are you really committed to getting her acquitted? Or do you know this is a lost cause and that's why you're taking in the son, too? Is this all your way of getting revenge on this woman who stole your husband and then killed him?"

"God, no. What do you think I am? And I didn't say I'm taking in her son. I'm just here to get some of his belongings. You're like vultures, aren't you?"

AMY IMPELLIZZERI

"Ok. Sorry. No one blames you for not wanting to take in the son of your husband's mistress and accused murderer out of the kindness of your heart. I mean only some kind of a super-hero could do something like that."

"What did you say?"

Angela just smiles at her with the microphone flush against Ingrid's face. Ingrid pushes the microphone away and turns again toward the door where the social worker is waiting for her with her child services tote bag, summoning her and shaking her head as she calls out, "No, Ingrid, don't talk to them."

Everyone seems to know more than Ingrid.

A police car pulls up then into the driveway and the press moves away from Ingrid to gather around the newcomer instead.

A muscular, good-looking man in a uniform gets out of the police car, ignores the questions about a newly found body and what it means to Opal Rowen's case, and makes it to the front door in just a few strides showing Ingrid how she should have made the same trip. Too little, too late.

"Margaret." The officer greets the social worker, and her own name makes her blush.

"Officer Tim." Margaret all but curtsies, and Ingrid rolls her eyes.

Sure, he's cute, but come on.

"Margaret, please tell me you weren't going to go in without me, were you? You know that's against the rules."

"Of course not, Officer Tim," Margaret giggles. "I was just waiting for you. And Mrs. DiLaurio, of course."

Officer Tim locks eyes with Ingrid like he's just noticing her standing there for the first time. "Ah, the famous Mrs. DiLaurio. Heard a lot about you. Haven't had the pleasure yet." He reaches out his hand. Ingrid leaves it there and nods at him instead. "Nice to meet you. If we could make this relatively quick and painless, that would be great. We'd like to go in and get some of the little boy's things to take with him to the next foster family."

100

"Well, of course. I'm simply here to make sure no one tampers with any potential evidence, which I'm sure no one was planning on doing anyway, right?"

Ingrid sighs. For God's sake, the man just *winked at her.*

"Right. Ok then. Let's just get going."

Margaret is still giggling annoyingly. She stops long enough to tell Ingrid. "I have a list of things Opal asked us to get him. A special toothbrush, some of his favorite pajamas, a spiderman action figure, and a stuffed teddy bear he loves and misses apparently."

Ingrid feels a pang for this little boy who was always so kind to her Drake. He's stuck with strangers now, without anything familiar, without his favorite things, and worst of all, without his mother.

As they enter the house, Ingrid sees the entranceway of a bedroom down the hall with yellow crime scene tape blocking it off.

"What's down there, Officer?" Ingrid asks out loud despite her best judgment.

"Opal's room."

Ingrid is tempted to run past Officer Tim and into that blocked off room. She's tempted to ransack the shelves and drawers. Right down to the underwear drawers, no matter how cliché.

She's tempted to look for evidence of Peter, traces of her husband that he must have left in this house when he was still alive. And Ingrid is suddenly glad that Officer Tim is here winking and flirting, if only because he and the crime scene tape are standing between Ingrid and the room of the woman Peter last loved in life. She looks away. Just as she didn't want to see Peter's dead body, Ingrid doesn't want to see where he was last truly alive. She doesn't want to know. She doesn't think she can stand it.

"Ok, where's the little boy's room?"

In CJ's room that is decorated haphazardly with basketballs, dinosaurs, and superheroes, Ingrid helps Margaret stuff the beige tote bag with the requested items, as Officer Tim stands in the doorway looking on. Ingrid surveys the room. She looks at the bookshelf and wonders if Peter ever helped CJ pick out a bedtime story or played dinosaurs with him. She wonders if Peter was more patient with CJ than he was with his own son. Whether he loved him more than he loved his own son. She shudders and turns her back on the bookshelf, ready to leave this whole place behind. Peter, it seems, is more present in CJ's room than she was prepared for.

Ingrid grabs Margaret's arm. "Come on, let's get out of here." Officer Tim leads the women back out toward the front door where, just on the other side, is the front lawn covered with barking, loud reporters.

In her jail cell, Opal has decisions to make.

Well, one major decision, actually. She has to decide who she will trust.

Ingrid has decided to take on her defense, but Opal fears she's doing it for her own selfish reasons. Opal knows better than to trust the woman she wronged. She hopes that Ingrid will put her best effort into her defense, because Ingrid is desperate that people stop connecting Opal with Peter even in death. But still, Opal doesn't trust her. She is growing certain that Ingrid is responsible in some way for Peter's death and now fears that she has made a big mistake trusting Ingrid with her defense.

Should she trust Peter? Peter told her everything would be all right. *If anything happens to me, everything is in place. Don't worry.* Opal is tempted to trust him. Even though he's gone. He promised her that he wouldn't let anything happen to her. But she knows better. He can't protect her anymore, and she's been down this road in the past. She's been betrayed by so many.

Her parents. The Mouse. Dean.

She's lost so many people in her life. She knows not to trust people who have gone and died on her, so she doesn't trust Peter either.

Opal stares down at the letter in her lap. This. This is what she will trust. This is *who* she will trust. The letter is crumpled and smudged through with Opal's tears. And it's not the content of the letter that has convinced her he's the one to trust. Because the letter itself is poorly written and littered with lies. But the truth is, if she doesn't let him help her, then she may never get home to her son. And that is simply not an option.

Officer Tim stands on the lawn amidst the noisy reporters, and smiles and waves at Ingrid and Margaret as they pull away, as if they are headed off on an adventure. Ingrid notices Angela from Channel 62 standing by his side pushing the microphone toward him, but he just pushes it gently away and continues smiling and nodding.

As she drives away from the house behind Margaret's sedan, Ingrid replays Angela's words in her head.

Only some kind of a superhero would do something like that.

Ingrid lets herself think about her first superhero, her mother, doing what she considered noble work. Work that got her killed in front of a women's clinic less than a mile from their home.

"Fifteen is too young to lose a mother." Roy Barton said it often and it was the only thing Ingrid and he seemed to agree on after Judy's death.

Roy took an early retirement, allegedly to take care of Ingrid, but his attention was devoted to a growing whiskey habit and not on Ingrid at all. Ingrid tried to bring him out of his grief. She planned projects around the house: cleaning out closets and reorganizing the kitchen pantry. She tried to keep him busy.

Sometimes he humored her. She thought maybe it was working.

But then on Ingrid's 18th birthday, he put a towel in the exhaust hose of his running car, leaving an empty bottle of Wild Turkey and a note to Ingrid on the kitchen counter. He explained that he'd waited until she was 18, so she wouldn't have to "go to foster care or anything like that. I couldn't live with myself if you had to be raised by strangers." It seemed Roy wanted to die with his sense of irony well intact.

The slow fuse of anger Ingrid had felt toward her father following Judy's death erupted into a burning blaze that day. She had suspected many times after Judy died that she wasn't enough to live for and she hated Roy for confirming that fact on her 18th birthday.

Ingrid used the small pot of insurance money her mother had left her to pay for college and later, law school, where she hoped to redirect her quest for fairness and justice that seemed stilted in the wake of her mother's death. Where Judy's world was grey, Ingrid sought a world much more black and white. While her father had failed her spectacularly, Ingrid was determined to succeed.

At a stop sign, staring at Margaret's tail lights, Ingrid thinks about how she's now working on this completely ridiculous case and suddenly, every single line in her life is blurry, an unfamiliar feeling that has created a posthumous kinship with her mother, long gone. Ingrid thinks about Drake sitting at home working on homeschooling lessons with no father, while his mother, who used to be home all the time and doting on his every move, is now running around town, studying in coffee shops, and eating at the Law Club, cleaning out crime scenes, and bartering with white collar crime attorneys so she can clear his father's name in death. She thinks about the little boy, CJ, who was once so good to her son that he created a friendship out of Ingrid and his mother: two unlikely companions. She thinks about what is being asked of her.

Maybe it's a reasonable request after all.

At the first stop light they encounter after leaving Opal's home, Ingrid flashes her high beams on Margaret ahead of her. On and off. On and off. She sees Margaret look up in the rear-view mirror at her and Ingrid waves her hands in front of her to signal to Margaret, who simply shrugs and looks over her shoulder as if to say: *I have no idea what you want.*

Ingrid's phone is in a holster plugged into the dashboard and she reaches for it, quickly scans for the last incoming call and returns it. Margaret's voice comes on the Bluetooth speaker.

"Hello?"

"Margaret, what would it take to transfer CJ to my care tonight? Just temporarily, of course. Is that something you could make happen?"

"Absolutely. Thank you, Ingrid!"

Margaret's words fill Ingrid's car over the speakers and the deadening silence after she immediately hangs up to start the process fills Ingrid with dread.

There's a chance she's gone too far. She knows this. But she doesn't know how to undo what's already been done.

CHAPTER 12
It's Just a Teddy Bear

Drake is much happier than CJ about the sleepover, Ingrid thinks wryly.

Drake has to now share his bedroom and his things, for God knows how long, and CJ gets to stay in a friendly, beautifully appointed home, with a built-in playmate and not a single ex-stripper in sight, and yet, *he's* the one who is throwing a tantrum.

And it's a full-on temper tantrum, at that. For the last half hour, he's been crying and yelling about having to put his pajamas on, about brushing his teeth, about having a bedtime at all, and about "that stupid teddy bear" which he threw across the room with a loud thud, when Ingrid held it out as a peace offering to him.

Margaret has come home with Ingrid to help get CJ settled into his first night in his new location, holding herself out as a facilitator, but now Ingrid is beginning to wonder whether Margaret hasn't been playing her all along. Maybe CJ's last foster family kicked him out because of his terrible behavior. Maybe CJ isn't at all the sweet, friendly boy she remembers from Mrs. Lopez's classroom. After all, three years is a long time. People change.

And how. Ingrid thinks about her, Peter, and Opal as Exhibits A, B, and C to the "people change" argument.

But Margaret assures her that CJ's just exhibiting some very typical behavior for the situation even though it's not typical behavior for *him*. She keeps repeating that CJ is a resilient and pleasant child who will feel much better in the morning and who just needs some love and patience. Drake offers him toys and books and while CJ is gentler with him—not throwing things like he did when Ingrid handed him the teddy bear—he is turning down every attempt at friendship that Drake is holding out to him.

Nevertheless, Drake seems happy he's there and unfazed by the yelling and crying. He gets in his own favorite mismatched pajamas and clears out a drawer in his dresser and tells CJ it can be his. He clears off the top shelf of his cluttered bookshelf as well, where CJ places the only possession that he's held onto the entire time he's been in Ingrid's home. It's a crumpled piece of poster board. Ingrid notices it's some type of school project. Various photos of live and dead plants make a dizzy line across one wrinkled side and after the state he's been in all night, it's good to see CJ show such care for something, even if it is a nearly destroyed poster with pictures of mostly dead plants.

CJ finally calms down and agrees to get in the bottom bunk of Drake's bunk bed, clutching his superman figure, albeit fully clothed and without brushing his teeth. Margaret heads out, and Ingrid says good night to both of the boys, hoping everyone will get some needed sleep. As she leaves the room, she hears CJ ask Drake, "Who's that man in the picture with you?"

She leans against the hallway wall afraid of what's going to happen next.

How could I have been so stupid?

Of course, CJ knows Peter. He's going to recognize him in that fuzzy picture of him and Drake from a fishing outing that she had blown up and hung on the wall for Drake's birthday last year. It's the only picture of Peter that's hanging in the house. They weren't ones for big family portraits. The house is covered in pictures of Drake at various ages, but that's the only picture of Peter in the whole house and it's hanging directly over where she's now put CJ to sleep. The picture is blurry and a few years old, but still.

Ingrid debates whether she should rush in and yank CJ out of his bed and drive him directly to a new home before he traumatizes Drake even more than he already has.

But Drake's cool answer stops her lead-footed outside the door.

"That's my dad. He's dead. He went to heaven."

"Oh, he looks like my Uncle. But he's not dead. He's just gone."

"Oh. Ok."

And then Ingrid hears Drake say, "Tomorrow I can help you put your stuff away."

It's a long, complicated sentence at the end of a full conversation and Ingrid has to cover her mouth to avoid gasping or crying. She decides to leave the picture of Peter hanging on the wall and leave CJ in Drake's bed and to just let things fall where they fall from this point forward.

Ingrid heads to the living room couch to assess the damage. The few belongings CJ brought with him are still strewn about the room where he's left them, because he refused Ingrid's and Margaret's instructions to pick them up. Ingrid debates whether she should leave them there and make CJ pick them up himself in the morning after he's had some sleep; and hopefully has returned to the sweet-natured boy she remembers from long ago. While she debates, she pulls up a news feed on her phone, realizing that she needs to catch up on what it is the reporters think they know that she doesn't.

Remains of a body have been found in a trash bag in back of an empty lot by the old DIVAS dance parlor on Route 92. Cause of death has not yet been released, nor has the identity of the body. Sources say it's a male, around 50 years old, and that it's being treated as suspicion of homicide, occurring 5-7 years ago, based on the advanced stage of decomposition. Police are investigating a link between this case and that of the death of Peter DiLaurio.

Ingrid reads the article twice trying to understand. What the hell would a dead body behind DIVAS have to do with Peter?

Is he now going to be linked to that damn dance club and its disgusting history forever? *Is she?* Ingrid rubs her eyebrows. Now she's going to need to spend the morning researching motions *in limine* to make sure the prosecution doesn't try to introduce any evidence about this new body to cloud the case against Opal. Those damn reporters. Then again, she can't resent them too much. She wouldn't even know about this without them. She needs to keep her head in the game and not get distracted by CJ, or Jane, or even Opal.

Ingrid shuts her phone off and surveys the room again. She decides not to make CJ's transition to a new foster home a difficult one and instead walks around the room picking up his things. While CJ did honestly seem happy to see his special toothbrush (although he refused to use it) and his superman action figure, the teddy bear made him angry, violently so. Why on earth did Opal want the social worker to make a special trip back to her house to get an item that CJ clearly didn't care about, as he spent quite a bit of time screaming that it was just a "baby toy?"

Ingrid holds up the teddy bear and examines it as if it is a clue. The truth is, it isn't even a cute teddy bear. He has a misshapen stitched face, as if someone has torn him and then put him back together again. More like Frankenstein than a child's toy. As Ingrid stares at him another minute, she thinks maybe the teddy bear wasn't really for CJ. Maybe Opal wanted him for another reason entirely. Then she shakes it off.

Ok, Ingrid, this is not a freaking John Grisham novel. It's just a teddy bear. You're letting everything and everyone get in your head.

Ingrid tucks the teddy bear under her arm and gathers up the other strewn items, tiptoes in to check on CJ and Drake, who are, finally, asleep, and heads to bed herself.

As she drifts off to sleep, she thinks about her mother's final days taking up a cause that she didn't understand. Ingrid wonders if her mother would be proud of her for taking up the cause of Opal Rowen when she had no one else truly on her side.

But no, Ingrid has to admit as she gives in to sleep.

This isn't the same at all. My mother died defending women she was fighting for even as she disagreed with them. I'm just fighting for me.

By 3 am, Ingrid finds herself in the kitchen with a pair of sewing scissors, and the Frankenstein teddy bear. She can't sleep, and she wants to know why Opal stitched together a ripped up ugly old teddy bear and insisted that Margaret retrieve it from her home. Ingrid hopes it's nothing, because she wants to believe that Opal isn't actually hiding anything from her that she doesn't already know, but she needs to see for herself that it's nothing so she can go back to bed.

Admittedly, reading about an unidentified decomposing body just before bed has messed with her head a little bit. It was either open up the teddy bear or warm some milk and she hates warm milk.

Ingrid snips a few stitches on the teddy bear's face and sees immediately that the reason he's misshapen is that his stuffing is two different colors and two different textures. Clearly someone has tried to repair this sad-looking guy. Ingrid pulls out his stuffing, a clump at a time, reasoning that she can put him all back together even better, like new, and maybe CJ will actually get some comfort out of this stuffed guy the way Opal intended.

If that's what Opal intended.

It doesn't take long for Ingrid to discover that's not what Opal intended at all.

Near the bottom of the hollowed-out teddy bear carcass, Ingrid puts her fingers on a folded-up piece of paper and pulls it out. She unfolds it carefully, and reads what is titled as a "Codicil"—a pretentious legal term for "amendment to a will"—signed by one Peter DiLaurio. Ingrid rubs her fingers over Peter's signature. Next to her husband's familiar signature is a signature of Tobin Rue, and it's dated two months before Peter died. The

Codicil amends a document referenced only as "The Last Will and Testament of Peter L. DiLaurio, dated March 4, 2015." The will is a document that Ingrid is familiar with. It's a document that has been kept in their bedroom safe next to Ingrid's own will since the day they signed mutual wills on Drake's 1st birthday, when they realized they needed to do grown up things like probate plans and health care proxies.

No life insurance.

That's where Peter drew the line when Ingrid insisted they needed a collection of legal documents. Peter insisted he wouldn't bet against himself, but he agreed to sign a "Last Will & Testament" on Drake's birthday, and according to this document, a few months ago, someone else got him to agree to sign another legal document amending that will. The Codicil states that a property located at 354 Route 92, will go to Opal Rowen in case of Peter DiLaurio's death. All other terms of The March 2015 Last Will & Testament are to remain in effect.

Ingrid stares at the document, trying to piece together this puzzle.

354 Route 92 is the DIVAS club and lot. What the actual hell?

Ingrid remembers the real estate documents produced by the prosecutor. the ones she's been putting off reviewing and pulls them out to flip through them. She finds a deed easily. Apparently, Peter's company purchased the property.

Actually, no.

As she reviews the papers more carefully, she realizes that while the other documents reflect transactions made by DiLaurio Development, the transaction involving the Route 92 property was not made in the business's name, but in Peter's name directly. Peter bought DIVAS. She looks back at the Codicil.

And then he left it to Opal in case of his death.

Ingrid's brain races past the reasons Peter might have bought the property and settles on the newly discovered fact that Opal has *inherited* the lot. That means, Opal has inherited real estate *as a result of* Peter's death. Clearly she knew this and wanted to keep it a secret; hence the Frankenstein teddy bear move. This is motive. This document is the smoking gun for the elusive motive in this case. And it's still here, which means the police didn't find it. No one has collected it for evidence. Yet.

Ingrid is about to re-stuff and stitch back up the teddy bear when she feels something else at the bottom of the teddy bear carcass. She peers inside and two shiny objects catch her eye. She pulls out a small rock and a flat red pocket knife.

Jesus, you've got to be kidding me, Ingrid thinks as she scoops up the small objects and puts them into the pocket of her robe. Then she rips up the Codicil into tiny pieces and flushes them down the garbage disposal.

As she drifts back to sleep in her room, Ingrid rubs the rock, its smooth, small surface with "BREATHE" hand painted in purple and with visible specks of blood on it, and she realizes, for the first time since Opal called her from the jail on the night of her arrest, that this bloody rock—and not a myriad of other reasons—*might be why Opal believes that Ingrid owes her something.*

CHAPTER 13
You Can't Win, Ingrid.

Over coffee the next morning, Ingrid mentally wrestles with the new developments. The purchase of the DIVAS lot by Peter, the will codicil, the new body. Are any of these things connected to Peter's death, or are they just more things to distract her from the matter at hand? The matter at hand being the need to wipe Peter's legacy—Ingrid's legacy—clean of this whole sordid mess, get Opal back to her son, and get Ingrid back to focusing on her business and her son. She's determined not to let Peter's death and the ensuing circus consume her the way her own mother's death consumed her father and ruined him from caring for his only daughter.

Ingrid decides that a little self-care is in order and since there's nothing that helps Ingrid think better than cleaning and decluttering, she calls Jane and arranges to head over later that morning to get started on their work together.

The night's sleep *does* seem to have improved CJ's mood. The two boys are watching cartoons together on the living room couch but Ingrid decides she wouldn't dare leave CJ with a babysitter yet. There's still something unpredictable about him. Something wild in his eyes and she doesn't really want to leave him alone with Drake for too long right now.

"I'll have to bring the two boys with me," Ingrid informs Jane without waiting for a response. When she arrives, she says "I brought the boys with me," again without waiting for permission or response, even though it's clear from the expression on her face that Jane isn't exactly thrilled. Ingrid has a collection of coloring books and Lego blocks. She sets up the boys in a corner of Jane's massive living room and, after surveying the museum-like quality of Jane's home, points a finger at the boys and says, "Don't you dare, either of you, touch a single thing," and then to Jane she says, "Ok, where do you want to start?"

"Rowen, you have a visitor."

"What day is today?" Opal doesn't bother rolling over on the cot. She faces the wall; she feels foggy like she's taken a sleeping pill or a shot or something stronger.

"Tuesday, Rowen. You losing your marbles or something? Don't do that, Rowen. Don't lose it on me."

Carla is Opal's favorite corrections officer. She seems to have taken pity on her and she gives her near daily pep talks. Or maybe she just does that with all the female inmates, but still, she has made Opal feel special, and for that, Opal is grateful. The smallest kindnesses feel huge inside these walls.

Tuesday. He comes every Tuesday now.

She thinks about his letter. About the promises made. But promises just get broken. Opal has learned that lesson over and over.

Opal shakes her head without turning around.

She doesn't want to see anyone today.

"No. Tell him to go away. Tell him I'm sick today."

"Ok, Rowen, but just promise me you won't lose your marbles today. You need them when you finally get the hell out of here."

Opal rolls over and looks at Carla. "I'm going to get out of here eventually, right?"

Carla's smile is broad even though her teeth are yellowed and a few are broken. There's a reckless optimism in her smile that warms Opal through the bars. She grabs onto it.

"On second thought, I'll go talk to him after all."

✧

Jane stands on her stockinged tiptoes to pull something down from the top shelf of the linen closet.

"Do you want help?" Ingrid asks, but Jane just shakes her head and carries something wrapped in an old blanket to a bench at the foot of the bed.

They've been going through Jane's professionally decorated home, room by room, closet by closet. Apart from a small box they've assembled of items to be donated, the home appears to contain very little clutter, actually. Ingrid is starting to wonder why Jane has even hired her.

Jane sets her wrapped bundle down on the bench. "This. This is something I really need to get rid of so no one finds it after I die."

For a moment, Ingrid wonders if it's all been a ruse. She wonders if maybe Jane has actually hired Ingrid to help dispose of a murder weapon for some unsolved crime, and then she quickly dismisses the thought.

Just because I'm involved in a murder trial, she thinks, *everything doesn't have to be about murder all the time.*

"What is it, Jane?"

In response, Jane just unwraps the old blanket solemnly to reveal a brass-colored box underneath with thick latches on all sides. The front latch has a padlock and Jane flicks her fingers around it until it pops open with a small click.

Ingrid comes and sits next to Jane on the bench and watches Jane sift through the box's contents. It's mostly photographs, piles of them. Jane sorts through to the bottom and pulls out a piece of crystal, holding it out to Ingrid who takes the gift in her hand. It's heavy and ornate and appears to be some sort of paperweight. In spite of herself, Ingrid examines it for dried blood in case it *is* a murder weapon after all.

On the flat bottom is a silver plaque with an inscription. *To Jane, You did it. With love, C.*

"Well, it's beautiful." Ingrid says while still examining the heavy crystal.

"It was a gift on the occasion of my making partner at the firm."

Jane pulls out a photo and hands it to Ingrid. In the photo is Jane about 20 years younger wearing Bermuda style khaki shorts and a navy blouse with her arm around a tall lean woman, her head tipped slightly to the woman, a smile captured that is easy and real. She's in love in this picture. They both are.

"Christine."

Ingrid looks up and sees Jane's expression as she says her former love's name. The smile now is forced and full of grief, nothing like the one in the photograph.

"She was killed in a car accident, about a year after that photograph was taken. I can't say I ever really recovered. Certainly, I never loved again that way."

"Oh, I'm so sorry. What a heartbreak."

Ingrid stares at the picture, trying to understand why it's something that has to be discarded. "Jane, I certainly understand why you've kept these old photos. I even understand why they might be painful to look at. But why is it important that no one find these things after you die? Your niece and nephew might enjoy these photos of you. Look at you, here. You look radiant. Happy. I'm sure they'd like to remember you like this."

"Actually. That's not likely to be true." Jane continues to flip through the photos in the box. She hands another one to Ingrid. Jane and Christine are in this photograph, too. But they are surrounded by more people. A young boy and girl and a handsome man who bears a striking resemblance to Jane herself.

Jane points to the figures. "That's Tom, my brother, and his children. Christine was his wife, and their mother."

CHAPTER 14
Woo Woo Magic

In the kitchen, Jane has poured them both some tea and the two women sit together silently. The boys are still playing relatively well in the next room, but Ingrid realizes she's really on borrowed time here before they all start to wear out their welcome.

Jane breaks the silence.

"Your first name? Is it a family name?"

"No. My mother was a huge Ingrid Bergman fan."

"Ah, so you're named for her."

"Well, for both Ingrid Bergman and her daughter the writer, Ingrid Rossellini."

"Interesting," Jane responds. "And conflicting."

"What do you mean?"

"Well, one woman was best known for portraying many different characters and many different stories, while her daughter is best known for her epic work in the book titled 'Know Thyself.'"

"Yes, well, my mother was a layered, interesting woman, I suppose. We didn't have that in common when she was alive. I have come into my layers only later in life."

Jane nods, and Ingrid dives into the subject still looming in the room.

"So, you never told your family? No one has ever known about you and Christine?"

"Christine and I, when we realized we were in love, we

talked about telling everyone but it would have been messy and traumatic. I'm not sure anyone would have actually survived it. I'm not sure I could have survived it. I told her I couldn't go through with it. That I couldn't do that to my brother and my niece and nephew. I rejected her and then she died shortly thereafter and I have had to live with that all these years. Now I'll die with it."

"I'm so sorry, Jane."

Ingrid wants to return the gift Jane has given her by sharing Christine. But selfishly, she just wants to share her burden with someone else, too.

"She was my friend," Ingrid says without a proper segue.

"Who?"

"Opal Rowen. My client," Ingrid looks over her mug at the kitchen window. The tree-lined river is visible in the distance. Spring is climbing onto the scene in the form of crabapple blossoms and forsythia blooms.

"She was my friend for a whole year. We had become very close. She helped me through some medical issues with my son and listened to me talk about my marriage problems and how much I missed my late mother and even how I missed bits and pieces of my law career, and well, in a very short time, we just became very close."

Jane nods. "Well, then. That makes sense as to why you'd take the case on despite what she's accused of doing."

"Yes and no. We're not still friends. We had a falling out. Actually, that's not fair. We just literally stopped talking. I stopped calling her back and so we stopped talking. It had nothing to do with my husband and her. That came later."

Jane sits silently, waiting, and for that Ingrid is grateful. She hasn't said these words to anyone out loud. She isn't sure what they will sound like to her own ears. "She confided in me about her past. The strip club, the prostitution, all of it. And how she'd gotten out. How she was a success story. Built her life back up, went to nursing school, created a new life for her son, all on her own. She told me that she still gets looks, still gets shunned by men who remember her from those days, and are afraid of her. Afraid she'll tell their wives, even though of course she wouldn't."

Ingrid looks over her shoulder to make sure the boys are still out of earshot as she continues telling the story in a low voice. "I told her nothing would change. I hugged her and I thanked her for sharing her story and struggle and her triumph with me. And I told her nothing would change between us."

Jane nods. "And you thought it wouldn't."

Ingrid slumps in her chair. "Right. I thought it wouldn't. In that moment, when I was saying it, I thought I was telling the truth. I hoped it wouldn't. But I just couldn't unknow it. If my mother was alive, I would have sent Opal to befriend her instead. My mother was much better at compartmentalizing than me."

"I'm sorry about your mother. When did you lose her?"

"I was 15."

"Oh, that's a terrible age to lose a mother. Although, is there really a good age? I lost my own mother just two years ago, and I was absolutely gutted. Still am."

"Ah. I'm so sorry, too, Jane."

A pause and then Jane asks, "Was she sick?"

Ingrid sighs, "No. Perfectly healthy. She was holding a week-long vigil at a newly opened women's clinic. Helping women cross the picket lines to get medical care, and you know, abortions, too. She was shot by a zealous protestor who was apparently sickened by what she was doing. He turned the gun on himself then. We never got to have a trial. No justice. Just death. Lots of death."

"Oh, Ingrid. How tragic."

"Yes, well the ironic thing is that, I was sickened by what she was doing, too. My father was also horrified by what she was doing. My mother herself was deeply conflicted. She was fiercely pro-life, but also fiercely pro-woman. She had so much trouble having me. I was a late-in-life baby, so you know, the idea of ending a healthy pregnancy was very abhorrent to her. But, she was just so distressed at how terribly these poor vulnerable women were being treated, and so she joined the cause, and she was the one who ended up dead by the end of the vigil. The center was closed and shuttered the day after the shooting. It all ended up being for nothing. Our lives were destroyed by a monster who killed her in the name of preserving life. Completely twisted thinking."

"It certainly was not for nothing. Empty words to you, I'm sure. But your mother's death was not in vain. It sounds as though your mother died knowing herself. Knowing exactly who she was. And that is a very powerful thing. Do not underestimate it. I tell you this coming from an old woman working valiantly to know her own damn self before it's too late."

Ingrid grabs hold of her words. "That's a beautiful thought. I never thought about it that way. I just thought my mother was so layered, so complicated, and that that's what got her killed. And I was determined to be less so. I went to law school because I wanted to believe there was just right and wrong. Answers. Yes or no. Black and white. I was so sick of the grey areas that my mother had shined a light on. But, of course, practicing law turned out to be very grey indeed. So I left, and started this podcast where things felt a little more in control."

"I've always been curious. Where did that title come from? *Too Busy To Die*? It's clever, if not a little cumbersome."

Ingrid can't look at Jane after she asks that question, so she stares into her tea instead. "Yeah, well, it's a long story. Let's save it for another time, ok?"

Jane concedes and changes the subject. "So, you've found the hard answers you've been looking for?"

"God, no. I mean motherhood provided some. But then Opal came along and shook everything up all over again with her revelation of overcoming her dark past. God, it was just the sort of story my mother would have loved. I remember thinking that very thing as Opal was talking. It almost distracted me from her story. the thought that my mother would have actually embraced her whole heartedly if only she was there. But I am not my mother. I couldn't believe what Opal was telling me. DIVAS was a haven for drug dealers and sex traffickers. And she'd been all wrapped up in it before she got out. After she told me, I couldn't get my head around it and I couldn't sit at the coffee shop or my kitchen island with her any more, sharing and talking like we used to. I thought about calling her back so many times, but I couldn't. I just couldn't. I'm embarrassed to admit all this out loud."

"What you're doing now? It's good. It's redemptive for both of you. You won't have a box full of secrets and regrets to discard when you're dying. And you won't have lived in vain. You will know yourself. After playing many different roles over a lifetime. That, my friend, is the goal by the finish line. Your mother had the right idea."

Ingrid reaches over and puts a hand on Jane's in gratitude. "I used to have this meditation stone. Opal actually gave it to me, back before, well before everything fell apart between us. She said she'd gotten it at some artisan craft fair one summer. It was allegedly from a monastery in Nepal with all this woo woo energy infused into it. She said it had changed her life when she needed it. Helped her kick some demons and all sorts of things. I don't know. I didn't even think I believed in that crap until I held that stone, rolled it over and over in my palm and felt something. It got to the point that I had to have that stone with me every minute of every day or I thought something was missing. Isn't that crazy?"

"I'm a dying woman. Nothing sounds crazy anymore." Jane smiled wryly.

"Well, anyway, I lost the stone and I actually didn't even miss it and when I found it again, I realized the stone was holding me back, not pushing me forward."

"What'd you do with it?"

"I threw it into the river so I wouldn't be bogged down by it ever again."

That last bit is a lie. But Ingrid thinks the lie is warranted right now. Under the circumstances.

Jane laughs. "Should we throw my box into the river then? Is this some sort of fable?"

"No. What I'm saying is we should give the box of mementos to your brother and niece and nephew and let them decide if they want to throw it into the river or believe in its woo woo magic or not."

Just then the boys come running into the kitchen to interrupt the women. "We're starving," CJ speaks for the group. "Can we eat something?" Jane looks startled and then jumps up. "Oh of course, let me make you some sandwiches or something."

Ingrid puts her hand up. "Absolutely not. We're heading out. I think we've gotten a good start here today. Look at your calendar and let's schedule a 4-hour block next week. I'll get the boys a sitter, and we'll crank out the last of the closets."

Ingrid and Jane say a quick goodbye. At home, over grilled cheese sandwiches and carrot sticks, Ingrid sees her phone light up with Jane's number. Thinking she's already prepared to make their next appointment, Ingrid takes the call while scooping food onto two hungry boys' plates.

"Ingrid. I don't feel right about keeping something from you."

"What is it?" Ingrid thinks about all she shared over the afternoon, how vulnerable she was. How vulnerable Jane was in return.

"I've heard things around the Law Club. The judge that's assigned to Opal's case. He's, well, he's never been one of my favorites, but he's popular among the Bar. The rumor around the Club is that he's retiring and he's quietly—behind the scenes—endorsing the Prosecutor in the next judicial election. Apparently, the Prosecutor is the son of a fraternity brother. You know how these things work. Anyway, they seem to have worked out a deal that the Prosecutor is going to win this case.

A big win on a splashy murder trial just before the campaign is announced will do wonders for his election bid. It's all rumors, as I said. But rumors at the Law Club, well, you know, they often have a fair amount of truth in them."

Ingrid thinks about Tobin's admonition to her when she first took the case. He was trying to warn her, too. This flimsy murder case against Opal with holes galore, with no motive (that they know of) or weapon (that they know of), and still everyone is trying to warn her.

Ingrid sighed loudly into the phone, and Jane continued.

"You need to know that there is a good chance you can't win, Ingrid. From what I understand, there's a fairly strong case against her, and with the prosecutor in cahoots with the judge, well, it's more than a good chance, actually. After what you shared with me today, I think you need to understand that your redemption might not come by getting her acquitted. You need to make peace with that. It's enough that you've taken on the defense. It's enough."

Ingrid listens to Jane's words and watches the boys eat lunch and talk quietly to each other over lunch. Drake's been more comfortable than she's seen him in years. Since CJ was last in his life, as a matter of fact. They have an easy, beautiful friendship. Not dissimilar to the one their mothers used to enjoy as well.

You can't win, Ingrid.

Jane's words ring in her ears and Ingrid feels dizzy.

She can't win. This is quite possibly the worst mess she's taken on to clean up and she's going to fail. This isn't a matter for organic solvents or decluttered closets. CJ's mother is going to spend a long, long time in jail, and CJ will go into the system and her son will lose his friend, yet again. CJ will lose a mother. A mother will lose a son.

Ingrid presses end on the call and lowers herself into a seat at the table with the boys.

Drake looks at her questioningly, but offers no words; he

just takes another bite of his grilled cheese soundlessly.

It's not just that Ingrid can't win.

It's that everyone is going to lose.

CHAPTER 15
Always One Step Ahead

On the following Tuesday, Ingrid's post office box that she's opened for communication relating to the case is full. It seems the prosecution has made another discovery drop and there's also a notice confirming the date and time for the upcoming preliminary conference. Sure enough, the Judge that Jane warned Ingrid about is listed right there on the notice: Lance Regan, his name, boxy and large, barely fitting on the space allotted, is inked on the signature line.

Ingrid flips through the new papers produced by the prosecution while she's walking from the post office to her car. What could the prosecution have found out that helps their case? They're so sure they have more evidence that they've decided they need to produce it under the rules of evidence? Still nothing regarding a murder weapon or a motive to kill Peter as far as Ingrid can see with a quick flip of the pages. Instead, it's a coroner's report and a police report about the additional body found in the lot behind DIVAS.

The body has been identified as William Russo, former owner of DIVAS. The fact that the prosecution has felt it necessary to produce these documents means they believe this body has something to do with the current case. Real murder trials are nothing like the ones on television. There are no surprises at trial. If the prosecution wants to offer evidence, they have to show the other counsel first. They have to give Ingrid everything they have. When she gets to her car outside the post office,

Ingrid pushes the seat back and studies the documents in more detail.

The body of William Russo was heavily decomposed. Ingrid moves the photographs produced to the bottom of the pile and focuses on the written report instead, equally gruesome, but more palatable than the photographs. The coroner classified the death as a homicide, and estimated the time of death as approximately six years earlier based on the decomposition of the body.

The police report added details to the narrative, including that William Russo was the sole owner of record of the DIVAS Club and the adjacent lot in 2016, the year he suddenly went missing. Apparently, there was a very short investigation into his disappearance in 2016, as not too many people actually missed Mr. Russo, other than some questionable characters, including creditors, drug dealers, and sex traffickers. The case was closed quickly, with resources needed for other missing persons. His home and surrounding area were searched for clues about his disappearance. The bar was searched for evidence, but apparently no one thought to actually look for a body on the premises at the time. He was still presumed missing, not dead. The recent discovery of Russo's remains was the result of an anonymous tip just a week earlier.

Within the prosecution's package is also a pretrial motion *in limine* to allow the coroner's report and the police report relating to the discovery of Russo's body. While it is somewhat unorthodox for a party to file a motion to *allow* evidence (usually, motions *in limine* are meant to *preclude* evidence) Ingrid figures that the prosecution must see how tenuous their evidence and case is and that they anticipate an argument from Ingrid so they want to get a preemptive attack on the record.

Damn right I'm going to object, she thinks. Reading through the motion papers, Ingrid gleans more about the prosecution's plan to link Russo's murder to Opal's case. In 2016, at the time Russo disappeared, DIVAS was barely making a profit on the books, and was thought to be just a front for a drug and trafficking ring. In fact, DIVAS was the subject of an active police investigation, based on the bartered testimony of several drug dealers who had been arrested with connections to DIVAS just before Russo went missing. But then, once Russo disappeared, all of the state's key witnesses suddenly got amnesia. Everyone refused to testify about what they knew of the drug and sex trafficking at DIVAS. The trail to the missing Russo went cold quickly, and it was believed that he had skipped town, leaving his creditors high and dry. With no owner, and the drug gangs apparently tipped off, DIVAS became just a shell of a building, abandoned and useless. The police stopped paying attention to it and so did everyone else. The bar was looted and vandalized and the building became a property of the bank that still held a small mortgage on it when Russo disappeared. Apparently, the bank remained the owner for years, until the building and accompanying lot was bought for cheap in the last year by a private developer, Peter DiLaurio.

Ingrid closes the file. The next part she already knows based on her discovery at the bottom of CJ's teddy bear. Peter bought that damn building and the accompanying lot and left it all to his mistress, a former stripper named Opal Rowen.

Ingrid leans her head against the car's steering wheel, wondering whether this thing is even worse than she originally thought.

Why would Peter have bought that run-down property? Surely, he didn't have anything to do with the club and its sordid business back when it was still operational? Peter didn't have anything to do with Russo's death, did he? Was he going to develop it just like the Russell Street property where he was killed? Were Peter and Opal going to build luxury apartments and stuff Russo's remains in one of the walls, Jimmy Hoffa style?

Ingrid sighs and puts the car in drive to head home. Well, whatever the case, the prosecution can't just spring this new body discovery on her without a fight. Its link to the case against

Opal is tenuous at best. It's not motive to kill Peter. And it's not a weapon. But it *is* disgusting.

The prosecution wouldn't have been so bold as to already put this tenuous motion together if they didn't think they could win. Jane must be right about the deal between the prosecutor and the judge.

Is there no way to get ahead of this thing?

Ingrid thinks about calling Jane, or Tobin, but she's not up for conversations with either one right now. And then she thinks of someone else to call. Someone who seems to be one step ahead of Ingrid. Maybe it's time to catch up. Ingrid pulls the car over, and fires off an email through the Channel 62 website including her cell phone number.

Angela calls back while Ingrid is still in the car on the way home from the post office.

"I'd love to meet. When and where?"

Ingrid puts a turn signal on and starts to make a turn away from her house instead of toward it. "No better time than now, I guess. I can be at the Riversedge Main Street Café in 15 minutes."

Angela is already there when Ingrid arrives.

Of course. Always one step ahead.

Ingrid is wary but realizes she needs information and this woman seems to know some things. Ingrid launches the meeting with a question. "So, what about this new body that was discovered at the lot behind DIVAS? What do your sources tell you?"

Angela laughs. It's a deeper, heartier laugh than Ingrid estimates would have come from this lean, well-coiffed woman. "That's it? You're going to come in here and ask me what I know? And you're not going to give me anything in return? I'm not sure you really know how all this works."

"How it works?" Ingrid puffs up with a confidence she

doesn't actually feel. "I'm trying to clear an innocent's woman's name and get her home to a sad, troubled eight-year-old boy, and now the prosecution is trying to pin a second, very old, very stale murder on her with absolutely no evidence. Excuse me for taking the moral high road here."

"You're something else." Angela gets up and for a moment, Ingrid fears that she's actually walking out of the coffee shop, but instead she heads to the counter and orders a black coffee and comes back to sit across from Ingrid. "I didn't realize we were going to sit here and pretend. I'm going to at least have coffee with my show."

The two women sit in silence for a few more minutes.

Ingrid is still thinking about how to break the stalemate, when Angela leans forward. "Have you even asked your client what she knows about this new body?" Ingrid shakes her head and immediately regrets showing so much of her hand to Angela.

"This is some weird ass arrangement the two of you have, isn't it?"

"It's a lawyer/client arrangement. I'm not sure why that's a strange arrangement." Ingrid looks over at the counter. Maybe she should be ordering a coffee too, she thinks. Maybe she should have met Angela at a bar so they could be drinking something even stronger than black coffee. Ingrid feels the tension in her back rising all the way up to her neck. She decides to try another tactic.

"It's just that all you reporters were asking so many questions about this new body discovery behind DIVAS the other night, and I'm not sure I see the relevance. And I'm sure as hell going to argue there is no relevance if the prosecution makes even a peep about it, but I'm savvy enough to realize that lots of issues will be tried in the court of public opinion, rather than the court of law, so I'm curious what you think I'm missing."

Ingrid knows she is appealing to Angela's ego and admitting a vulnerability. As she sees Angela sizing her up, she thinks, *What do you think I'm missing, Angela? Go ahead. Spill your guts. Show off.*

"Your husband was sleeping with this woman. And then he bought a building where she used to strip and an adjoining lot. The same lot where a long-ago murdered body has just been discovered. And then he ended up dead."

Ingrid flinches and acknowledges that these are all true facts. "Right. But still none of this shows a motive or proof that Opal killed Peter."

"Well, she probably killed Russo. Can we admit that?"

"Of course not. It sounds like Russo had many enemies. Powerful enemies. Drug cartel enemies. I think this is one of those instances where the simplest solution is most likely the answer."

Ingrid tries to recall something from the back of her memory. Opal *did* tell her about Russo's death back when they were still friends. He was her boss. The local pimp. He was called by a bizarre nickname. What was it?

Mouse.

In those last few moments of their friendship, Opal had told her about the Mouse, too. Something about a drug deal gone wrong. And another thing: she told Ingrid that he *died*. Not that he was missing. It was all caught up in her admission about being a stripper and a prostitute. In hindsight, Ingrid knows that her brain was reeling with the new information revealed at the time, and she can't quite remember all the details. She tries to recover them, but they're lost. She's going to have to talk to Opal about all of this. About her past. About Peter. About all the things she's been avoiding up until now. Given that the prosecution has indicated they are going to make Russo's newly discovered body part of the case, or try to anyway, Ingrid is going to have to bite the bullet and raise all of these things with Opal.

Angela seems to hear something unspoken or reads it in Ingrid's face. "You two used to be friends, right?"

Ingrid takes a sharp breath that actually hurts. "Our boys were good friends when my son was still in school. Before I—

before I decided to homeschool him. We sort of lost touch then. But I was always impressed with Opal that she had pulled herself up by her bootstraps. A single mother, who had made some bad choices early on, but had straightened things out in time to turn her life around for her son. That's the Opal I want the jury to see. That's the one who would never have killed Peter. Or Russo, for that matter. She took advantage of a situation that came her way when Russo died, and got away from that life, sure. But good for her."

A smile teases across Angela's lips. "Right. She's some success story. But how do you think Opal just managed to get out from under her complicated past, when she had literally no support system and no family and only one very innocent, starving baby to feed at the time?"

"Hard work and chutzpah. Certainly not by murdering her boss, like you think she did."

"Oh come on, Ingrid. Don't be naïve. Women don't just leave careers like that and end up as suburban nurses, you know? At the very least, she had some help. Even if she didn't outright murder Russo. Have you given any thought to how she managed to claw her way out after he died? And whose toes she might have stepped on—or worse—on her way out?"

Ingrid sits silently. She has not. She has given very little thought to Opal in the last three years or so, ever since she confessed her former life to Ingrid hoping for solidarity and support, and that fact has come back to bite Ingrid again and again.

Angela folds a square napkin into a rectangle and then a smaller rectangle and then a smaller one still. "Well, here's where I'm with you. I don't think any of this Russo story, even if all true, helps explain why she murdered Peter. I mean, it looks to me like Peter was trying to protect her. Buying up this old property and helping her hide the body for good. He was on her side, right? Why on earth would she turn on him? She needed him."

Ingrid thinks about the amendment to the will she ripped up at the house. Angela's wrong. Opal certainly had some security in place with Peter alive *or* dead.

Angela stands up. "Well anyway, if you come up with anything else, let me know. We can work together, Counselor. As you said, public opinion is going to be quite important to this case. I can help you. I can help gauge public opinion."

And you can help sway public opinion, too, Ingrid refrains from saying. She knows she doesn't want to make an enemy out of Angela. And she's proven right by the fact that Angela jots some numbers down on a coffee shop napkin and hands it to Ingrid.

"Call this number. Apparently, the guy doesn't really understand how to block his number before he calls. I haven't met with him yet, but you might want to. I'm pretty sure he's the guy who led the police to Russo's body. Let me know if you have any luck with him. My experience with him has been kind of squirrely."

Ingrid accepts the napkin, but wonders if she's being led into a trap. Why would she cold-call Angela's anonymous tipster?

As she leaves the coffee shop and says goodbye to Angela, Ingrid thinks about the fact that even though the prosecution knows about Peter's purchase of DIVAS, they don't seem to know about the will codicil, at least if the motion *in limine* they prepared is any indication. There's not a word in there about any codicil. And Angela, who knows so much, isn't mentioning it either. So maybe no one knows that Peter was leaving the dance club to Opal in case of his unlikely demise. But if they did know, Ingrid realizes, things would be different.

If anyone gets the last piece of the crazy puzzle here, they might actually be able to put something together that looks like motive.

CHAPTER 18
Running

Opal has been sleeping too much. Lots of the women on her hall complain that they can't sleep at all, but she has the opposite complaint. She's been sleeping too much, and she hates it. She can't stand sleeping, because it's then that she dreams about him.

In her dreams he's not facing her at first. She can see him up ahead. She wants to see him, until he turns around, and then his eyes are hollowed out and his expression is dead and lifeless, and then she doesn't want to see him at all. She doesn't want to know him at all.

But she does.

It's her brother, Dean.

He's trying to say something to her that she can't hear. But he wants something that feels like revenge.

Whenever Opal dreams about Dean, she wakes herself up and then she stares at the ceiling until morning comes, willing herself not to go back to sleep.

She feels muddled by all this time alone. Time to think about things. Things like Dean selling her out to a sex trafficker and drug dealer. Things like Billy Russo bleeding out on the floor of DIVAS. Things like Dean disappearing without a trace.

Things she buried away in a place she planned never to retrieve them from.

Until Peter gave her no choice.

Opal waits for Ingrid behind the plexiglass, and looks down and picks at her fingertips. The last stripes of coral nail polish from a manicure a few days before her arrest are the last memories of freedom she still has in this awful place. Everything else is pretty much gone. She can barely remember what it's like to sit in her home and have a normal evening, one in which her worst problems are overdue bills and CJ's science poster project.

Even CJ feels like a blur, like a dream really. Opal doesn't want him to come visit her. Not in this awful place. When she comes to visit, Ingrid brings pictures from him. Pictures of himself that he's drawn. Bold strokes of brown and gold outlining the figure of a boy in shorts and tees, holding hands with a larger figure with long, dark brown hair and no other features drawn in. These crayon pictures are the only real memories of CJ she has right now. Her brain has shut down in an act of self-preservation, keeping her from filling in the lines.

Sometimes she wonders if she should just tell someone what she believes, that Ingrid killed Peter and that they should let Opal go. But Opal is in jail and Ingrid is not, and Opal is smart enough to know that the situation isn't just going to disappear because Opal shouts loudly. Besides, Ingrid is still defending Opal, and that fact alone gives Opal reasonable doubt about Ingrid's role in Peter's death. Whatever Ingrid did, she seems adamant that she doesn't want Opal connected to her husband, even in death. Opal *needs* Ingrid and her righteous, indignant, arrogant anger. She doesn't trust her, but she sure as hell needs her.

Ingrid is all business when she arrives. She wants to talk about the preliminary hearing which is apparently just a week or two away. Opal realizes she has already been in this God-forsaken place for nearly two months. Ingrid says to prepare for another six months more, although she's working on getting a trial date as soon as possible.

"So what exactly is this preliminary hearing?" Opal looks up from the coral flecked nails.

"The prosecution is going to set out what they have so far. Try to prove they have a case. So they can get a real trial."

"And what do we do?"

"Nothing."

"Nothing? What are you talking about? Won't I at least testify?"

"Dear God, no. You won't even testify at trial. If this gets that far. I'll be filing a motion to dismiss at the preliminary hearing. They have a pretty shitty case as these things go. No motive. No weapon."

"Well, that's good then."

"No. Don't get your hopes up. I don't think we're going to get off easy here. We have to act like it's going to trial and prepare for that. Seriously."

Opal nods.

"And so, in that vein, we need to discuss some things the prosecution is going to bring up at the preliminary hearing. I'm working on a motion to exclude certain so-called evidence. But you need to know that the prosecution is trying to bring another murder into this case. That of William Russo."

"Billy? What does he have to do with any of this?" Ingrid detects a nervous elevation in the pitch of Opal's voice. Maybe it's just the idea that her past is most definitely going to be part of this trial. A past she believes she rose above and left behind. But Ingrid needs to find out exactly why Opal is nervous at the mention of Russo's name.

"Russo's body was found in a shallow grave on the grass lot behind DIVAS. According to the police, he was murdered. They had been treating his case as a missing persons case until the discovery of the body. Apparently, no one really knew what happened to Billy. It's been a cold case. Until now."

"What do you mean? They're going to say I killed Billy *and* Peter?" There's no mistaking the nervousness in Opal's voice now.

"Well, here's where it gets tricky. The body is so badly decomposed that they seem to be at a loss right now. The coroner has ruled it a homicide, but they can't pin that homicide on anyone right now. And they haven't amended the charges against you just yet to include Russo's murder."

"Ok. So I don't get it."

"Well, they *do* have evidence of Russo's suspiciously dead body being found on an empty lot. The same lot that Peter bought only recently. It seems they are trying to tie you to Peter's murder through this body."

"That makes no sense."

"Well, that's what I would have thought, too."

"But?"

"But, the prosecution seems to believe they have something here. They've filed a motion before the preliminary hearing ruling that Russo's body should be evidence in this trial. It's a pretty bold move, and I think they must have something in their back pocket that gives them confidence."

"What do you think they have?"

"I was hoping you'd tell me if you can think of anything."

"Nothing." Opal says it far too quickly.

Ingrid sighs. She doesn't want to admit there was a will amendment. She doesn't want to admit she destroyed it. She takes a gamble that they can go about this another way instead. "Opal, I know Peter discussed transferring the ownership of the DIVAS lot to you."

Opal's eyes grow wide.

Ingrid stares at her waiting to see who blinks first.

And it's Opal. She leans back in her chair and summons the security guard keeping watch over everyone. "I want to go back to my cell now. We're done here."

On her jailhouse cot, Opal tosses and turns. Her dreams have been replaced by memories and they aren't much better.

Memories of stumbling in on Mouse and Jessie arguing. Jessie was a frequent patron of the club and seemed to have some business dealings with Mouse that she wanted no part of. She was trying to get her paycheck from Mouse and get out of there. But she'd had too much to drink and it had been a long night. Longer than usual. When she stumbled in on the fight, she noticed there was a large bag of white powder sitting between Mouse and Jessie. Mouse looked nervous, which made Opal nervous. She wasn't used to seeing him like that. Usually he was so cool and controlled. But not that night. Opal looked at him and saw something in his eyes that scared her and whenever Opal replays the fuzzy scene in her mind, she knows that was the moment that she should have turned and ran.

"Opal," Jessie had put his arm around her with a cool, slow smile. He was the only one in the room smiling. The only one in control.

"I got an idea, Mouse. How about you throw in this little girl, along with my money, and I forget how you just tried to double cross me with some shitty diamond powder?"

"Jesus, Jessie. I tested the stuff myself. It's not my fault. Give me a couple of days to sort this out."

"A couple of days?" Jessie had barked a laugh, and pulled Opal tighter. "What do you think, Sweetheart? Should I give this asshole a couple more days to come up with my money? The money he stole from me in return for an entire cargo of weak coke?" Jessie pointed to the bag of powder on the table. "I put that shit out on the street already. You made me look bad, Mouse. I don't like to look bad. I ain't leaving without my money. Not in a couple of days. *Today*."

"Sure, sure. Let me get it out of the safe." Mouse started to walk toward Jessie.

"The fuck you doing? You stay put." Jessie pulled out a gun and trained it on Mouse. He let go of Opal and she drifted away from him. She was still standing between him and Mouse, but drifting closer and closer to Mouse. Opal felt like she was watching everything from outside her body. She'd drunk so much. Her feet were numb. Mouse put his hands up.

"Jessie, I don't want any problems here."

"You and me already got plenty of problems, Mouse."

"Jessie, why don't you go in the back and relax. You're all wired. Opal will help you relax. Won't you, Sweetheart?"

Her head was blurry and numb, and she looked at Mouse who was offering her up like she was a door prize. She was tired of being bought and sold. By Mouse. By Dean. She was stumbling and drunk, but there was a fire starting inside her again. Something she'd long forgotten was there. She thought about her son at home sleeping in his crib. She had to get home to him. If she got home to him, she promised to someone that might have been God, she'd never leave him for this shithole again.

Opal drifted closer to Mouse. She nodded at him.

"Sure, I'll help Jessie relax," she murmured, but all the while still looking at Mouse. She was wearing her jacket over her bikini. She hadn't even finished getting dressed yet, just threw a puffy jacket on over her red dancing bikini. It was winter and she was cold and the jacket wasn't much use against the winter weather. But it was enough that night, because inside the puffy jacket was her dad's pocket knife. She reached in the pocket and fingered it gently, opening it with a click, and then she jabbed it in Mouse's neck while he was still standing there, with a gun trained on him and a bag of bad coke on the table.

The next thing she remembers is running. Something she's been doing ever since.

CHAPTER 17
Investors

When Mary arrives the next day so Ingrid can go to the coffeeshop and work on the case, she is tempted to drive directly to the courthouse and file a withdrawal of counsel. Who could blame her? Her client is not cooperating at all. She's hiding things and playing games. Dangerous games. She might get punished in this trial for another crime altogether.

Why did I ever think I should help this woman?

But Ingrid looks at CJ and Drake eating breakfast together in quiet camaraderie, and reminds herself what's at stake. She doesn't know who killed William Russo. But she does know Opal didn't kill Peter. And Ingrid has enough of her mother in her to still err on the side of justice even when all the lines are pretty blurry. So, Ingrid is determined to stay the course.

Ingrid stops for gas in town, and checks her voicemails. Would-be podcast guests are few and far between right now. It seems people are still wary about getting involved with Ingrid right now. She's messy right now. Not on brand at all.

To compensate, Ingrid is recycling old taped segments and despite the stale content, her website is seeing a slight uptick in traffic so her advertising revenue is still intact. She assumes the website traffic is actually from voyeurs who have now learned through the media that she's handling the murder trial of her dead husband's former mistress. People are vultures, after all. But she just keeps pushing out her website metrics to advertising prospects and it looks like, financially, anyway, she'll be able to stay afloat through the trial. Ingrid doesn't have a clear life or business plan for afterward. She'll cross those bridges when she gets there.

She doesn't want to lose everything she worked so hard for. When she first left the law, Peter didn't believe she'd ever have a second career. Part of her drive to ensure that *Too Busy To Die* succeeded was actually to prove Peter wrong.

Revenge can be a great catalyst for action, Ingrid thinks.

After all, it helped her build a company from nothing.

Well, not nothing.

There were "investors" along the way. That's what Ingrid has always thought of them as. She never told Peter where the initial money came from, and he never asked. He didn't take any great interest in her or her business. He never really seemed to think too much of Ingrid at all after she left the law. Her value to Peter was as an identity that she'd long ago given up to focus on being a mother and a new entrepreneur instead.

Peter complained that Ingrid didn't make time for him in her new life. There was that one night, early on in her entrepreneurial journey, that he asked, "You're reinventing yourself in every way. But what about us? Where do we fit in?"

"Stop being selfish, Peter. I'm trying to build a new career here. And I'm raising our son. I don't have time for your childish temper tantrums."

"There's no new career. You're a lawyer, for God's sake. This podcast business is just silly. It can never be anything but a hobby. You'll see."

His lack of faith in her reminded her of the first man in her life to fail her long ago. Her father.

I'll show you, Ingrid thought.

She'd shared these conversations with Opal. Opal hadn't exactly gotten on the same page about Peter, and Ingrid realizes she should have known even then that Opal had a soft spot for Peter. "He just sounds like he's trying to manage your expectations. He's used to thinking of you as a lawyer. He'll come around."

"No, he's a selfish ass. He's only thinking of himself, not me and Drake. He's not much better than my own father, to tell the truth." Opal had shrugged, like she wasn't quite sure she agreed with Ingrid, but she jumped on the train to support Ingrid nonetheless.

"Well, I can help you get some needed funds for the podcast business. Then you can build the business, and hopefully show Peter that this is more than a hobby. Like the law was."

"Really, how?"

Turns out it was the same way Opal had gotten herself through nursing school and pulled herself out of her past. It wasn't technically illegal, what Opal helped Ingrid do, but it was certainly unsavory. It wasn't anything Ingrid would want going public, and Opal knew that.

Opal helped Ingrid get "investors," and when she first took on her case, Ingrid thought Opal was holding those "investors" over her head. She thought that was what Opal meant when she called her that night from the jail saying, "You owe me, Ingrid." But now, Ingrid knows Opal has a full deck of reasons she believes Ingrid owes her, not the least of which is because she's found Ingrid's BREATHE rock with Peter's blood on it, and stashed it away in a sewed-up teddy bear that she doesn't know Ingrid has already uncovered.

After the gas pit stop, Ingrid drives in circles for a while, knowingly avoiding the coffee shop, the murder case file, and home. Drake and CJ are with Mary working on the lessons she laid out for them in the morning before leaving. CJ has been a handful, no doubt about it. Ingrid knows it's not easy for him being separated from his mother, being forced to homeschool alongside Drake and Ingrid, who are essentially strangers, but she hasn't relished being a constant disciplinarian. He gets along fairly well with Drake and Drake isn't the least bit put off by his constant rambunctious behavior, but Ingrid is pretty exhausted by CJ. It's been good for Drake to have CJ back in his life for a time, but it will be even better for both boys to have their own *mothers* back. She's looking forward to the end of this trial for many reasons, not the least of which will be handing CJ back to his mother, or so Ingrid hopes.

CJ hasn't mentioned his "uncle" again since that first night, at least that Ingrid is aware of. And he hasn't yet realized that his "uncle" is a shared connection that binds all of them.

He is so unlike Drake. CJ and his mother are loud and bold and the complete opposite of Ingrid and Drake's pensive, thoughtful, careful selves. And after she finally gets both boys in bed each night, Ingrid can't help but stare at the ceiling and wonder if that was why Peter was going to leave them and choose CJ and Opal over Ingrid and Drake.

Tired of driving in circles, Ingrid pulls over on the side of the road, and reaches into her bag for the coffee shop napkin Angela had given her.

She dials the numbers and when she gets a robotic voice mail message, she leaves her own. "Hello. I'm an attorney working on the Peter DiLaurio murder case. I'd appreciate a call back at your convenience. You can reach me at this number."

She makes one more call then, to a potential podcast guest she's been playing phone tag with. Other than the fact that she's one of the rare potential guests who's actually returned Ingrid's calls lately, she's also a woman with a fascinating background. She's developed an all-purpose cleaning rag and solvent to use on nearly every surface of your house that will repel dust and fingerprints for up to seven days. The Reboot Cloth and Spray will restart your home to new," @AskLillyP claims on her voice-mail message. "And I should know, I have a background in forensics with a special expertise in fingerprint detection."

CHAPTER 18

It's Always on a Tuesday

"You have a visitor, Opal."

"My attorney?"

The guard shakes her head no. Yesterday was the preliminary hearing, a pretty uneventful occurrence, in which Ingrid saved all her talking for the Judge and spoke to Opal very little. At the end of the hearing, the trial date was set for two months out. Ingrid was right to prepare Opal for the eventuality of a trial. The Judge spent about a minute considering Ingrid's motion to dismiss, and then said brusquely, "Denied," before opening his calendar to schedule a trial date. Opal wasn't really expecting Ingrid to be back today, but she asks if it's her attorney out of habit.

She only has two visitors. So if it's not Ingrid, that means it's him. Right, and it's Tuesday. When he shows up, it's always on a Tuesday.

Well, why not? What else does she have to do? Opal nods her head and follows Carla out to meet him.

"You look like shit, Opal."

"Good to see you too, Christopher."

"So what are you on a hunger strike or something? You're too skinny."

"Sorry to let you know it's not exactly Applebee's in here or anything. I don't even think the burgers on burger night are made with real meat."

Christopher's laugh is smoky. The nurse in her wants to tell him to stop smoking. The girl in her wants to tell him he sounds sexy.

Christopher showed up out of the blue after her face hit all the local media and asked to be put on her visitors' list. He sent her that letter telling her he still loved her, all these years later, and that he'd do whatever he could to help. She's held onto it like a life preserver in this place. He's the only one she trusts right now and she feels badly that he seems to trust her in return. She's lying to him constantly.

She has to admit it was nice to see a familiar face, but now she sees the danger in having let him come back into her life in even a small dose. They hadn't seen each other since she broke up with him after high school. After she realized she was pregnant, and after she decided she would never ever tell him about his baby.

At that first jailhouse meeting, she filled him in on her resume since they last spoke. He wasn't put off at all about the fact that she'd worked at DIVAS. "You always did have a great ass, Opal," he'd smirked. But then he fast forwarded to the nursing career.

"No surprise, there. You were always tough as nails. I'm proud of you."

She basked in his pride. It was like a handful of crumbs to the starving woman she'd become.

"So, did you do it?" he asked point blank after they got through the niceties at their first meeting.

She shook her head matter-of-factly, and he said, "Yeah, I figured you didn't. Didn't really seem like something you'd do. Not the Opal I knew and loved way back then. I wish I could help you get your name cleared. It's not like I'm an attorney or anything. Still, I wish I could help somehow. I'd do anything for you, Opal."

Well, I'm not the Opal you knew and loved anymore, Christopher.
He repeats a familiar mantra again today.

"You ok? I'd do anything to help you, Opal."

He still has that sort of doting puppy dog look in his almond-shaped eyes that Opal remembers well from the years together in high school. She had always known her power over Christopher was strong. That's why she left him the way she did without telling him about his baby. She wanted to cut ties with him, cleanly and finally. But now? Now things are different.

"How's your kid doing?"

"Fine. Good as can be expected." Opal keeps the details about CJ as blurry as she can, not even daring to tell Christopher his name. The papers left out CJ's name and his age, so Opal lied and told Christopher, "He's five," at that first meeting when Christopher asked, "How old's your kid?" Even with rudimentary math skills, Christopher couldn't think Opal's son was his. Opal just wants to let him believe he's "Opal's kid" and that he was a product of those seedy dance club days that she'd pulled herself out of.

"You busy with jobs this week?" Opal makes small talk.

"Just one big one keeping me busy. So that's good. Still get Tuesdays off so I can keep visiting you. So that's good, too." He winks at Opal and she smiles back at him.

Christopher is in construction now, and Opals has a vague fantasy of enlisting his help if she ever gets out of here. *When* she gets out of here. She knows that she needs to think positively. But she also needs to stop thinking Christopher can be part of her life when this is all said and done. He's a nice distraction right now. With Peter gone and CJ gone, Christopher is literally the only genuinely caring interaction she's even getting these days.

He's nothing like Peter, of course. But who was? Peter was smooth and charismatic. She was used to dealing with rich men when she was a dancer at DIVAS. She was used to them thinking they were cool when in reality they were pigs. She could see right through them and never got sucked into their lies.

You're so beautiful I'd leave my wife in a heartbeat if you'd run off with me, baby.

When men used to say that to her at DIVAS, she'd whisper promises in their ear and coax their money out of their wallets. When Peter said it to her, it felt real. Different. Like they could really be something. Opal feels foolish in hindsight.

How could this have ended any other way than it has?

That night she first called Ingrid from the police station, Opal was desperate. She just wanted a real attorney, and yes, she wanted a friend. Part of Opal still believed that Ingrid would have forgiven her by now. That because she didn't love Peter, she wouldn't mind much that Opal did. It was all so misguided, of course. Ingrid wasn't her friend and Ingrid probably took this case to make sure Opal got sent away for good. Ingrid really threw her when she asked about Peter transferring ownership of the lot. Opal called Margaret shortly after that meeting. "Did you get CJ's things I asked you to take from the house?"

"Of course, Opal. Everything you asked for. Officer Tim let us pack a tote bag for CJ from his room. His superman figure, that teddy bear, his favorite toothbrush."

"So CJ has all his things now?"

"Yes, he does. Don't worry, Opal, he's in good hands. Ingrid is taking good care of him. I stop by weekly for home visits."

"And he seems happy?"

"He likes Drake. They seem very comfortable together. He misses you so much. But he's a brave little boy. He's always got that superman figure every time I see him."

"What about the teddy bear?"

"The teddy bear sits in a place of honor in the living room. I always see it, every time I'm there. I'm sure it comforts him having some belongings from home while he waits for you."

Opal's heart hurts. She closes her eyes. The teddy bear. It's there in Ingrid's house. That's dangerous, but necessary.

Ok. She only thinks she knows something, Opal thought as she hung up with Margaret that day.

Now, she stares through the plexiglass at Christopher's pleading eyes.

I wish I could do more for you, Opal.

Maybe there's a way Christopher can help her out of the mess she's created for herself after all.

CHAPTER 19
DiLaurio's Old Lady

Angela's anonymous tipster calls Ingrid back a few days after her voicemail message. She sees "blocked number" come up on her screen, picks up on the first ring anyway, and the greeting is abrupt. "How the hell did you get this number?"

His voice is coarse but there's a timidity behind the gruffness that relieves Ingrid and encourages her to keep going.

"A mutual friend. I'd like to meet in person."

"In person? You nuts?"

"Possibly."

A long, breathy pause by the coarse voice emboldens Ingrid. She's still got him. He's not going to agree to meet in person, but she's still got him.

"How did you know where Billy Russo's body was buried?"

"The hell?"

"I know it was you."

"I didn't agree to be public about this. I did my civic duty and all that. I helped the police do something they should have done years ago. But that's it. I can't be arrested just for knowing something, so don't try to threaten me."

"Threaten you? I'm not trying to threaten you. You know how I got your number? You didn't block your number properly just one time, and now your number is being shared. You have to be careful. If you're trying to stay anonymous, I'm just trying to help you."

"Shit."

Ingrid pictures an aging drug dealer, cleaned up after a lot of years, suddenly having a 12-step moment, and deciding to reveal where he buried Russo's body. She realizes it might help her case to have another character with a seedy past to help deflect light away from Opal.

"Listen, you certainly did the right thing coming forward about Russo's body. I guess the big question is why now? Why would you come forward after all this time?"

"After all this time? But I literally just found the body. What are you talking about?"

Ingrid is taken by surprise. How did this guy just find the body? Who is he if not a drug dealer or sex trafficker from the good old days? DIVAS is private property. What was he doing? Jogging on an old strip club off the highway one morning? Who the hell is this guy?

"So you weren't there when Russo was killed? When his killer hid his body?"

"Jesus, no. What do you think I am? I never went to that place when it was open. I'm a married man. I got a wife and kids, and that's why I didn't want to be mixed up in any of this stuff. I told Mr. DiLaurio that myself."

Ingrid sucks in a breath at the reference to Peter. Yet another reminder of how deeply involved her husband was in this whole sordid business.

"Of course you didn't. What did Mr. DiLaurio say?"

"Well, he said he just wanted me to pour concrete all along that grass border. As soon as possible. He wouldn't tell me what he wanted to do with that lot. He was just clear that he didn't want me to subcontract it out. Wanted me to do it myself. There was something, I don't know, not right, about the whole thing. I had my dog with me, and he kept barking right around the dumpster, and Mr. DiLaurio kept telling me to get him under control, put him back in the truck. I didn't feel right about any of it. I been working for Mr. DiLaurio for many years, on many different sites, but this one seemed different, and I told him I have a wife and kids and I don't need to get mixed up in any funny business."

Ingrid starts to understand this guy isn't a reformed drug dealer but a construction worker who has worked for her husband, including very recently.

"Ah, I see."

"So, you know, after Mr. DiLaurio turns up dead, I figure, I gotta tell the police to go look at that lot. There's something going on here that just ain't right."

"Indeed." Ingrid sighs. She changes her mind. She doesn't think this guy can help very much. She doesn't mind if he just stays hidden, after all. "Well, again, if you don't want to be summoned to testify— if you really do want to keep your identity hidden, you need to be more careful."

"You ain't going to subpoena me or anything? My wife, she says the prosecutor might just subpoena me as one of Mr. DiLaurio's former contractors. That I might get mixed up in this business even though I had nothing to do with nothing. I been dodging that reporter's calls. But I figure I can't dodge the law much longer. You work for the prosecutor?"

"Me? No, I—"

"But I thought you said in your message you're working on the Peter DiLaurio murder case."

"Well, yes. But I'm Opal Rowen's attorney."

"What the hell?"

"Sir, I—"

"No way, lady. I read the news reports. That means your DiLaurio's old lady. What are you trying to do? You trying to trap me or something?"

Ingrid is stunned. It never occurred to her that he didn't understand who she was. Or that she was someone's "old lady."

The phone line goes dead, and Ingrid shudders as she realizes she still doesn't know who the voice on the other end of the line is.

But he knows her.

CHAPTER 20
Fingerprints

Ingrid sets up the podcast equipment in her kitchen after a long hiatus. She has a call with @AskLillyP today, a sponsored appearance and a small influx of cash into the *Too Busy To Die* business and maybe even a little welcome distraction from decomposing bodies, anonymous tipsters, and motions *in limine.*

She sees @AskLillyP's face come up on her monitor.

"So nice to meet you."

"Same."

Ingrid shushes the boys in the adjoining room, and presses live on the recording.

Opal pushes the food around on her plate. She has no appetite anymore. She hasn't been this thin since she worked at DIVAS. She can feel her hip bones when she lies on the cot at night and the sharpness of her body is a reminder of a time she doesn't want to remember.

She didn't mean to kill Billy.

Or maybe she did.

After she dug the knife into his neck, there was a moment when she hesitated. But only one. Jessie howled, laughing like it was the funniest thing he ever saw. Billy bleeding out on the floor and Opal standing there with her pocket knife and a puffy jacket over a bikini was apparently better than any stand-up routine.

"Get the hell out of here," he barked at her.

"Oh my God. Oh my God." She kept repeating.

"Listen, sweetheart. You just did me a pretty big favor. And this ain't the first body I ever had to get rid of. So get the hell out of here or I'm going to make you help." With that her moment of hesitation ended. She ran as fast as she could. She ran all the way home. When she saw a small news story a few days later about Billy being missing, she held her breath, waiting for someone to come find her. But they never did.

She never really knew where Billy's body had ended up. Not until Peter bought that lot. There was a shallow grave under the dumpster when they moved it and emptied it for what seemed the first time in years, and it wasn't hard to figure out that it was Billy's likely burial ground. Peter was going to put cement over the area and seal Opal's fate for good. Make sure she could breathe easier.

Opal keeps pushing food around on her plate, wishing she could stop remembering. And stop running for good.

@AskLillyP is animated and friendly and open, the kind of woman who ends up giving you way too much when you ask her how her day is going. The kind of woman who responds to small talk conversation starters by telling you about her ex-mother-in-law's bunions and that her sex life is sort of stale at the moment, and that she has a standing appointment with her therapist on Mondays.

This is why she is so popular. She has a sort of tell-all personality that makes her a darling on social media. Ingrid has barely done any talking and she doesn't mind. It feels wonderful to be in a conversation about something other than a murder trial for the first time in months.

"So your Reboot Spray? You use it on countertops and windows and appliances, and it will actually repel fingerprints?"

"Yep, much cheaper than those fancy fingerprint proof appliances people are trying to sell these days. Oh! And you know those spots your dog makes with his wet nose on your kitchen windows and your back door? Gone! I had a dog once that used to pee in every corner of the house once a day. Talk about a mess! My first husband told me it was just because I made him nervous because the pitch of my voice is too high. And let me tell you, that was only one of the reasons I left him. Not too great in the sack if you catch my drift."

Ingrid laughs, and is immediately shocked to hear the sound come from her. She hasn't laughed in a long time. It feels good. She hopes @AskLillyP makes her laugh again.

"So how does a forensics expert make the switch to cleaning supplies?"

"Oh honey, you know. I got so sick of always working in houses where bad stuff had happened. I wanted a way to help people who were just, you know living in their homes with normal stuff happening."

Ingrid glances over her shoulder and sees Drake building something on the floor.

Yes, normal stuff would be nice, she thinks.

"So you know, I developed the Reboot System so people could get rid of those pesky fingerprints that are always messing up your house and making your kitchen look dirty just a few hours after you've cleaned it. After a lifetime of retrieving fingerprints from murder weapons, now I get to coach people through removing fingerprints on refrigerator handles. Much less stress at night!"

"I would think so," Ingrid says without laughing this time.

Her mind wanders away from @LillyP back to the bloody rock and the pocketknife in the safe, covered in fingerprints: including her own. She pulled them right out of the teddy bear, without gloves before she hid them. Ingrid thinks about wiping them down and removing the incriminating evidence still on them. But it's not only her fingerprints on the knife and rock, and so she needs them. She definitely still needs them both.

According to the coroner's report, William Russo was killed by a stab wound to the neck, the size and shape of which was consistent with a small knife, likely a pocket knife. And according to the other coroner's report Peter was killed by a head wound caused by a small sharp object, likely a rock. If Ingrid does manage to get Opal acquitted, she needs the fingerprints on that rock—all of them—to keep herself from becoming the next suspect in Peter's murder.

CHAPTER 21
Grey

A month before jury selection is scheduled to begin in Opal's case, Ingrid makes a date at Jane's posh apartment to finish the project they started together. Between homeschooling the two boys and getting Opal's defense ready, Ingrid has sketched out a plan for getting Jane's estate in order. She knows she has the biggies in place like a will and a health care proxy, but it's the fine details that she needs help with: cleaning out the rest of the storage spaces in the apartment so that Jane's niece and nephew won't be burdened with that process; pre-selection of auction and estate sale companies to sell the property and personal effects the niece and nephew don't want to keep for themselves; and possibly even putting the Riversedge apartment on the market. That's something she wants to discuss with Jane today.

Ingrid shows up again with the boys in tow and is immediately sorry she brought them, because already Jane looks frailer and weaker than last time Ingrid saw her.

"Ingrid." The smile that accompanies Jane's greeting is forced and plastic. Ingrid thinks about turning around and leaving but Jane waves them in feebly and she doesn't want to be rude. Also, she wants to talk to Jane about some other things. Things having to do with the upcoming trial. She settles the boys in the massive living room.

"Would you like a cup of tea?" Jane asks.

"Yes, yes, let me make us both a cup of tea. Have a seat. I

made a chart that I want to go over with you."

Over tea, Ingrid goes over the print-out of the organizational chart she made for Jane, who sits mostly silent the whole time, and Ingrid starts to worry if maybe she's overstepped some line.

Finally, Jane says, "Yes, this is exactly what I'd hoped for. I just can't focus on details like this anymore, and I don't know how to admit that to Antonella and James. This is a tremendous help to me. I'm going to give some thought to putting the apartment on the market. There's something appealing about having that detail tied up when I'm gone but if I'm being honest, I think I'm not quite there yet. Give me a few weeks. We can re-visit after the trial?"

Ingrid nods and pats Jane's hand affectionately. She can feel every single bone under her hand and she has the fleeting fear that this will be the last time she sees Jane.

"Sure. Of course. This is all just to get us started. We don't have to rush. There's no reason to rush." The words are all wrong. Ingrid knows this as soon as they come out, but she can't retrieve them now. Jane nods slowly and changes the subject.

"I've been listening to the old replays of your podcast. It's such an entertaining program, you know."

"Thank you. I haven't exactly had the time to devote to it lately. But I'm looking forward to getting back to it. It's been a real labor of love."

"*Too Busy To Die.* You never did tell me where the name came from."

Ingrid looks down at the chart she's created for Jane full of auction agencies and to do items. "It was just something my dad used to say after my mom died."

"Oh?"

"He'd constantly accuse me of trying to distract him with cleaning and reorganizing projects. He always said I was trying to keep him too busy to die."

"Oh, how poignant."

Ingrid sighs and stands up. "Yes. I just wanted to be enough for him, even after my mom was gone. But I never was."

"Ingrid, I'm sure—"

Ingrid waves Jane off. She doesn't want to do this now. She wants to clean out Jane's closets and put all of her affairs in order. "Come on, let's get to work."

Jane nods and stands to join Ingrid. "Ok. I was thinking about my box of photos and mementos of Christine and I know now what I want you to do with them after I'm gone."

"What *I* should do with them?" Ingrid is startled by Jane's choice of words. Jane heads over to a kitchen cabinet and retrieves the box. She brings it back and places it in front of Ingrid with a flourish.

"Yes, I want you to take this and burn everything inside. I'll pay you of course."

"Jane. That's preposterous." Ingrid looks over her shoulder at the massive wood-burning fireplace that is the center of Jane's living room. It seems that Jane could handle this task on her own without paying anyone. And Ingrid is insulted that Jane thinks she might need money badly enough to take it just for burning a bunch of letters and photos.

"No. Listen to me. There's more. When I'm gone, I want you to get the ashes to the funeral home, along with this letter, that I'm going to ask you to witness and notarize. It states that I want my own ashes commingled with the ashes you present to the funeral home on the day of my death. In a sense, Christine and I will finally be together, and yet no one has to be hurt by the decision. It's perfect.

"Jane. Do you really think the funeral home, or your niece and nephew for that matter, are going to let a stranger just waltz in with a letter demanding your ashes be commingled with some foreign substance? There's no way this will work." Ingrid worries that Jane has progressed beyond rational thought. She shakes her head as she looks at the letter Jane has pushed across the table at her. A letter demanding the funeral director do her posthumous bidding.

"They will if we make this a legally binding document. Together."

"Ok, but even assuming Antonella and James decide not to contest this, what is it you want them to think the ashes are?"

Jane smiles triumphantly. "Just tell them it's sand from a favorite beach or ashes of a wood fire from a favorite forest. Or tell them nothing at all."

She's not sure at all that this will work, but Ingrid nods in agreement in spite of herself at this woman who would have everyone think she is absolutely bonkers when she is dead rather than simply a woman who once loved and was loved.

"Ingrid. Can I ask you something?" Ingrid is reluctant to say yes and agree to some other bizarre plan of Jane's. But it turns out the question is something else entirely.

"Why did you leave the law?"

Ingrid resorts to a familiar and impulsive response. "I was pregnant. I was having a baby."

"Well that's not a reason. Lots of pregnant women, lots of mothers, in fact, continue to practice law."

"Really? Because I'm not sure I saw all that many of them at the firm."

"Fair enough. But still, that's not a *reason*. So, tell me, honestly, why did you leave?"

Ingrid looks over her shoulder at the boys still quietly playing in the next room. It doesn't appear that they are going to save her from this conversation any time soon. She'll have to dive in. Lie or come clean. She decides to come clean.

"I heard you talking to some of the male partners one morning as I stood outside a conference room."

"Me?" Jane asks, but nods as she says it, like she knew this was coming. Like she's been waiting to see if she was caught or not.

Ingrid continues. "Yes. You were discussing which associates to staff on a big case that had just come into the office, and my name came up from one of the male partners. And you cut him off, and said, 'No. Not Ingrid. She's having a baby and she's not even likely to come back after maternity leave. Frankly, she's lost that litigation mojo lately. She's not one of us. I need someone else. Someone dedicated 100%.'"

Jane nods unapologetically. Ingrid wonders if Jane really remembers that particular conversation, or whether it was simply one of many.

"So you decided to prove me right?"

Ingrid smiles. "Something like that. You were just putting into words something I was already feeling. I figured I didn't have it in me. After the law, I needed to put that energy into the baby and another project altogether. I started my podcast from home shortly after Drake was born, during his nap times, really, and alongside a website and a blog in the beginning. It started generating enough traffic a few years ago to solicit some modest ad revenue. So you know—the rest is history.

"You found a passion to replace what you'd lost in leaving the law?"

"Yes, I suppose. I never really considered it a loss leaving the law. It didn't seem to define me the way it did so many others. I mean, you sort of got it right, when you said I wasn't one of you. At the time, I just didn't understand the greyness of it all."

"The greyness?"

"Well, you know, I wanted the world to be black and white. That's why I originally went into the law. After what happened to my mother, I just wanted to sort the world into categories. It seemed there were right answers and wrong ones and that appealed to me. But when I started working at the firm, I saw how utterly grey everything was. I was supposed to represent companies no matter if they had done something wrong or not. I was supposed to help write motions that would get them out of trouble, no matter whether they deserved it or not. Suddenly all the reasons I'd chosen law were revealed as wrong. The podcast has brought me back to a world I'm more comfortable in:

right and wrong. Clean and dirty."

"Interesting. How are you feeling now that you've dipped your toe back into the legal water?"

"Well, I've evolved a lot in the last eight years, since leaving the law, so it hasn't been as difficult as you might think."

"How so?"

"I guess I'm just much more, you know, *grey* now."

Jane pats her hand. "Well look at that. Turns out you *are* one of us, after all."

Ingrid laughs wryly. "Well, since I'm in the club, then maybe you could help me get past this Judge."

Jane smiles weakly.

Ingrid continues. "He's denied my motion *in limine* to preclude completely irrelevant evidence that really could get Opal convicted for all the wrong reasons. I know he's hell bent on letting this Prosecutor win at trial. Do I just concede that fact? Do I just keep creating issues for appeal? And how do I do that?"

Ingrid locks eyes with Jane and is hopeful. Since Jane first revealed the case was stacked against Ingrid, Ingrid has believed Jane knows more than she is letting on. She hopes that Jane will take pity on her given Ingrid's revelation that she overheard Jane sabotaging her career eight years ago. There's a long pause while Ingrid wonders whether Jane will reward her optimism.

She does.

"Ok, well, there is one way you might still be able to turn the tide a bit at trial. I did a little digging at the Law Club. And, since I've got nothing left to lose anymore, here it goes. It turns out the reason Judge Regan is retiring and leaving the bench sooner than expected is that he was going to be investigated on some wireless hacking charges, but the Prosecution has decided to let that investigation drop, pending the outcome of this case."

"Hacking charges?"

"Yes, apparently he was carrying on with a young woman who broke it off with him about a year ago. And he's been somewhat obsessed with her in the aftermath of the breakup. He's been trying to track her phone calls and find out who she's with now. She threatened him with a PFA, but never filed. And now I hear that she's actually left town, trying to get out from under Judge Regan's creepy spying, but not before meeting with someone in the Prosecutor's office with some proof that Regan was trying to hack into her phone records and even illegally shadow her text messages. They've made a bargain with him to drop everything and in return he's to leave the woman alone and make this case go smoothly for them, supporting the election bid. Everything will be tied up in a neat bow."

"Dear God. That's horrible. But, why has *this* case become part of the deal for the prosecution?"

"Just bad timing, really. It's a fairly high-profile murder case, and the Prosecutor's office doesn't like to lose those, and it got assigned to Regan in the regular judicial case pool, so it was an easy pawn in the game they were already in the process of working out final details on."

"So that's it. He helps them look good, and they drop everything and save his reputation and he helps the Prosecutor's career?"

"I'm afraid so. Everyone wins."

Not everyone, Ingrid thinks.

"There's something else to consider, Ingrid."

"Which is?"

"No matter what good intentions you have, and no matter what the Judge and the Prosecutor have worked out, if Opal really did this thing—and I'm not asking you whether she did or not—but if she did, you have to be prepared to lose. There's only so much you can do for a truly guilty client."

"She didn't do it," Ingrid says too quickly and then leaves it at that.

CHAPTER 22
Mary Poppins

Gabby had arrived on Ingrid's doorstep, humming, with a duffel bag and an umbrella a year earlier.

Ingrid joked that she was just a carpetbag away from Mary Poppins. Gabby smiled and said she'd heard that comparison before. She swept into their lives much like the energetic babysitter from the musical, with one big exception. She didn't fuse their family back together like the Disney character: she exposed its breaks and fissures, and eventually split it wide open.

Gabby and Ingrid worked side by side a few days a week. Gabby helped Ingrid with Drake's behavioral therapies and helped cook dinner. She did more than Ingrid asked and while Ingrid always put extra money in Gabby's envelope, she was constantly returning the money back to Ingrid in the form of little presents for Drake and bouquets of fresh cut flowers for Ingrid. It was the closest thing Ingrid had experienced to real friendship since her relationship with Opal imploded years earlier.

She confided in Gabby, more than she should have, of course, but she couldn't help it. After she knew it was true, she told Gabby that Peter was having an affair with Opal and she told her about Opal's past.

"I'm just working out how to sit Peter down and let him know the gig is up. It's going to be time for him to leave, but I have to figure out what's best for Drake first. It's hard losing a father, no matter how shitty he is. Unfortunately, I know this from personal experience."

Gabby was wise, mature. She'd nod during these conversations as they folded laundry or put away toys together or re-organized the pantry shelves side-by-side. "You'll do the right thing, and at the right time, Mrs. D. I have no doubt."

Gabby revealed bits of pieces of her past. Small doses of intimacy revealed at the odd time. Her mother's neglect in Ohio. A pet dog that got run over by a car when she was nine, that ruined her for pets for life. A narcissistic boyfriend and a toxic relationship back home that she'd narrowly escaped.

In hindsight, Ingrid would come to realize how little she actually knew about Gabby, but if you'd asked her when Gabby was working for them, she would have told you Gabby was the closest thing she had to family.

The week before Peter died, Ingrid came home from running errands to find Gabby asleep on the couch. Drake was sitting on the floor building an elaborate structure out of his favorite Legos and Gabby was passed out cold. It was the strangest sight. Ingrid stood over her staring for a couple of long minutes, trying to piece together the unlikely vision in front of her.

Mary Poppins was sleeping on the job.

"Drake, did Gabby just fall asleep?"

Drake shook his head.

"Has she been sleeping for a while?"

Drake nodded.

"Did you finish your lessons for the day?"

Drake shook his head no again.

Ingrid felt a growing sense of alarm as she stood over Gabby whose sleep seemed deeper than just a midday nap.

"Drake, go up to your room. I'll be up in a minute."

Drake looked at his mother with his head crooked. She knew he was wondering why she was sending him to bed in the middle of the day. She pointed her finger up the stairs and looked at him firmly.

"Drake, please. Just go."

He abandoned his Legos and headed up the stairs silently. When Ingrid was sure he was out of view, she shook Gabby's shoulders, a little roughly, but she was suddenly afraid. "Gabby, Gabby."

Gabby's head lolled around in a circle, and she opened her eyes only halfway. "Mrs. D. You're home." Her words were slurred and she looked like she was trying to focus as she pushed herself up to a sitting position.

"Gabby! Are you drunk?"

"No, no way, Mrs. D. Just a little cold medicine. My allergies. Just need to sleep it off. I'll be fine. Headed home now." She started to stand up from the couch but slunk back down.

"Gabby! You're not going anywhere in this condition. Sit back down." Ingrid didn't need to tell her twice, though, because Gabby was back down on the couch, her head twisted uncomfortably into the arm of the sofa, her eyes shut tightly closed again. Ingrid looked around for Gabby's duffel bag that always accompanied her and ransacked it quickly.

Underneath a change of workout clothes and a water bottle like she was headed for the gym, was a brown pill bottle, for Naltrexone made out to "Gabrielle Connors." A quick Google search revealed that Gabby's prescription was for a drug prescribed to people trying to get off opioids.

Ingrid immediately called for an ambulance. "My babysitter is passed out on my couch. I think she ODd."

The paramedics were quick and efficient, and they took Gabby and her duffel bag to the hospital. Ingrid wished she had Gabby's mother's number in Ohio. She would have liked Gabby to have someone with her at the hospital, but she certainly didn't want to be that person. She felt betrayed and horrified thinking about all the times she'd left Drake with Gabby when she was high or worse, close to overdosing.

"Drake, does Gabby sleep a lot when I'm gone?"

"Sometimes."

"Why didn't you ever tell me?" Drake shrugged and looked embarrassed, and Ingrid hugged him fiercely, saddened that Gabby had stolen even more of Drake's words.

"It's ok, buddy, we'll get you a new babysitter. Gabby won't be back." Drake nodded happily, and Ingrid shuddered to think about how long this had been going on. She thought to herself that Gabby was now out of their lives without any concrete or lasting damage.

How wrong she'd been.

A week later, Gabby showed back up for her Monday shift like nothing had happened. She was manic and ready to work.

Ingrid was stunned as she opened the door and Gabby moved quickly past her.

"Gabby, what are you doing? We can't have you here anymore."

Gabby fluttered around folding and cleaning, while Drake stood in the middle of the room, wide-eyed and visibly anxious. Ingrid felt the same way and sent Drake up to his room where he fled willingly. "Gabby, you can't. You need to get help. I can't have you here."

Gabby stopped cleaning and looked up at Ingrid with tears in her eyes. "Please, just give me another chance. I promise you it will never happen again. I've had some crazy stuff going on recently. My old boyfriend got back in touch with me recently. He won't leave me alone. He's gone off the deep end. But I've got it all under control now. I promise you. It's really all under control, now."

"Gabby, I'm sorry. I don't know what's been going on with you. But I can't have you around Drake while you're using."

"No, I'm not using. The naxo, it's a prescription to help me stay clean. It's just that I started it too soon, and that's why it affected me the way it did. You're supposed to be off pills for at least 14 days before you start it. Mrs. D, please stop looking at me like that. It's not like I'm doing heroin or something. I was just on some painkillers for a bum knee, and my old boyfriend, he gave me a bottle of pills left over from an old prescription, and I just started to get too dependent on them. Really, it was a small misstep, and I'm back on track now. Mrs. D, please you can't just dump me. I've been a good friend to you and listened to a lot of your secrets."

There was something ominous about Gabby's words. Ingrid stood in the kitchen trying to piece it all together. She had crossed lines with Gabby, and Gabby was reminding her of that very fact. Ingrid was supposed to be her employer, but she'd confided in her babysitter as if she was a friend. She'd misled her. Now Gabby wanted to share personal information and stories with Ingrid, and it just couldn't work that way.

She was still standing in the kitchen trying to figure out how she'd gotten herself into this mess, when Peter walked into the kitchen, dressed for the day. He kissed the top of Ingrid's head absent-mindedly. It was the closest thing they ever got to affection those days. She was waiting for the day those quick exit pecks ended as well.

Peter nodded at Gabby, but looked surprised. Ingrid had told him, of course, about finding Gabby passed out on the couch the week earlier. He'd suggested they consider filing some criminal charges, but Ingrid had assured him she'd handle it, that Gabby wouldn't be back. Peter looked back and forth between Ingrid and Gabby, and Ingrid rushed him out the door. "Gabby and I are just having an exit interview, Peter. She's collected her final paycheck. I've got it covered."

Peter looked unsure, but still took his leave with a quick, "Ok, I'm headed to the Russell property on 35th Street. I have to do an inspection." Ingrid watched him leave, wondering how much of his day would be filled with the Russell property, and how much would be filled with his mistress.

Gabby seemed to read her thoughts. And then twisted them as the door closed behind Peter.

"You know I'm on your side, Mrs. D. With that husband of yours running around with a whore, you need an ally around here. You know, he left his phone out unlocked the other day, and I got her cell phone number. We could call her together. Confront her. Listen to me. I'm on your side. Give me another chance, Mrs. D. I need the money and—"

Ingrid shook her head, no longer distracted by Opal or Peter or Gabby's Mary Poppins feats, but consumed only with her own terrible error in judgment. *Gabby has hacked Peter's phone. She's calling Opal a whore. Dear God, what have I done?*

Gabby's eyes looked wild and suddenly her manic movements were revealed not as grand gestures of help, but rather drug-fueled motions.

"You're high, Gabby, aren't you? You're still using. You're not clean. You have to get some help. Take care of yourself first and then let's talk in a few months."

Ingrid was just bluffing. She hoped Gabby would forget all about them in a few months.

Ingrid reached in the pocket of the cardigan sweater she was wearing and brought out a familiar comfort item. Her "BREATHE" stone that Opal had given her years before.

"Gabby, take this, it's gotten me through some rough times and I hope it does the same for you. I'll help you find a rehab, but I'm not going to give you any money now. I'll pay you what I owe you in rehab time instead."

Gabby took the stone but turned hysterical. "What? No, no. I need cash, not rehab. Ok. I'll prove to you that I'm on your side. I'll prove it to you. Where'd that husband of yours say he was headed? Russell and 35th Street? I'll prove it to you."

Ingrid shook her head fiercely at Gabby. "Gabby, you're not thinking straight. You need to forget about us and our problems, and worry about yourself. Maybe go back to Ohio? Maybe reconnect with your mother or—"

Gabby laughed then. A wicked sinister laugh that chilled Ingrid and reminded her that not one of us knows each other. Not really.

Gabby stomped out the door, and Ingrid let her go.

She told herself she wasn't responsible for Gabby. She told herself she didn't really know where she was going or what she would do. She considered calling Peter and warning him that Gabby was high and bonkers and headed his way. But there was a part of Ingrid that didn't mind that Gabby was going to confront Peter about Opal.

Let Gabby confront Peter.

What's the worst that can happen?

It wasn't long before Ingrid got an unwelcome answer to that question.

Gabby overdosed that very day. A small buried notice on the police blotter on page 23 of the newspaper, spotted by Ingrid on the day of Opal's arraignment, revealed the not-so-surprising tragic result of Gabby's sudden and downward spiral. She'd died before anyone could connect the dots of her role in Peter's death.

Ingrid has been debating whether she should hire a forensics expert to put together all the evidence showing Gabby was at the 35th Street property that day. She wonders if she should offer up Gabby to create reasonable doubt about Opal's guilt. But that strategy has its own potential pitfalls and Ingrid isn't sure she wants to go there.

Am I any better than this corrupt judge? Ingrid wonders.

Ingrid knows she should never have been relying on a nanny hyped up on uppers. Ingrid knows she should never have confided in her or let her go confront Peter that day. Ingrid knows she should never have let Gabby do her dirty work.

But she did.

CHAPTER 23
True Say

The night before jury selection begins, Ingrid can't sleep. Jury selection (*voir dire*) is scheduled to commence at 9 am. A panel of jurors will be questioned by both Ingrid and the prosecutor, one at a time, until they can come up with a group that will sit and hear the evidence at trial.

Ingrid recalls a lecture from her early days of law school in which her criminal procedure professor had recited, in a very British accent: "Voir dire. The Literal translation of which is True Say."

Ingrid is up and ready early, a pot of coffee on at 5 am. She doesn't have to be at the courthouse until 8 am but she's wired. The boys are still in bed and she has told them that when they wake, she'll be gone as she has to spend the next few days at the courthouse. She and the social worker agreed to keep the details of the trial fuzzy for CJ. Best that he not get his hopes up that his mother could possibly come home in a few days. Best that he not get his hopes up for anything at all. Mary, the babysitter, is lined up for every day this week. It's unclear how long jury selection will last, let alone the trial. The boys' lessons are prepared. Meals have been frozen. Ingrid has tried to cover all the bases. She hopes she hasn't missed anything.

The judge is going to let in evidence that Peter and Opal knew each other. Countless pages of phone records and texts between the two dating back nearly an entire year before Peter's death. The judge is going to allow evidence also of Peter's purchase of the DIVAS lot, of the body that was found there, and while it's still not clear—won't be clear until opening arguments—how exactly the prosecution is going to use this bit of ridiculously irrelevant evidence, Ingrid assumes it won't be pretty. The jury will also get to hear about Opal's seedy past as a working member of the DIVAS club. Local witnesses who have bartered drug charges for thin testimony in this case, will testify that Opal was not just a stripper, but a prostitute and a drug trafficker as well, and that they had always known Billy was buried on the property, but that the police had never bothered to ask them. A busy body neighbor of Opal's will testify that he heard Opal and Peter fighting just two nights before he was found dead. That their voices were loud, elevated, and angry. That he couldn't hear everything, but that he'd been sitting outside on his porch, taking in the otherwise quiet evening with a glass of scotch, "neat," in his favorite rocking chair when he distinctly heard Opal say "I swear I will kill you, Peter."

The 911 call tipping off the location of Peter's body was traced to Opal's phone and the GPS function on her phone showed that she'd been at the Russell Street property during the window of time that Peter was likely killed. Opal killed him, left him for dead, and then later called the police in some sort of change of wicked heart, they will say.

Ingrid will poke holes in everything the prosecution has but she will also tell the jury that even if they believe everything the prosecution is telling them, it all proves nothing. Without a murder weapon and without a motive to kill Peter, the prosecution has strung together a case based solely on the bad deeds of one woman. Bad deeds that have nothing to do with the case at hand. She hopes the jury will listen to her. But she also hopes to preserve a record for an appeals court, if they lose at trial. If she has to stay on this case through an appeal, so be it. She wants to see this thing through. Her mother's legacy is strong in her. And her father's is not. She doesn't want Drake to suffer unnecessarily. If people are going to gossip about them, she wants people to talk about what a strong and wonderful example Drake's living parent is. She wants that message to overshadow (and eventually drown out) the salacious gossip.

And so she has to save Opal.

Voir Dire. True Say.

Although it's been a while, Ingrid has been through enough jury selections to know that jurors lie. They embellish the truth. Some of them make things up to get out of jury duty altogether. Others keep their biases and discrimination to themselves, in the hopes of actually ending up on the jury.

Will the truth come out? *Not likely.*

When Mary arrives, Ingrid heads out for her first day of the trial, but not before she pauses at the door of the boys' bedroom and sees their sleeping, dreaming selves, and thinks, *The only thing I won't do to save Opal is tell the jury the whole truth.*

The parameters of *voir dire* have already been hashed out in the pretrial hearing. Fourteen jurors will be selected. Twelve plus two alternates. The judge will question the prospective jurors and then each party will be allowed to ask a few follow-up questions. Each party will be able to strike jurors "for cause" if there is evidence in their responses to the questioning that indicates they cannot be fair and impartial for some reason. Each party will also have 20 so-called peremptory challenges they can use to strike jurors for any reason at all, including that they look at them funny or wear cologne that is too strong.

The first and second jurors are selected easily. A bland-looking white-haired woman and white-haired man who look like they might be a married couple or brother and sister, but who each indicate in preliminary questioning that that they are not related to anyone else on the panel or at the counsel bench and that they most certainly *can* be fair and have not heard anything about this case in the newspapers or elsewhere.

"I canceled my newspaper after the last election," the white-haired woman says.

"I try never to watch the news, or TV in general. It's depressing. I like that Millionaire show, though," the white-haired man says.

Judge Regan's law clerk keeps the whole process running smoothly as he repeatedly leans over to her and whispers. She never fumbles. She types quickly into a small iPad that goes everywhere with her.

Ingrid wonders if Judge Regan's law clerk knows about his upcoming retirement or the Prosecutor's election bid or the hacking charges that have become a bartered commodity by the Prosecutor.

After the early successes of the morning in placing the first two jurors with ease, Ingrid thinks maybe the jury selection will be easy. At the end of the first day of *voir dire*, however, there are still only two jurors sitting in the box. Both attorneys have used five peremptory challenges and Ingrid has used an additional four challenges for cause, all for prospective jurors who literally answered "no" when asked by the Judge if they could remain impartial and unbiased and be a fair juror on this trial.

"Is this usual?" Opal asks Ingrid just before the guard takes her back to her cell for the night. She's been allowed to dress in the same ill-fitting black pantsuit she wore to her arraignment. She smells musty and Ingrid calculates whether she has time to shop for new clothes for Opal to wear tomorrow on top of everything else on her plate right now. She guesses not.

"Nothing is usual or unusual. This is just how it goes. You can never really predict."

"Great. That's super reassuring," Opal says and rolls her eyes in what Ingrid has come to think of as Opal's signature move, as she heads back to her cell for the evening.

Ingrid takes a back exit out of the courthouse, trying to avoid press that are asking her for a statement. She and the prosecutor have agreed not to speak to the press now that jury selection is underway.

In her car, Ingrid takes a few deep breaths and tries to find a classical music station on the radio. Her nerves are fraught as she ponders how to put together a jury that can see through the evidence that is so clearly stacked against Opal by a judge who is seemingly motivated by his own selfish reasons to get this case over with quickly and easily.

Ingrid releases the sun roof on the car and starts driving around town trying to put some distance between her and the long day before heading home.

When she's passing Hemingway Park, she sees the car in her rearview mirror. It's black and shiny and it's keeping a good safe distance but it's definitely making every turn along with her even though her turns are haphazard and goal-less.

Ingrid makes a few more turns without a turn signal warning and the car follows every one of her moves. She taps her breaks and pulls over suddenly on the side of the road, letting the car go past her. She's breathless as a result of actually holding her breath the last few moments. The car is nowhere in sight, but the next morning when Ingrid comes out of her house to leave for court, she sees a black, shiny car pull out from the curb across the street and peel down the road. Apparently, someone is not only following her.

Someone is watching her.

CHAPTER 24
Nothing is Missing

Rattled by the knowledge that someone is following her and watching her, Ingrid stumbles through the first couple of prospective jurors during the second day of jury selection. She keeps one eye on Judge Regan at all times. She suddenly feels very exposed in his courtroom, wondering whether he's following her himself or having someone follow her, given what she knows now about him.

And because of what Jane's told her and what she's found out, Ingrid doesn't trust anyone. A phone call to the police is not likely to help. She thinks about tipping off Angela the reporter now that she finally has some news-worthy information to share, but she isn't sure she's ready to go public yet. She'd rather keep the information about Judge Regan in her back pocket until she absolutely needs it.

On the second day, *voir dire* ends with half of the necessary jurors selected. Ingrid says a quiet goodbye to Opal as the guard takes her back to her cell, and drives directly to her house with her eyes flitting between the road and her rearview mirror the entire time.

At home, Mary greets Ingrid looking a little more tired than usual. These trial days are going to take their toll on everyone.

"Your cabinet arrived," Mary says as she finishes cleaning up the kitchen while Ingrid says hello to the boys.

"My what?"

"Your cabinet." She waves to the corner of the living room

where a brand new, distressed wood cabinet has been placed in the corner.

"I have no idea what that is." Ingrid walks over to the cabinet and inspects it like it's a bomb. "Who brought this? And when?"

"This morning. Not too long after you left. I was going to call you and verify, but I knew you were in court, and the guy had a receipt and a delivery order with your name and signature on it. It all seemed legit. Did I do something wrong?"

Ingrid feels a wave of panic rising in her throat and spins around the room looking again at the boys as if they have been snatched from right under her nose. They are still there. Everything in the living room is right where she left it. If the delivery man was a kidnapper or a thief, he was a bad one.

"What did the guy look like, Mary? Think. This is important."

Mary looks even more tired and completely panicked as she stands in front of Ingrid trying to remember physical details from hours earlier.

"God, nothing special. A young guy. White. Scruffy. Needed a shave. I really spent very little time looking at him. I studied the delivery order, and thought I was doing the right thing not bothering you. I mean, he wasn't here to take anything. He just unloaded the cabinet from the box and then left with the box. He made no mess at all. I'm so very sorry, Mrs. DiLaurio if I did something wrong."

Ingrid takes a few deep breaths. No need to get Mary all worked up. She needs her. And the boys are looking at Ingrid now with wide eyes and growing panic as they are feeding off the mood of the only two adults in the room.

Ingrid spins around the room again a few times, taking inventory. Nothing's missing. "He was only here? He didn't go upstairs or in the boys' room, or the bathroom?"

"No, no. He was only there, in that one room. And then he left. I walked him out myself. He was just carrying the empty box the cabinet was in. Nothing else."

Ingrid starts to relax. It has to be a mistake. A strange coincidence. A mix-up. Nothing more. Nothing nefarious. "Ok, Mary. Don't worry. I'll sort this out tomorrow. I'm sure you're right. I'm sure it was just fine—just some weird mix-up—because he didn't take anything."

She pays Mary and walks her to the door, and it's only after Mary is gone and the boys are in bed, that Ingrid realizes something is missing after all.

The stitched up, empty teddy bear that was sitting in the corner of the living room where a distressed wooden cabinet is standing now, is gone.

CHAPTER 25
Yes, I Know, Too

After lunch recess on the third day of jury selection, Ingrid takes a good look at the jury members seated thus far. So far it's a jury composed heavily of conservative, older jurors: the perfect demographic for the prosecution, and Ingrid realizes that she only has a few more juror openings left and only one last peremptory challenge to try to place a few jurors on this panel who will be sympathetic to her client. She *needs* to use the information in her back pocket.

She approaches the newest prospective juror after Judge Regan finishes his rote and bland questioning that reveals the juror only as yet another conservative prosecution-friendly juror, and instead of asking a few predictable questions, Ingrid trots out a brand-new line of questions.

"Good afternoon, Sir. Thank you so much for being here. You mentioned you usually read your news online instead of in print."

A quick nod.

"You're not wary of internet hackers, then, taking over your computer and manipulating your whole news feed? Hacking is a pretty real concern these days, isn't it?"

The prospective juror looks at Ingrid like the question is stupid and shakes his head. But the question isn't for him. She looks squarely at Judge Regan who is boring through her with his eyes.

Ingrid stares back. *Yes, I know, too. So be just as careful with me as you are with that prosecutor.*

And then to test that her message is being received, she says, "You Honor, I move to strike this juror for cause."

The prosecutor looks up at her like he is noticing her for the first time. "That's ridiculous, you Honor. This juror hasn't said anything that would indicate he should be dismissed for cause. If she wants to dismiss him, she's going to have to use her last peremptory challenge."

The Judge never takes his eyes off Ingrid as he says "Motion Granted. Juror is dismissed." The prosecutor shakes his head at both of them, knowing as well as Ingrid does, that the message between the lines is "Well, I guess we're all playing the game now with the same information."

The rest of the afternoon sees a few additions to the jury panel that are as friendly to the defense as the early jurors were friendly to the prosecution, and by 4 pm, there are 14 jurors selected to hear the case of State of New York v. Opal Rowen. Opening statements are scheduled for the following Tuesday. Everyone has five days to prepare for the start of trial.

Ingrid walks out of the courthouse and takes the long way to the parking garage. She does a double take as she sees a woman turn the corner ahead of her that she's certain is Ingrid Bergman's daughter. She almost calls out to her.

Ms. Rossellini, it's me. I'm named for you. My mother would have loved to meet you.

She refrains and rubs her eyes, hoping this case isn't going to cause her to lose any more of herself than she already has.

As she drives home, Ingrid doesn't feel relief or success. Ingrid is smart enough to know Judge Regan isn't going to make this easy for her, and indeed by 7 pm, Tobin has already called her.

"Ingrid, we need to talk. I'm on my way over," he says, and Ingrid is not the least bit surprised that it's Tobin sent to do Judge Regan's dirty work. After all, Riversedge is a small town.

CHAPTER 26
Subpoena

Tobin shows up with a copy of the same will codicil that Ingrid ripped up and flushed away after finding the original in the teddy bear carcass. For a moment, she wonders whether Tobin was involved in stealing the teddy bear. Whether he was trying to get back the original, but he has a copy of the destroyed document so that theory doesn't really make sense. He holds the copy out to Ingrid.

"How many copies of these exist, Tobin?" Ingrid asks when she sees what he's holding out to her.

"I have no idea, Ingrid. Peter had the original."

Ingrid thinks back to the raised seal and blue ink signature on the version she ripped up. That was likely the original, but who knows how many copies Opal made before stuffing the original in her son's abandoned teddy bear. She isn't going to be able to keep this whole thing under wraps much longer.

Tobin apologizes, but Ingrid waves it off. "There's no time for apologies now."

Tobin knew about the document. He notarized it. He kept a copy in his files. He wasn't going to come forward with it, but the prosecution is subpoenaing his files as the dead man's former lawyer.

"This is obviously pretty sensitive," he says. He seems to be waiting for a reaction from Ingrid. She's busy thinking.

Tobin leans in as if getting a closer look at Ingrid. "Why don't you look surprised? You knew about it?"

She waves him off again and observes, "I guess the new sub-poena is because I pissed off Judge Regan today."

"Ingrid, you need to be careful with him. He's the one who really pressured my firm to take this case on from the beginning. And I've heard through the pipeline he wasn't too happy by the change of counsel. He's a bit of a loose cannon."

"How so?" Ingrid wonders how much Tobin knows. She wonders if he knows who is having Ingrid followed and who sent a delivery man to her home yesterday to steal a stitched-up teddy bear.

Tobin looks at Ingrid, and if he's thinking about disclosing more about Judge Regan, he doesn't let on. Instead he says, "I'll tell you what. I'm going to give you this—the only copy I kept. I simply notarized this document for Peter as a friend. Not as legal counsel. There's no reason for me to keep a copy if Peter wanted to keep the will codicil at his own home. You hold on to it. You decide who needs to know about it."

Ingrid takes the document. She doesn't rip it up, she just rubs her hand over the copied signatures of Tobin and her dead husband and wonders how many other copies of this document are out there waiting to be discovered. She wonders if whoever stole the teddy bear knows yet that the original is gone. She wonders whether they know now that the bloody rock and knife are gone, too. They won't have anything incriminating on Opal after all if that's what they are looking for.

Or on Ingrid.

The next morning, Ingrid is back at jail for a meeting with her client, with only one item on the agenda. She flattens the one-page codicil up against the plexiglass and asks, "How many other copies of this document exist?"

"I have no idea what that is."

"No? Well, I'll tell you what this is, Opal. This is what we lawyers call the smoking gun. It's the only motive they can possibly pin on you. Everyone knows that Peter bought that lot, and according to this legally binding document, Peter planned on leaving the lot to you in the case of his death. I got this copy from his former lawyer."

Opal shakes her head in response, and Ingrid keeps going. "Now, I don't believe you killed Peter for a rundown dance parlor. I don't believe you killed Peter at all. I don't know why he bought that decrepit building and property and left it to you and frankly, Opal, I don't want to know. But in the wrong hands, this document seals your fate. So again, I'll ask you. How many other copies of this document exist?"

Opal picks at her nails although the coral flecks are long gone along with most muscle memory of what it feels like to be free.

"Only one that I know of. The original. I swear it. I hid it somewhere and no one will find it. They won't. I promise. They haven't found it yet, and they won't."

Ingrid thinks about the teddy bear carcass. She's not sure she's willing to admit to Opal that she found the hiding place, because then she'd have to admit she knows what else is hidden there. She's also not willing to admit to Opal that her babysitter let someone break into the house and steal the hollowed-out teddy bear right from under her nose, either.

Ingrid nods. "This is bad, Opal." Ingrid lowers the document, and lays it out in front of her. One short paragraph and a few signatures that could alter the entire course of Opal's, and Ingrid's, life. So little and so much contained on this one page.

"I can't get ready for trial with any more secrets lurking out there. So this would be the time to get those all off your chest."

"Great. Where do I start?" Opal smiles half-heartedly at Ingrid and Ingrid shakes her head and looks away. Opal is right, of course. There are nothing but secrets between the two of them.

Opal brings Ingrid's gaze back with her next words. "Ingrid, I really want to testify. I want to explain why I was there at the scene. I want to give my side of the story."

"Opal. That's a disastrous suggestion. No defendant ever

helps themselves by getting on the stand."

Opal leans into the plexiglass. "Ingrid, destroy it. The will amendment I mean. Keep the deed, and destroy the will. Then the dance club literally goes to you as Peter's wife. No one will ever know that he was going to give it to me. It's the best thing for both of us."

"And what am I going to do with that decrepit piece of real estate?" Ingrid shivers at the memory of the boarded-up building with the rancid dumpster out back. Who knows what other bodies are buried there?

Opal whispers again. "You don't have to keep it. When I get out of here, when you get me acquitted, you just give it to me. When all is said and done."

Ingrid looks at Opal wide-eyed.

Is she crazy?

She's suggesting Ingrid work for free, suffering the humiliation of helping her husband's ex-mistress get acquitted, and then hand her a piece of real estate at the end as a reward?

"We can help each other stay safe and free and out of jail, Ingrid." Opal looks at her with eyebrows turned up. "I *know*."

Ingrid shakes her head at this woman who thinks she knows anything. She wants to tell her that she's found the teddy bear's secrets: the original will codicil and the bloody rock and the pocketknife. She wants to tell her, *You don't know everything, Opal.*

On Ingrid's way out of the jail house, she signs the old-fashioned exit log and she sees a name penned above hers. Ingrid was so focused on confronting Opal with the will codicil that she didn't even notice. She's not the first visitor Opal has had today. Ingrid flips the pages back. Opal's had the same visitor for weeks, in fact. Today is a Thursday, and he came early, but usually he comes on a Tuesday. He signs his name with a child-like signature that is clear and deliberate, every letter formed with care: Christopher Lance.

Ingrid goes home and Googles him. After a few rabbit trails of Christopher Lances in Miami and California, she comes up with some social media posts for a Christopher Lance who lives in a New York suburb about an hour away. Handsome, if a little shaggy. His eyes are striking, almond-shaped. Opal walks to the bedroom where Drake and CJ are playing and CJ looks at her with those same eyes, questioningly, and Ingrid knows who Christopher Lance is.

If her son's father is back in the picture, then Opal is up to something. Ingrid remembers clearly that Opal had told her in the past, she had nothing to do with CJ's father. That he never even knew CJ; that he took off soon after Opal got pregnant. She had told Ingrid that she raised CJ alone, bravely and without regrets.

But now he's back. Or maybe he was never really gone. And, interestingly, Opal has just inherited some real estate. What are those two plotting?

Or worse, what have those two already done?

CHAPTER 27
A Call That Can't Wait

"I'm sorry to call you so early, but it happened during the night."

Ingrid is holding the phone gingerly, waiting for the blurriness of sleep to fade completely. She shakes her head. In the haze, she feels like this is a call that could have waited—could still wait—but the voice on the other end is insistent.

Jane has died. Antonella is on the phone carrying out Jane's wishes, which included an immediate call to Ingrid to inform her of Jane's passing.

Ingrid knows she is supposed to start the charade now of bringing the Christine memento ashes to the funeral home so they can be commingled with Jane's. She's still not sure this will work, but she's committed to seeing the bizarre task through. As she sits up in bed and summons the alertness to make all the appropriate condolences to Antonella, she suddenly feels the prick of grief.

Jane has died.

They spent many years working together with absolutely no friendship or intimacy, but in the last few weeks, with just a few encounters and conversations, they had formed a bond that Ingrid has been relying on subconsciously. Jane had been her one lifeline in the world since Peter had died. Ingrid trusted her, and now she is gone.

Ingrid hits end on her call with Antonella, and before she knows it, she is sobbing into her pillow with uncontrollable grief.

Jane has died.

And now Ingrid has no one in her corner. Again.

CHAPTER 28
The Opposite of Déjà vu

At the funeral home, Ingrid feels the opposite of déjà vu.

It's the second time she's walked through these doors in less than a year, and yet, this time feels very unlike the day she sat with the director planning Peter's funeral.

For one thing, there are other people there.

Also, everyone is crying.

Even the funeral director is a little teary. He's apparently known Jane Stewart for many years, and for a man whose business is keeping it together for families who are grieving, Ingrid notices that he isn't doing too well today.

Jane's brother is flanked by his kids and they all have matching faces: purple and tear-streaked. They miss Jane already, and while Ingrid feels uncomfortable witnessing their grief, she also feels reassured to know that Jane is missed. That Jane's efforts to protect this family from her secrets worked. That they now grieve her wholly, and that her legacy remains intact. Ingrid allows herself to puff up a bit in pride at her own contribution to helping Jane.

She shakes hands with everyone and offers her condolences the best she can. "I knew your mother for many years. She was an incredible mentor to me both at the law firm, and after I left to forge a new life as well. She was instrumental in helping me make many of my formative decisions."

These are half-truths. Ingrid leaves out the part that it was actually Jane's original unkindness that drove her away from the law. And that pushed her to succeed in places—motherhood and the podcast—that had nothing to do with Jane. But still the words land where they were intended.

Antonella and James hug her squarely. "Thank you. You clearly had a huge impact on her in her final weeks and months. She spoke of you often when we'd see her."

Ingrid is startled to hear that. "Your aunt spoke of me?"

Antonella dabs at her eyes. "Well of course. You were among the first people we were to call."

Ingrid remembers then why she is here. "Yes, yes. I'm not sure you know this," Ingrid turns to the funeral director, thinking this will be easier news to deliver to him than to Jane's actual kin, "But Jane had assembled some sand and ashes from wood fires at some of her favorite locales around the country. From traveling over the last few years. And she made a request to have these commingled with her ashes."

Ingrid offers the box to the funeral director.

He looks puzzled, but he takes it from Ingrid. With her hands now free, she reaches into her bag and withdraws the legal document the two of them prepared and offers it to Antonella and her father.

Antonella looks similarly puzzled, but reviews it quickly, and hands it over to the funeral director.

"Hunh. Well, it's an odd request, right, but ok, can you do that?"

The grief-stricken funeral director nods his head once, and then Antonella points to a small marble box with two compartments that sits on the table in front of them. Apparently they'd been discussing urns when Ingrid came in and that had prompted the tears just before her arrival.

Antonella appears to be in charge. Her father and brother, and now Ingrid, sit quietly and allow her to direct the plans.

"As I was saying," Antonella sniffs, "I'd like to secure a double urn like this one. I'd like to transfer some of my mother's ashes from the family urn and have them next to Aunt Jane. They loved each other so much. It's only right."

Her brother and father nod and sniff and dab their eyes as does the funeral director.

And now it's Ingrid's turn to be startled, and she can only assume that if there is an afterlife, Jane is somewhere looking down at all of them, saying something like, "Well, I'll be damned. They knew all along."

CHAPTER 29
Not One of Us

After Jane's funeral two days later, stately and solemn, there is a reception at the Law Club. Ingrid is starting to forget she's not a member. She's here so often.

In the bathroom, a woman makes small talk. Ingrid recognizes her from the Park Avenue law firm as a mousy legal assistant who worked often with Jane. But the woman seems to know Ingrid only from current media reports. "You're Ingrid DiLaurio, right? Nice to meet you. I've been impressed with your story. I recognize you from the papers. How fascinating that you'd take on this woman's defense."

"How so? Because she was a stripper? Who turned her life around? What do you think, because she had a colorful past, she's not one of us?"

The woman looks stricken. "Well, no, because she's accused of killing your husband. I don't even know what that means: *not one of us*. Who's us, for heaven's sake?"

The stranger walks out of the bathroom too quickly, and Ingrid is left to wonder the same thing. She splashes cold water on her face and warns her reflection to hold it together.

This is no time to lose your mind, Ingrid.

After she leaves the Law Club, Ingrid takes the long way home and feels a little sorry for herself. Losing Jane has reopened a fresh wound. She's never really been able to find her place. Not in this town, or with the moms at school, or at tee ball, or at the Law Club. She's not the last woman her husband loved before he died.

She really is alone.

Ingrid adjusts the rearview mirror and thinks, *Well, except for the black car that's following me and that never seems to leave me alone these days.*

Opal is thinking about that red flat pocket knife. Christopher says the teddy bear is in a safe place. She is worried he might open it up and find its secrets, but he doesn't seem that smart, and she keeps telling him how much it means to her. How much it means to her son. She knows she's leading him on. She plans to have nothing to do with him when she finally gets out of here. But she doesn't know how else to keep him around to help when she needs it.

That knife. She should have gotten rid of it, not sewed it up in the bottom of the teddy bear where she'd later stash the will codicil and then, only hours before she was arrested, that stone as well.

She was glad she'd kept those other items. But the knife? It was the only gift her father had ever given her. An odd choice of birthday gifts, but still, he'd presented it with a flourish on her 13th birthday as he was on his way out the door to the local dive bar. He already smelled like cheap beer when he hugged her and presented the gift. It wasn't wrapped up or tied with a bow or anything like that. But it was a gift, nonetheless.

Happy Birthday, Sweetheart. 13. Wow. You're a real little lady now. You need something to keep you safe. Here you go. That there was mine when I was a little boy, not much older than you.

"Don't you need it, Dad?" She'd seen him use it to cut fishing lines and pop caps off beer bottles.

But he just laughed and said, *Oh, no, Princess. I've got better ways of taking care of myself now. You hold onto that. Self-protection. You don't ever take shit from anyone, you hear me? Promise me that.*

Opal had nodded hungrily, eager to please, eager to agree. And that was that.

It was the first and last present she'd ever gotten from her father. So no, she couldn't just get rid of that pocketknife, when it was the only thing her father had ever given her, and she'd used it to do the very thing she'd promised him she'd do.

CHAPTER 30
A Money Pit

Partly because she's trying to lose the black car, and partly because she isn't ready to go home, Ingrid detours to the highway after the funeral luncheon.

She calls Mary from the highway to check on the boys. "They're fine," Mary reassures. She holds the phone out to them and yells, "Anyone want to say hello to your mom ... I mean Mrs. DiLaurio?" Two boys in unison shout out, "Hello!" but don't appear to come any closer to the phone. Mary offers to stay with them for the rest of the afternoon so Ingrid can run some errands and work, and Ingrid accepts the offer, saying, "Thank you. I have so much to do to get ready for this trial."

Free for a while longer, Ingrid drives out to the dance club.

There's some crime scene tape set up around the grass lot and the dumpsters in the back of the property, but otherwise it looks the same as the last time she was out here a few weeks ago.

Actually, scratch that. It looks even worse.

This place is decaying in real time, day by day.

Why on earth would Peter want this place? Ingrid wonders, not for the first time.

The site is in a complete state of disrepair. It wasn't like him to buy a money pit. He was a sophisticated and successful real estate developer. This makes no sense.

Did he really want to restore it to its old glory and put his mistress back on the pole? It seems unsavory. Even for Peter.

Ingrid considers something for the first time. Opal has certainly lost her nursing position by now. Perhaps even if she gets acquitted she won't have any gainful employment to support her and her son. She's been quite resilient in the past. Is she planning a creative return to work after this is all said and done? If his social media profiles are to be believed, Christopher Lance is a construction worker. Are Opal and her son's father planning to carry out Peter's plans to restore the club now in light of his early demise?

As Ingrid walks the perimeter of the building, she notices that it seems to be closing in on itself, as if it could soon disappear altogether. And as she watches the building sink into the ground, she wonders anew, *How can I ever win this case?*

Ingrid took this case on for a host of reasons. She wanted to undo the damage Peter's affair and messy death had caused her, Drake, and even her growing business. Opal was her husband's (and Ingrid's) dirty little secret, and she intended to keep her that way. But look at what she's learned from Jane. After a life filled with all sorts of success and wealth, Jane Stewart has now died leaving a legacy of a sizable estate, a clean home, and a box full of secrets and regrets. Even Jane didn't really know how to dispose of those secrets in the end.

Maybe Ingrid doesn't want to die with her secrets intact either

Everyone seems to know now that Opal was indeed Peter's mistress. But all who have heard the story of Ingrid defending her husband's ex-stripper mistress, have commended Ingrid along the way. Jane, Josie, even Angela. She thinks about the two boys yelling hello into the phone not an hour earlier. Drake is not just surviving in the wake of his father's death and a new disruptive little boy in the house, but thriving.

In the end, Ingrid's legacy won't be a cheating husband and the ex-stripper mistress that Peter left behind. It will be that she defended Opal and took in her son.

Wouldn't my mother be proud? Ingrid can't help but think by the fourth lap around the building.

But what about Opal? And CJ?

Judge Regan isn't going to let Opal prevail. He has a reputation to protect and Ingrid fears that going up against him at trial is going to be an insurmountable task.

Not unlike the final task her mother took on.

Ingrid fears this crusade might just destroy her.

As she walks the lot thinking and reflecting, Ingrid sees something out of her peripheral vision. A black car pulls into the parking lot and heads directly toward her.

CHAPTER 31

I'm Worse

The black car pulls up alongside Ingrid and parks neatly and parallel against hers in the old DIVAS lot as if there are painted lines, which there are not, and as if there aren't deep divots in the asphalt all around them, which there are.

A young woman gets out of the car. She has a new hairstyle since Ingrid last saw her a few days ago, ashy blonde, with expensive-looking highlights, but Ingrid sees that her face is still entirely familiar.

"Miss Jenner."

She nods a silent hello.

Carly Jenner is Judge Regan's law clerk, his right arm on this and all his cases.

Ingrid made it a point to learn her name even though everyone else pretty much treats Jenner like she's invisible in the courtroom. Ingrid knows how important Jenner is to everything that's happened so far and everything that will happen in Opal's trial.

Ingrid herself spent a year as a law clerk between law school and joining the Park Avenue firm. Law clerk positions like Jenner's are highly coveted gigs gobbled up by the brightest and most ambitious of each law school class. They run their judge's docket, handle all the paperwork, the scheduling, and if the judge is generous (or lazy), share in the research and analysis of the cases as well. They get, however, very little credit for their hard work. Judge Regan's name is on every decision and every order in the case. Carly Jenner will be a silent worker bee in the background of this and all of Judge Regan's cases, content to work on the sidelines for a very small stipend and even less recognition, because at the end of the day, she'll hopefully parlay that year of anonymity and hard work into a prestigious and lucrative position at a firm like Ingrid's Park Avenue law office.

Ingrid knows the drill. She performed it as well, clerking for a now retired judge in New York City, Sylvia Mather. At the time of Ingrid's clerkship, Judge Mather was new to the bench, and unwilling to share any of her caseload with Ingrid. Ingrid tried to insinuate herself into the Judge's good graces, but ended up getting coffee and doing mostly *pro forma* orders for a year. Judge Mather didn't even bother to throw her a goodbye party at the end of the year, just commissioned her to train the new law clerk for two unpaid days after her term was up. Ingrid had waved her hand over the empty desk and said to the new law clerk, "Congratulations on landing your clerkship. As you can see, she won't let you actually do anything. So you'll have to make it up as you go. Best of luck to you."

Ingrid has figured out that Carly Jenner is the kind of law clerk who is running the show. It's not that Judge Regan is a better mentor or a more generous, industrious judge than Judge Mather was, but rather, he's lazy. He's a veteran, content to collect his judicial salary and attend black tie dinners and long liquid lunches at the Law Club. He's happy to be called "Your Honor" when he's off the bench and happy to fill his time on the bench with as little work as he can muster. Given what Jane told her, Ingrid has figured out that Regan's reputation means everything to him, despite his transgressions, and that he has distractions in his personal life that seem to take up more of his time lately than actual jurisprudence.

Carly Jenner is in charge and by the fall, she'll be headed the way of all former law clerks. Ingrid has wondered often, as she's seen Carly working behind the scenes on this case, where she's headed with her judicial clerkship lined resume tucked under her belt.

But now she's wondering why Carly Jenner has been following her for days. And why she's come to find her here at this, of all places.

Is she here to do Judge Regan's dirty work?

Ingrid doesn't get a chance to ask any questions before Carly thrusts a yellow envelope her way. Ingrid notices Carly is wearing clear surgical gloves, and wonders if she's a germaphobe, or if she's trying to keep her fingerprints to herself.

"You can do with this whatever you wish. Just leave me out of it, ok?"

"Should I open it now?" Ingrid treats it like it's a gift at a child's birthday party instead of a mystery package that's been handled with latex gloves. Carly nods.

Ingrid unfastens the clasp on the envelope and pulls a stapled packet out of it. Several pages of short docket sheets are clipped together. Each docket sheet is fairly short, with little activity.

Ingrid scrolls through the docket sheets for party names that will look familiar, but none of them do.

She notices that each one has something in common. The last entry on the short docket sheet is an order sealing court records, signed by a Judge Regan. That means these cases and everything in them are not for public consumption: an outcome reserved for cases where the safety of the parties is an issue, or trade secrets might be divulged, or really a host of other reasons. Sealing case records is firmly in the judge's discretion. And Judge Regan seems to have used his discretion liberally.

"I don't understand."

"Yeah, I didn't either when I found the Judge working late one night shredding the contents of about 25 bankers' boxes. Let's just say he's not exactly one to burn the midnight oil, if you know what I mean, so his late-night working binge sort of surprised me."

Ingrid snorts a little laugh at Jenner's barb.

"It's been killing me to watch him re-write my decisions in this case."

"Re-write your decisions? What do you mean?"

"The orders on your motions *in limine* to exclude the evidence of everything that happened here." Carly waves gruesomely over to the crime scene tape.

"And the body found here? Evidence in a completely unrelated case? It's all ridiculous. Those were no-brainer motions. I didn't even spend that much time on the research. I wrote orders granting all your motions and gave them to him for his signature. But he re-wrote every single order I wrote. When I saw him working late that night on the bankers' boxes, I took a few pictures of the sides of the boxes where docket numbers had been stamped and I did a little digging in the court clerk's office.

"It seems that Judge Regan spent about 4 years on the family court docket before getting the criminal docket. And you want to know something odd? In all those years, he never once granted a TRO. Not once.

"TRO" is the shorthand for Temporary Restraining Orders. Ingrid remembers her days working as a clerk, also on a family court docket. Motions for TROs were filed, generally on an emergent basis, by parties who were seeking protection from abusive spouses, partners, and others. They were not always meritorious. Sometimes they were even frivolous. Spouses and parties trying to use children and lies as tools in a heated and nasty divorce and custody case. Ingrid had become quite jaded during that time. But she'd also learned that many of them were indeed warranted. And when in doubt, her judge had advised her that they'd grant the TRO, and schedule a hearing quickly to sort out the details. It seemed odd that Judge Regan had the opposite approach of denying every last one that arrived on his desk over the course of four years.

Odd, but not necessarily worthy of the cloak and dagger game Carly was now playing.

"Interesting," Ingrid offers cautiously. "But I'm not quite sure why you've been following me for days, waiting to deliver this information to me. He denied a bunch of TROs and then sealed the court records? It's not that unusual to seal records in these types of cases. They're highly sensitive." Ingrid wonders if maybe she's mis-judged Carly. If maybe she isn't as smart or ambitious as Ingrid had pegged her for.

"Those aren't the TRO cases that are sealed, Ms. DiLaurio. Each of those docket sheets you're holding is for a murder case."

"With a docket sheet this short?" Ingrid flips through the pages again. "This makes no sense." Ingrid knows the docket sheet on Opal's case is about 4 pages long by now and it's not even a complicated case. Murder cases aren't generally resolved with such little activity.

"Each one of these cases involves a murdered woman."

Ingrid looks up at Carly and feels a chill despite the summer temperatures.

"And each woman had previously filed for a TRO before Judge Regan. He's got control of the calendar and he takes every single murder case filed in that courthouse right now. So he knows that if anything goes wrong in any of those cases he dismissed on the family docket, he'll just get rid of it on the criminal docket now. Those are powerful men on the other side of those cases. The richest and most successful men in Riversedge. They wield their power any way they like, including threatening and in some awful cases, killing the women they claim to love."

"Jesus." Ingrid flips through the docket sheets whose brevity suddenly speaks volumes.

"He killed those women—Judge Regan did—with his laziness and his misogyny. He dismissed those cases before they even got started and sealed the files, all to protect his cronies, and himself. Again and again, it's happened over the years without any remorse. And honestly, Ms. DiLaurio, there's more. But—"

Carly looks over her shoulder and Ingrid is left wondering what more Carly knows about Judge Regan because she suddenly just clams up in silence.

Ingrid studies the docket sheets some more and then looks up at Carly. She takes a chance. "What do you know about the hacking allegations against Judge Regan?"

Carly shakes her head but doesn't look surprised. "Not much. I've heard him talking in hushed tones with the prosecutor. I try to stay out of his personal life as much as I can. He's separated from his wife, so she calls every once in a while trying to get access to his personal calendar. I figure the less I know, the less I'll have to lie to her. It's all very awkward."

"Well, I think he has a vested interest in making this case go easily for the Prosecutor."

"Good God. You don't think he had something to do with murdering your husband, do you?"

"No, I don't. But he has everything to do with feeding Opal Rowen to the wolves. He doesn't seem to care too much about people who can't do anything for him. But he seems to care eminently about people who *can* do favors for him." Ingrid holds up the packet of docket sheets as proof to Jenner.

"He's awful."

"Ms. Jenner, are you going to deliver this information to the authorities?"

Carly laughs. "What good would that do? I wouldn't even know who else to give it to that's not already in his pocket. That's why I brought it to you."

Ingrid sighed. "I don't know what to do with it either."

Carly sighed loudly. "So, I guess Judge Regan wins. He gets to keep his hands clean and Opal Rowen will take the fall for this murder and he and his cronies can just keep wielding their power in this town and taking down anyone who steps in their way."

"Ms. Jenner, I'm sorry—I just—"

"Listen. I've been working for this man for nearly a year and he's been nothing but a pig to me. But me? I'm worse. I handed in his letter of recommendation on embossed official judicial stationery when I interviewed for my New York City law firm position just last week. I'm not sure how long I can keep up the charade that this law thing is all about good guys and bad guys. I want to believe I can still do some good with my law degree. But I couldn't leave this clerkship without passing off this information with the hope that some good could come from it."

Carly points to the docket sheets in Ingrid's hand. "No matter what happens. Appeal this case on the clear judicial abuse. The denied motions alone are grounds for appeal. And then use this information and get him off the bench for good. Save even more women from his circle of destruction. Start with saving Opal Rowen and then save even more."

Ingrid continues to flip through the docket sheets, shocked. "I guess I'm still a little confused. Why me? Why are you giving this information to me?"

"Because you're defending that woman who, let's face it, is at least guilty of having an affair with your husband. And you're doing it because you're outraged over the misogyny of bringing up her past life as a means of convicting her. You know the lines are blurry. You're trying to navigate them as well. I knew I saw a kindred spirit in you. Don't let the Judge Regans of the world win."

And with that, Carly Jenner gets back in her shiny black SUV with her new expensive suit and highlights, all of which are probably purchased with her fancy new law firm signing bonus and heads away, leaving Ingrid alone in the DIVAS lot. As she watches Carly drive away, Ingrid exhales loudly.

Carly has her all wrong. Ingrid is no one's champion. No one's hero. She's not Judy Barton. She's just herself. She's simply trying to keep the world from talking badly about her. And she's trying to control the narrative around Peter's death. She has nothing but selfish reasons for doing so.

Ingrid flips through the docket sheets one last time and stuffs them back into the manila folder. She is tempted to do nothing with this new information. She just wants her own secrets to stay buried. She wants to forget the fact that she let Gabby head off to confront Peter high as a kite, not knowing and not caring what would happen next. She wants to forget how she grew her business, and how she decided long ago she'd rather Drake have no father than a shitty one. She wants to forget how her own father didn't even think she was worth staying alive for.

Ingrid fears she is more like Jane Stewart, and even Judge Regan, than she would have thought.

After all, when you take a deep breath and come clean about your past, when you open your heart to trust someone fully and completely with your past, you might just end up like Opal Rowen: friendless and on trial for murder.

CHAPTER 32
Second Chapters

At home, Drake and CJ are fighting over a Minecraft game. It's uploaded to the only iPad in the home and CJ wants it. Also Drake wants it. Mary looks like she's ready to run out the door when Ingrid walks in.

Ingrid takes the iPad that is volleying between the boys and puts it up on top of the refrigerator. "Ok, if this is going to be causing this much fighting, we're putting it away."

Both boys look stunned, as if each one was certain she was going to validate *his* claim.

CJ starts to scream, "I want it, I want it, I want it!"

For the first time since he arrived, Drake looks like he's over CJ's tantrums. He puts his hands over his ears and shakes his head and runs out of the room.

Ingrid tries soothing CJ in a gentle voice. "CJ, that's not how we work things out. You'll have to stay off the game for the rest of the night."

"I hate you, I hate you, I hate you!" CJ starts screaming over and over until Ingrid is wondering why his voice isn't just giving out. She's not used to all this screaming. The silence between her and Drake is uncomfortable at times, but this is no better at all. She reaches down, takes CJ's hand and tries to lead him out of the room but he slaps her hand away and sits down in the middle of the kitchen screaming, "I hate you," while Drake is still running in circles in the living room with his hands over his ears. Ingrid walks away from both boys up the stairs to the bathroom, where she sits on the edge of the tub and cries loudly, in a way she can never do when it's just Drake, because she doesn't want him to hear her in the silence. But now the house is so loud that her tears are disguised. She is able to cry completely unnoticed.

✦

Opal is playing chess with one of the other inmates. It's a game she hasn't played in a while and she has to re-learn it on the fly. There isn't much to do here, and she's figured out this is a good way to pass the time. CJ taught her to play chess when he was in kindergarten. He looked up how to play on YouTube. She is always surprised at how clever that kid is until she remembers that he is her kid after all.

As she moves her bishop diagonally across the board, she thinks about the trial. Opening statements are tomorrow. Ingrid has told her to be prepared for a relatively short trial. There doesn't seem to be that much evidence, and Ingrid expects the case to present and finish within a week. Maybe a verdict by the weekend. Hopefully, Opal will be back with CJ by the weekend.

Opal is trying not to get her hopes up, but hope is all she has in here, and she definitely feels a lightness to her step. Christopher has helped, of course, but soon it will be time to cut him loose. He's got the teddy bear, he keeps telling her gleefully. Does she want him to bring it here to the jail? She shakes her head. "Of course not, Christopher. Just keep it somewhere safe until I get out of here." She hasn't told him why she wants it. She hasn't told him what's inside.

Opal doesn't want him back in her life on the outside. She doesn't want Ingrid back in her life either. She's been thinking she'll take what little savings she has (*maybe request a bit more from Ingrid given the contents of the teddy bear?*), buy a bus ticket for herself and CJ, head as far west as her money will take her, and restart her life in a place where no one knows her. She is looking forward to being in a place where she'll never run into a man from her past again. She doesn't know what she was thinking, believing she could reinvent herself right here, in the same place, right down the road from where all her secrets were buried. After the trial, there will be absolutely no reason for her to stay in Riversedge, or in New York, or anywhere on the East Coast, for that matter.

Because now even Peter's gone.

Opal's mind has been too scattered to even allow herself to properly miss Peter since she's been here. But lately, as she's permitted herself to conjure up an image of what it will look like when she gets out, she can't help but miss Peter. Because when she gets out, he won't be here. And their plans have all gone up in smoke.

Sometimes she thinks she could take the original of the codicil out of the teddy bear when she gets out of here, and she could make her claim after all and go through with Peter's and her original plans. But other times, the thought of going through with it all makes her violently sick. She's not sure she has the strength to go through any of it without Peter.

Peter was the first man she'd ever been with who was comfortable with all of Opal. He wasn't put off when he found out about her past, and he wasn't obsessed with fetishizing it either. When Opal told him one day, more of a test than anything else, to see if Ingrid had already told him, he was unfazed.

"I have something sort of shocking to tell you," she started.

He waved her off and said, "Yes, yes, I've heard all about that. It's just one chapter of your story. What else?"

And so she told him more. About Dean. About Billy. About her neglectful parents. About her makeup counter job, and her nursing degree. She shared all of herself with him: her fears, her vulnerabilities, her strengths and victories, and he accepted them all.

One day while they were driving into the city for a dinner date, she asked him not to take the well-known shortcut using the Route 92 bypass

"Why not?"

"I never go that way. I just can't bear to drive past the old DIVAS building." He had looked at her then, tenderly, questioningly, in a way that was so completely unfamiliar to her, and he pulled the car off to the side of the road, put it in park and took her face in his hands. "I hate that you think you have to run from that part of your life forever."

Opal had been speechless. Much as she had been when he came to her with the deed for the lot, a fancy notarized legal document, and a plan.

"I'm going to make sure you don't have to run away ever again, Opal."

That was the Peter she knew. He was so different from the one Ingrid had described all those years earlier. She didn't think Ingrid had been lying. Instead, she thought, *He's changed, too. Like me. He's put his past behind him and everyone deserves a second chance.*

That was why they found each other and connected so easily. Because they were both in their second chapters and together they planned to find their way to the next ones.

CHAPTER 33
It Was Worth It

With CJ and Drake finally calmed and fed, Ingrid puts them both to bed without baths and without stories. She's spent. She feels dangerously close to some new breaking point: a different line than she's already crossed. She needs to expedite this trial. She needs this all to be over.

Jane's death, caring for CJ, the murder trial, all of it has taken a toll on her emotional state, already weakened in the aftermath of Peter's death, and she doesn't think her reserves are going to last much longer than one week.

She cues up taped podcasts to replay for the week. The podcast is getting stale. She hasn't had a new guest in six weeks. Advertising revenue is down. She knows she's put her business, her labor of love, on the backburner, and it, like everything else—like everyone else—is suffering right now.

Was it worth it? she wonders.

For the first time in a while she hears Gabby's voice in her head, unbidden.

Silly goose. Of course it was worth it.

Oh Gabby, Ingrid thinks of her late babysitter with affection in spite of herself.

Gabby was always saying things like "silly goose" and "lickety-split." She was truly a modern-day Mary Poppins spitting out words and phrases that had rhyme and rhythm but that sounded like a mouthful of ridiculous. Peter was usually dismissing her, making faces at her behind her back as he passed her on his way out the door.

But one day, not too long ago, Ingrid noticed that Peter actually started speaking to her more gently. More kindly.

Ingrid had come home from running errands and Peter was already home. They were all sitting together in the living room, playing a board game together: Gabby, Peter and Drake. Gabby was giving instructions, and Drake was playing silently, but still there was a serene glow to the scene Ingrid walked in on that day. She stood in the entrance hallway, observing the three of them playing together and smiling, and it was unsettling. Ingrid had watched them for a beat more, almost like time had stood still, and felt a wave of nausea come over her.

Ingrid knew what it was like to live with a man who was only biding time. She'd worked hard to keep her father distracted and busy in an effort to keep him in her life after her mother died. Ultimately it hadn't worked, and that wasted effort had very nearly derailed Ingrid, too.

With a heavy mind Ingrid falls asleep and tosses and turns and eventually does something she hasn't done once since Peter died: she dreams about him.

He's standing on the edge of a cliff and he's looking at her wide-eyed and clear-eyed.

He seems to be saying goodbye. Ingrid wants to say it back. She wants this to be over. She doesn't want to be connected to him anymore. She opens her mouth, but the words don't come out.

"You're like Drake. You can't speak," Peter says quietly in the dream.

Hearing her son's name like that, even in a dream, is enough to motivate her.

In her dream, she reaches out her hands and she deliberately pushes Peter off the cliff. She stands on the top and watches him fall. It's a long way down and when he arrives at the bottom, he lays there, staring back up at her. And finally, finally, he mouths the words she's been waiting to hear for so long now.

"I'm sorry, Ingrid."

In the middle of the night, Ingrid switches on a light and looks around at her bedroom, covered in laundry piles that need to be folded, and clutter that has mounted up. Even her usually neat and clean home is a mess. Her Mary Poppins, along with everyone else in her life, is gone.

With the light on and sleeplessness a given, Ingrid starts sorting the piles in her room, hoping the organization will bring her some calm. Maybe even some sleep. She sorts and files some recent mail and invoices for the business and as she does so, Ingrid thinks about the early days of the business, when her big plans for *Too Busy To Die* were scoffed at by Peter. She got the ball rolling while Drake was still an infant, but she had even bigger plans to get it to the next level. As Drake started preschool, Ingrid decided to make the business a full-time venture.

Peter laughed at her.

But Opal didn't.

She encouraged Ingrid to keep following her dreams, to invest in herself.

"Well, that all sounds great, but without my law firm salary, I don't have any income coming in to invest. Peter is adamant that I can't use what he affectionately calls 'his money' to fund the business. He says I need to find a way to do this completely on my own."

"So do that."

"Sure. You make it sound easy," Ingrid had laughed. But Opal had been serious. It was still months away from the day she'd make her big strip club revelation, but on that day, Opal revealed another secret altogether. She told Ingrid about the way she'd raised some capital when she needed cash for nursing school.

"I started a 'HelpFundMe' account."

"What do you mean? Like one of those crowdfunding plat-forms?"

"Yep. I set up a profile. I made a video. I said I was down on my luck, no parents, a recently deceased brother, and a small boy I needed to support on my own. I posted it on the main website page and I raised $15,000 in just two weeks."

Ingrid looked at her. "Just like that? You've got to be kidding me."

"I'm not. But I—" Opal paused.

"What?"

"Well, I embellished some of the details. I made it a little more, shall we say sympathetic? Most of it was true, don't get me wrong. But there were details: a sick boy, a mother looking to make sure he had the best possible medical care while pursuing her own education. Things like that."

Ingrid had looked at Opal with wide eyes and an open mouth.

"You insinuated that CJ was sick?"

Opal shook her head. "It was all on the up and up. CJ had strep throat when I posted that video, and I had no insurance so his medicine was costing me a fortune, and so you know, none of it was an actual lie. It was just packaged together in a way that made my story a lot more sympathetic than it might have been otherwise."

Ingrid had smiled then. The greyness of Opal's story had appealed to her. For a moment—a brief shining moment—she thought maybe she wanted to be more like her mother and less like herself. Of course, it would be months before she'd learn the truth about Opal's sordid past. At the time of the HelpFundMe revelation, she still thought Opal had just moved from makeup counter clerk to nursing school. She thought the small embellishments in her story were harmless.

Opal had said then, "I can help you. I can help you package your story, too. You can make a video. Post it on HelpFundMe. Raise some money. Build your business."

"But do I have to check in with the investors regularly? How would this work?"

Opal laughed heartily. "Investors? Oh that's perfect! Yes, call them investors, but no, they just donate money, and go on their way. They are strangers. It's a completely anonymous transaction. You don't even have to be in the video if you don't want to. I could make the video for you. I could use my story again, frankly. It worked so well the first time, let's try for an encore. I'll make a video, raise the money, give it to you as a gift, and you use it as you'd like."

"Are there seriously no rules for this?"

"Everyone is free to ask for help, Ingrid. And everyone is free to decide who they help. That's how the world goes round. Well, that and money."

The women had laughed then. Ingrid had never really said yes, and never really expected Opal to go through with it. But a month later, when Opal gave Ingrid a check for $17,000, and said "Take it. No, really, it was my pleasure. Someday you'll repay me with a favor," Ingrid had taken the check hungrily, and bought sponsored guest time and podcast equipment, and a month of publicist time, and she had never looked back.

Of course, Opal had cashed in on that favor in a big way. First she'd taken Peter. Then she'd gotten him killed. And then she'd made Ingrid clean up the whole damn mess. Ingrid makes a decision before she goes back to sleep. She's going to give in to Opal's misguided insistence to testify on her own behalf. It's not likely to help her get acquitted, but Ingrid is starting to care less about getting Opal acquitted, and just getting this trial done.

CHAPTER 34
The Blue Poppy Lady

Opal can't sleep. Ingrid has given in to her request to put her on the stand.

She wonders if she's been tricked. And if so, is it the way she tricks CJ into eating his vegetables by pretending they're candy? Getting him to devour them in whole bites when he thinks he's getting one over on Opal but she's really getting him to do something that's good for him?

Or is it the way she used to bribe CJ to go to bed early so she could be alone with a glass of wine and Peter in the family room? Getting CJ to embrace an early bedtime with the promise of actual sweets in the morning, for something that was ultimately bad for them all?

The prosecution is resting their case today and the defense will be able to call their first witness. Ingrid has said it will be Opal.

In the opening statement, the prosecutor said that he would prove that Peter and Opal hid the decaying body of Billy Russo on the grounds of the old DIVAS strip club after they purchased it and made plans to build on the property together. He said he would further prove that Opal wanted that body's existence to remain hidden. That they'd argued about whether to come forward with the body. They'd argued loudly, and that a neighbor had heard Opal threaten to kill Peter if he did come forward. That Peter hadn't had time to report the existence of the body, because Opal had killed him first. The so-called evidence to prove all these points had been tenuous at best. The neighbor was a terrible witness on the stand and Ingrid was able to poke holes in his memory and hearing. And not one of the witnesses battling old drug charges was able to say why exactly Opal would want to keep Billy Russo's body hidden. The implication was that she'd killed him, but since the coroner's report itself was vague on the details of Russo's death, and there were no pending charges against Opal Rowen for the homicide of Billy Russo, Opal is certain the case should fall apart on itself.

There is one problem.

The white-haired lady who was empaneled on the jury first, has started scowling at Opal. She wears a light blue cardigan with an embroidered poppy on it every day of the trial, and while Opal had started the trial believing her to be a sympathetic juror, she has shifted in her seat since the trial began. Despite the fact that no hard evidence of a motive or weapon has been presented, she has started glaring at Opal over all the circumstantial evidence: the bloody footprints, the neighbor's overheard argument, the anonymous 911 call. Each time the prosecution finishes questioning or offering a document into evidence, she turns a cold hard stare at Opal.

Even if the rest of the jury decides to do the right thing, this white-haired lady seems hell bent on being a potential hold out. Ingrid says all it takes is one juror to turn the whole panel. Opal isn't sure she believes her. But she isn't sure she can afford not to at this point.

As Ingrid and Opal meet at the counsel table the next day, they confer briefly before court starts for the day. Opal sees the blue poppy lady sitting in the corner, observing her and Ingrid. Opal smiles at her and the lady looks away, as if she's been caught.

"You haven't changed your mind, right?" Opal turns back

to Ingrid. "No. I'm still putting you on the stand today," Ingrid whispers.

Previously, Opal asked whether they should role play or practice in case Ingrid gave in to her requests to testify. Ingrid has always looked at her like she's made an obscene proposal. One time, Opal said, "I'll even play myself," to make a joke and lighten the mood, but Ingrid just responded by shaking her head.

Now Opal feels nervous that Ingrid has finally given in. "Are you going to ask me about the property? About Billy? About Peter? What do you want me to say? What do you want me to hold back on?" she whispers at the counsel table.

"The truth, Opal. I just want you to tell the truth."

"You sure?" Opal asks just as the judge comes in and everyone rises and faces front.

"Yes, Opal, I'm sure," Ingrid says without looking at her.

The prosecution starts the day by resting. They have no more witnesses. It's time for the defense's case. Ingrid makes a motion first to dismiss based on the lack of evidence in this case. It's a motion made simply to preserve the record now, because Judge Regan has made it clear he won't be granting a single of Ingrid's motions. Carly Jenner purses her lips as the Judge murmurs predictably, "Denied. Carry on with your case now, Counselor."

Opal gets sworn in and sits with her back straight, and with her legs crossed at the ankles, even though the jurors can't see her legs behind the wall. She's been watching the prosecution's witnesses sit all week, and they look like slouches. Leaning forward, backs hunched. Police officers, 911 dispatcher, forensics expert, they have all looked ridiculous. She's hardly been able to concentrate on a word they said. The jurors, on the other hand, have been sitting up straight, with polite attention.

Especially the lady with the blue poppy cardigan. Opal is determined to get her back on her side. The white-haired Juror Number One sits with her legs crossed at the ankles, and Opal emulates her as she takes the stand, meets her gaze, and holds it.

Ironically, the one who taught her all these tricks about posture and holding an audience's attention was Billy Russo. Part of his initiation for the new girls was a kind of manners class; the girls always referred to it affectionately as "strippers' finishing school." Opal was a student and later a teacher many times over as turnover rates were high over the course of the years she worked at DIVAS.

As she sits with her ankles crossed, answering bland questions like her name, date of birth, and current place of employment, her mind wanders to Billy and her prior place of employment and she wonders why a place that she has largely tried to erase from her memory has suddenly become all that defines her these days. From her posture to her reputation.

"And how were you related to the deceased, Peter DiLaurio?"

"Related?" Opal is brought out of her daydream. "But I wasn't related to him. You were."

Ingrid flinches, and Opal shudders with the realization that her guard has been completely let down. It's almost as if she's forgotten how to talk in polite company. *What is wrong with me,* she wonders, as she shakes off the misstep.

It's Ingrid's fault for not letting us prepare for this first, she thinks.

"I mean, we weren't related. We were friends."

"Were you intimate?"

Opal widens her eyes at Ingrid. *Is this what she wants to talk about? Right here, right now? Why on earth would she ask her that?*

Ingrid asks the question again, and this time, she nods while asking it. Opal realizes Ingrid meant it when she said she wanted Opal to tell the truth on the stand.

This could get interesting. And not in a good way.

"Yes, we were intimate."

"And how long had your relationship with Peter DiLaurio been intimate?"

"For nearly a year."

Opal looks at the blue poppy lady. She looks like something smells funny in the courtroom. Opal finds herself inadvertently sniffing.

"Did you previously work at a club named DIVAS located on Route 92?"

Opal looks at the jurors and then looks away as she answers. "Yes."

"Were you aware that Peter DiLaurio had recently purchased from the bank, the property where DIVAS is located, on Route 92, along with the adjacent lot?"

"Yes, I was."

"Do you have any idea why Peter DiLaurio would have purchased that property?"

"Objection, your honor. Calls for speculation on the part of the witness."

"Sustained."

Ingrid levels a cool look at the prosecutor then turns back to Opal.

"Did Peter DiLaurio tell you why he purchased that property?"

"Yes."

"And what did he tell you was the reason?"

"Objection, your Honor. Hearsay."

Judge Regan sighs loudly. Ingrid sees that he wants to hear the answer. Especially, since Opal has already said yes. She gives him a reason to overrule the objection.

"Your Honor, hearsay is only excluded if it's used to prove the truth of the statement. We can't know the truth of why Peter DiLaurio bought the property. He's dead. But Opal Rowen's belief about why he bought the property will go to her state of mind, a key issue in this case."

"I'm going to allow it."

The Prosecutor sits down defeated, and Ingrid looks over at the jury who is looking at her with renewed respect. They may not be sure exactly what legal issue she argued, but she argued it successfully. She might just be winning them over.

"Go ahead and answer the question, Miss Rowen."

"I'm sorry, can you ask it again?"

Ingrid notices how confused Opal looks and wonders if maybe she *should* have prepared her for the witness stand. Ingrid shakes it off.

"Sure. Ms. Rowen, what was the reason Peter DiLaurio gave you for buying the property?"

Ingrid watches the confusion lift from Opal's face. Her eyes well up with tears and her face has a timid smile through the tears.

"To put up a parking lot." Opal sings the words instead of saying them. It's a line from an old song and Ingrid watches in shock as the lyrics transform Opal's face completely.

"He was going to level the remains of the building and put a parking lot there. It was for overflow parking from the commuter rail down the road that has an express train into the city. He was going to have a shuttle running continuously through the daily rush hours. He figured he could turn that neglected site into a profitable site within a year or two."

"A parking lot?" Ingrid is as surprised by this as the jury is. She has violated one of the key rules of trial strategy: *Don't ask a question if you don't already know what the answer is.*

Opal nods. Her guard is down. She keeps talking. "He said it was like an engagement ring. But better."

Dear God.

Ingrid takes a deep breath and keeps going. "An engagement ring? How so?"

"It was his way of making sure I was taken care of. In case

anything ever happened to him. He said he really didn't believe in life insurance. Didn't believe in betting against himself. But this way, I'd have something after we got married that would be mine, and it could take care of my son and me. It was his way of turning my past into something good."

Ingrid looks at the jury. They are looking carefully at this woman. They believe her. She would have no reason to kill this man for the property. He was buying it *for* her. He loved her.

"You've heard the testimony of your neighbor about an argument you and Peter had a few days before he died, correct?"

Opal looks down at her hands.

"I did. I hate thinking about that argument. I hate thinking we wasted any of Peter's last days fighting. Of course, I didn't know those were his last days. If I did, I would have savored them. I wouldn't have fought with him at all. I wouldn't have let him go to that Russell property. I would have done whatever I could."

Opal's voice is breaking on the stand, and she looks so genuine and real. Ingrid feels a little guilty for not preparing Opal for her testimony, although she can't help but notice that the lack of preparation has helped her to look genuine and sincere on the stand. Opal has turned out to be a great witness. Yet, her genuine heartbreak over Peter's death unnerves Ingrid. She has to clear her throat. She looks down at her legal pad, and pretends she's reviewing something. A wave of unwelcome guilt rises up and threatens to overtake her. She thinks about Jane Stewart's dying advice that the goal in the end is simply to *know yourself*. She thinks, too, of her mother and wonders if taking on this difficult case might just have made her the type of woman Judy Barton could be proud of. She knows Judge Regan is going to do everything in his power to stop her, but she can't give up now. She looks up at Opal with renewed determination.

"Yes, well, as painful as it is to remember, I'm going to ask you to do just that. What were you and Peter fighting about?"

"It was stupid, really. It was about the parking lot. Peter was adamant that he wanted to get construction going as soon as possible, and he wanted me to come with him and watch the concrete be poured, and I just wasn't ready. I wasn't ready to go back to that property again and relive all those bad memories, and I didn't want Peter and me to be, well, seen together just yet. And Peter started saying, he didn't care. It was time for us to come out in the open and start living in the open. To come forward, he said. And—"

Opal looks at Ingrid, her eyes questioning.

"Do you really want me to keep going?"

Ingrid nods.

"And, he said he was going to come home and announce to you that he wanted a divorce, and that he was leaving for me. And I just said, 'Peter DiLaurio, that's not at all the right way to handle this. It's not fair to me, or to your wife, or your son, and I swear if you do that before I'm ready, I'll kill you.'"

Ingrid glances at the jury. They are leaning into Opal. Their brows are collectively furrowed. They believe her. She's baring her heart in front of the woman she wronged. They want to believe her and so they do.

"I didn't mean it, of course. I was upset and angry, and frustrated. It was just one of those things people say. You know what I mean, right?"

"I do," Ingrid whispers softly. And the juror with the blue poppy nods along with Ingrid and Opal.

Ingrid relaxes, but only partly. She has to tie up one more loose thread before she lets Opal leave the stand.

"Opal, where were you on the day Peter died?"

"Well, I was working at the hospital, until I got a really troubling phone call."

Ingrid realizes if she's going to let Opal shine on the stand after all, she's going to need to flesh out her current position. She detours from her original line of questioning.

"Opal, let's back up for a moment. Let's talk about your

work at the hospital, and then we'll come back to where you were on the day in question."

"Ok."

"You're a nurse?"

"Yes. I've worked on the pediatric unit of Suburban General for five years now."

"Five years? So, you became a nurse after your son was born?"

"Yes. I took classes, mostly online, and then did my clinical work during the day while I had a sitter. At night, I worked on a cleaning crew at the hospital and did medical dictation work from my home while my son slept to help make ends meet."

"Those must have been hard years for a single mother."

"Objection, your honor. Is there an actual question there, or just a sweet sentiment?"

The prosecutor sounds sickened by Opal's story. His ill-timed objection, just when the jurors are really starting to warm to Opal, is not a good idea. Ingrid sees in their eyes as they glare at him, especially the woman with the blue poppy.

Ingrid jumps in before Judge Regan can and says, "My apologies, Your Honor. Let me ask it another way. During those years when you were getting your nursing degree by day, and working by night, and caring for your toddler-aged son, who did you have to help you?"

"Well, I'm a single mother, so I was on my own. I paid a babysitter, a neighbor, for some assistance three days a week while I did my clinical work. And the hospital had a nighttime daycare for those of us on the cleaning crew. But other than that, I was on my own."

"And you said you work on the pediatric floor?"

"Objection, your Honor. Asked and answered."

Ingrid hears the jurors actually groan behind her. They are turning on the prosecutor. How can he object to the fact that Opal works with sick kids? They hate him. Ingrid would like to keep Opal on the stand a while longer just so the prosecutor can keep destroying his own credibility.

Judge Regan gives him a look. It seems to say, "You are shooting yourself in your own foot here, and I can't help you anymore."

"Move it along, counselor," Judge Regan says to Ingrid.

"Of course, Your Honor. Miss Rowen, can you tell us what a typical day on the pediatric floor looks like?"

Opal begins talking animatedly about her work. She clearly loves it. She's clearly good at it. Ingrid watches as the prosecutor sits slumped in his chair. The jurors are all on the edge of their seats. They like Opal. They are rooting for her.

It's time to finish.

"Ok, so Opal, you said you were at work when you received a phone call on the day of Peter's death?"

"Yes, I got a call at the nurse's station, and it was a woman's voice, and she didn't identify herself and I didn't recognize it. It sounded muffled, you know. Like she was disguising her voice."

"What did the woman say to you?"

"She said I better go check on Peter. She gave me an address, and said I better go check on my "supposed boyfriend" and that he was hurt. That was all she said."

Ingrid tries to keep from flinching. She didn't know Gabby had called Opal. For a moment she worries that Gabby might have said something to incriminate Ingrid. But Ingrid shakes off her fear and keeps going. She is almost there. She doesn't want to lose sight of the finish line now.

"Do you know who called you?"

"I never figured it out, actually."

"What did you think she meant by that phone call?"

"I had no idea. But I was worried about Peter. I pretended I was coming down with a migraine and I took a half sick day to leave work. I headed straight to the Russell property. I walked around and around and that's when I saw him."

"What exactly did you see?"

Opal's face clouds over. "Peter was lying at the bottom of a pit."

"Was he alive?" Ingrid tries to keep her voice level, but it's getting harder.

"Honestly, I don't know. I was screaming and screaming, and he wasn't moving, wasn't responding at all. He was just staring at me with his eyes open from the bottom of the pit and there was blood—so much blood—all around the top of the rock pit and—and—"

Opal looks at Ingrid, her eyes asking if Ingrid wants her to go on. She doesn't. She shakes her head.

"What did you do?"

"Well, I was in a state of shock, and I was scared to death. I didn't know who was on the other end of that earlier phone call—I still don't—but I was certain that Peter was murdered, and I raced out of there to go find my son. I wanted to make sure he was ok."

"Where was your son at the time?"

"He was with the sitter. I was supposed to be working late that night, so he was going to be staying overnight with the sitter I pay. She's a retired teacher and she babysits in our neighborhood. She's been watching CJ for years."

"So, when you got to CJ, what happened then?"

"Well, I was just petrified and shocked and scared, and I took CJ home and locked all the doors and windows, and tried to keep everything as calm as I could so he wouldn't know anything was wrong, and then after dinner, just as I was putting him to bed, I realized, in all my panic, I never called 911 or anything. I didn't want Peter to be out there all night. I knew he was gone—"

Opal breaks down, and Ingrid lets her. She takes the time to collect herself as well. The jurors are nodding sympathetically at her. She's become the most sympathetic mistress in the history of other women.

"I called 911, and told them about Peter, and well, tucked CJ in bed, and that was it. Of course, I expected the police to show up and question me. I'd even taken the next day as another sick day expecting that. I didn't expect them to arrest me, however. I didn't kill Peter. I loved Peter."

Ingrid lets the words settle over the jury and the courtroom. Opal has managed to win them over, and Ingrid has let her come clean about everything. Part of the reason Ingrid took on this case, to clear her own name and that of Drake's from any connection to this woman, are moot now. Opal has done a pretty good job on the stand and there's a strong chance the jury will believe her, but she's also tied a bow around her and Peter's love story. The two of them will be linked forever. Ingrid has helped her do that instead of stopping it.

There's a moment when Opal is leaving the stand where Ingrid feels both proud of what she's done and extremely horrified. She wonders if that's how her mother felt in her final moments on this earth.

The prosecutor gets up to cross-examine Opal, but the jury is hardly even paying attention. Ingrid doesn't bother to object to his ridiculous questions. He's digging his own hole deeper and deeper. She decides to let him.

"So, you're saying you didn't even bother calling 911 after you found Mr. DiLaurio's body?"

"I did, but later."

"Your first instinct was to run?"

"Yes, to run to my son. It was clear that Peter had been murdered. I had just received a threatening phone call to my work place, and I needed to make sure my son was safe. He is my number one priority. I'm all he has. I think I made that clear already."

Ingrid sees blue poppy lady nod her head enthusiastically. She thinks, *We've got this. There's no need to do anything else.*

Ingrid stands and says, "The defense rests, Your Honor."

A proverbial hush falls over the courtroom. Everyone knows that Ingrid's husband was going to leave her, and that he, in fact, bought the disgusting dance club where his mistress once worked and that he had presented it as an engagement gift to the love of his life. He was going to marry Opal Rowen. As soon as he left his wife and son. Peter's legacy is firm now. And Ingrid's is very much in question.

The judge calls a recess and says he'll charge the jury when they return. They can start deliberating that very afternoon. Opal turns to Ingrid. "How did I do?" she whispers. Ingrid nods and smiles through clenched teeth. "Good. Pretty good."

The judge calls both of the attorneys into his chamber during the recess.

"Counselor, pretty bold move putting your client on the stand."

Ingrid isn't sure what he wants her to say so she just nods.

Judge Regan turns to face the prosecutor.

"And you weren't doing yourself any favors objecting to that woman's hard luck story, Counselor."

The prosecutor looks sheepish.

Ingrid is feeling bold, and then Judge Regan blindsides her.

"Ms. DiLaurio, I'm going to ask you to put together a proposed deal for the prosecutor to look at before I send this case to a jury. I don't think you want to take the risk of letting the jury decide this case, do you?"

Ingrid is stunned, and looks over at Carly Jenner, who is sitting in the corner of Judge Regan's chambers with a legal pad on her lap. Her expression is as stunned as Ingrid's.

How dare he?

Ingrid is actually winning the case. There is still no motive and no weapon. The jury was eating out of the palm of her hand during Opal's testimony. Why would she back down now? He's obviously still being blackmailed by the prosecutor. Ingrid gives him a steely look.

She thinks about that manila folder of dismissed cases in her bag of docket sheets. Is it enough to change his mind? And what about all the appealable errors in this case? Are they enough? Maybe they are exactly enough. The judge knows he's screwed up this case left and right. The denied motions, and admitted evidence would be enough to raise issues on appeal if this jury was crazy enough to convict Opal. It wouldn't stick. Judge Regan would be called out for all his incompetence in any Appeals Court decision. It will be hugely embarrassing. But of course, this case only gets to an Appeals Court if Ingrid loses. If the jury actually convicts Opal. But they won't. Ingrid saw them during Opal's testimony. They want to acquit Opal. Ingrid wants to let them. Now that her dirty laundry has been aired for all to see, the only redemption she can possibly get by taking on this case is to *win*.

"No deal. We want to go to the jury."

"You need to ask your client first, Counselor."

"I already have," Ingrid lies.

The judge looks at her coolly. She holds his gaze. She sees Carly Jenner smile at her out of the corner of her eye. Carly still thinks Ingrid is one of the good guys.

Ingrid heads out of chambers and they all go back to the courtroom where the judge gives the jury their instructions for deliberation, and then everyone settles in to wait for the verdict.

Ingrid sees the judge's shoulders slump as he dismisses the jury to the deliberation room. The prosecutor glares at him, and Ingrid thinks about how the prosecutor has promised to retaliate if they lose this case. For a moment, thinking about how much embarrassment this case has brought her, Ingrid feels almost sorry for Judge Regan. Almost.

Ingrid is winning, she knows. But no one is going to come out of this whole thing victorious.

CHAPTER 35
The Verdict

Not guilty.

It takes the jurors 3 hours and 43 minutes to decide Opal's fate.

Opal turns to Ingrid and looks like she might hug her. Ingrid takes a step back just in case.

"Congratulations, Opal. You get to go fill out some paper-work, and then you'll be a free woman. You can pick up CJ at my house when you're ready. I'll call the sitter and tell her to expect you."

Opal takes a deep breath. There are fresh tears on her face. Tears of loss and grief and gratitude. Ingrid feels those same emotions. Opal's victory is so very much Ingrid's defeat, and suddenly Ingrid wonders if she, like her mother, has made choices that have simply been in vain. If her legacy will be going down for championing a cause that wasn't even hers to take up.

"Thank you, Ingrid," Opal whispers.

"Do you have someplace to go?" Ingrid fears the question as soon as it leaves her. She does not want to take Opal in. She's already given up so much.

Opal nods quickly. "Yes, yes, my house, the rent was paid up for the two-year rental term. Peter, he took care of it."

Ingrid flinches and looks away. Opal has assumed that since Ingrid encouraged honesty on the stand, she'd still want all that honesty now. Opal assumed incorrectly.

Ingrid nods quickly, and turns away from Opal, gathering

up her things, thinking about all that this trial cost her in the end. Ingrid remembers Jane's words of encouragement. "Your mother knew herself in the end. That's a powerful thing."

Do I know myself?

Ingrid looks at Opal being led away by the guard to process her release from jail and thinks, *not quite.*

Outside the courthouse, Ingrid faces a swarm of reporters. There are microphones and cameras inside her comfort zone. She realizes she forgot about this part. About having a statement ready. She was so prepared for the trial, she forgot about what would come next.

She puts a hand out and says simply, "Justice was served today. A woman was put on trial, based solely on bad decisions and indiscretions of the past that had nothing to do with the murder of Peter DiLaurio. What Opal Rowen has suffered at the hands of this community was wrong. Dead wrong. And now it's over."

Ingrid sees Angela in the crowd. Angela gives Ingrid a knowing smile and nods and jots down a few notes and then scurries away to deliver a soundbite into an oversized microphone outside the courtroom.

Ingrid walks away from the reporters. A few follow her, but she's smarter now. She doesn't give in. She just holds her hand up and repeats, "No more comment. It's over now."

She's still making her way to her car when her phone lights up with Tobin's number and a message.

Hey, Counselor. Why don't you meet me at The Law Club? I heard the good news. I'd love to buy you dinner to celebrate.

Ingrid thinks about Drake at home studying and playing with CJ one last time before his mother comes to take him home. Mary has promised to make them grilled cheese for dinner tonight, which is the favorite dinner for each of them. Ingrid doesn't want to interrupt them on their last night together. She doesn't want to be there when Opal picks up CJ and when Drake turns to ask Ingrid when they will all see each other again. She types a quick response.

Yes, I'd love to.

In her car, Ingrid looks in the rearview mirror, and realizes she hasn't been able to look at herself in the mirror lately. Her eyes have been so tired and her hair needs a coloring. She feels she's been aging at warped speed in the last few weeks and months, but today, she flips down the car visor mirror and studies her face up close, lines, circles, and all. This trial nearly broke her. It was every bit as hard as she knew it would be. She wishes that, like her mother before her, taking on this cause would make her a superhero. In reality, it's made her like her father instead. A shell of a person.

Even though she's exhausted and broken, walking up the steps to The Law Club feels different, fresh after her victory in Opal's case. The marble, the columns, the club's ornate lettering on the façade, none of it seems as intimidating or unwelcoming as it did just a few short months ago.

Even the hostess cannot deter her today. Ingrid gives her name and asks for Tobin, meeting her gaze head-on. Tobin is not there yet. The hostess walks her to their table anyway. Ingrid is aware of the eyes on her as she walks into the dining room.

She folds her napkin on her lap and sips her ice water while she waits for Tobin. A few people stop by her table while she waits. "Congratulations, Counselor. One hell of a case, there. Genius move putting your client on the stand."

They congratulate her and press their hands into hers, and she smiles and greets them but inside there is a war waging between the part of her that is proud and the part of her that knows they wouldn't have given a damn about her if she had lost.

She feels her eyes welling up with the attention, and embarrassed, she decides to use the restroom while she's still waiting for Tobin to arrive.

Along the hallway on the way to the restrooms are portraits with small brass signs underneath. Birth and death years separated by a small line and one-line epitaphs. Ingrid lingers in front of the wall reading the brass plates.

A zealous advocate for his clients.

A brilliant legal mind.

A pioneer on the bench.

She walks slowly down the hall to the end where there is an empty space waiting for a new portrait apparently. The brass plate has already been hung. It reads:

Jane Stewart, 1950-2022, A relentless warrior for the truth.

Ingrid thinks about Jane's last months of cleaning out her closets so those closest to her would never know her truth.

A relentless warrior for the truth? Hardly.

Ingrid looks over her shoulder where the dining room is full of judges and lawyers jockeying for positions Ingrid no longer wants to be in. Ingrid takes a post-it out of her bag and writes in sharpie and sticks it over the brass plate there waiting for Jane Stewart's commissioned portrait.

As she walks out of the restroom, she passes by the empty space in the hallway and her post-it note that reads: *"Jane Stewart knew herself."*

When she arrives back at the table, Tobin greets her with a flurry of apologies and accolades. "Sorry I was late. Wow, Ingrid, that was a fast verdict. Congratulations. Sorry again."

Ingrid dismisses him and orders. They are halfway into their entrees when Tobin says, "You know, Ingrid. I'm going to make partner next year at the firm. I'll have some hiring responsibilities. We could use a fierce litigator on our team, someone like you. No, no, don't answer me now. Think about it. And Ingrid, in the meantime, I'd be happy to sponsor your membership to The Law Club if you'd like. After today, I'm sure we'll be seeing much more of you around the courthouse. You should really be part of things around here. It will make your life easier if you can have meetings right here."

He waves his hand around to signal the very room they are sitting in. "After all, this is where all the real magic happens."

Ingrid feels something then. There is a moment of belonging. She tries it on. She nods at Tobin, and thanks him. "Yes, that's wonderful. Thank you for the offer. I'll think it over."

Out of the corner of her eye, she sees the prosecutor and Judge Regan across the room, heads leaned in together, locked in their own private battle of blackmail and retaliation. It occurs to Ingrid that she needn't have worried; she was never going to get in the way of their deal. They'll renegotiate terms now. A new murder case, a new deal. Ingrid wasn't part of their game. She was never one of them anyway. And, by the time the check arrives, Ingrid already knows what she's always known: Tobin's offer doesn't fit.

CHAPTER 36
Know Thyself

At home, Ingrid pays Mary and thanks her profusely for all she's done. She pretends they will see each other again next week but she gives her a goodbye gift: a monogrammed leather case for her laptop and an extra wad of cash.

She will call her sometime later in the week and explain that she and Drake have left town for a while, and that she won't need her babysitting services for a few weeks. Then she'll just stop calling. Ingrid is not good with goodbyes, frankly.

Opal has already picked up CJ. Drake is sullen and asking when they will all see each other again, as predicted. Ingrid is tempted to shush him, an impulse that horrifies her and makes her realize that she needs to get away from all of this; away from Riversedge and all it means, as quickly as possible. She pats Drake's head and whispers, "Soon enough, sweetie," as she lets Mary out.

Drake retreats to his room, giving Ingrid a chance to head to the safe hidden in the back of the closet in her bedroom. She'd left the safe off the listing when she'd helped the real estate agent prepare the house for sale weeks ago. In between helping Jane, and getting ready for trial, Ingrid decided to put the house up for sale. The agent assured Ingrid that it would sell quickly.

Ingrid grabs a bag out of the closet. It's already packed with a few necessities for Drake and her. She packed during the last few nights in a sleepless, manic state. She has decided to travel light for the new chapter in their lives.

They will have a fresh start, literally. She isn't sure exactly where they're headed, just away. The brief moment in the Law Club with Tobin in which she wavered, in which she thought about staying, even though it passed, scared her enough to expedite her plans. She called her agent from the car on the way home, and told her the house would be ready for the market the very next day.

Wonderful! How much advance notice will you need for showings? The agent asked.

"None. The house will be empty. Just add a lockbox, and handle the whole thing on your schedule." The agent had sounded surprised: relieved, but surprised.

From the safe in the back of the closet that wasn't on the listing and will simply be a bonus to whomever ends up living in her house next, Ingrid pulls out a stack of bills and a cashier's check, assembled over the last few weeks from withdrawals after selling off Peter's final real estate holdings, one by one. She and Drake will be able to start over, somewhere new, without financial worries. The podcast business can help fund their new life or be a hobby. It will remain to be seen how Ingrid feels about being connected to *Too Busy To Die* in her next chapter with Drake.

She also grabs the bloody rock and the shiny pocket knife she removed from the Frankenstein teddy bear. She types out a note, prints it out, and takes Drake's hand as she leads him out to the car.

"How about some ice cream?" she suggests. Drake nods, smiling.

"I know you miss CJ," Ingrid says over ice cream sundaes.

Drake shakes his head. "I've missed *you*, Mommy."

Ingrid reaches over and tousles his hair with tears in her eyes. Four words. Four *huge* words. "I've missed you so much too, buddy. We're going on an adventure. Trust me, it will be so much fun."

When she pays for the ice cream sundaes, she remembers the letter she printed out. She will mail it to Opal from the road.

✧

At home, Opal leads CJ through the front door hand in hand. She is trying to talk herself out of the nervousness she feels as she crosses her own threshold at long last. The house smells of mildew and the crime scene tape remnants are still littering the floor, especially around her bedroom.

CJ seems oblivious to the dust and mustiness, as he runs around the house, reclaiming his things. His room, his television, his video game, his iPad. He circles the house again and again with glee, and Opal tries to mimic his excitement and relief, hoping someday soon, she'll feel it again.

Christopher had been waiting for her outside the jailhouse, like he was a hero in a romantic Hallmark movie. Leaning against his beat-up car, with a bouquet of wilted flowers, and that damn teddy bear, like this was how it was supposed to end now.

She'd been tempted, but only for a moment. "Christopher, no. It's not going to be like that for us. I'm sorry." She'd hugged him, taken the teddy bear he'd stolen back for her and walked away toward the bus station where she'd waited for the next bus to head to Ingrid's. She'd picked up CJ, and left everything else behind.

At home now, she puts the teddy bear in her own room where she resolves to deal with it later, after she gets CJ settled. It feels different, lighter, and she fears what she'll find when she cuts it open, which is part of the reason she decides to wait until later to open it back up.

✧

Ingrid and Drake are stopped at a look-out point along the river's edge: the one the town is named for. In front of them is

New York City and behind them is the small town where Ingrid has made her home for over a decade without once feeling at home.

She holds the rock with the hand-stamped word on it, "BREATHE," the one she gave to Gabby on her way out the door that fateful morning.

She rubs the rock like she did so many days and nights over the last year, when Peter left her each night to go to Opal. She tried to accept her fate. Tried to accept that this was the way it was going to be. It was hard, but she thought she'd succeeded.

The small flecks of blood are the last bits of Peter she has, and she is done holding onto them. If anyone had studied the rock carefully, if it had made its way into the hands of anyone competent enough to check for fingerprints deep in the now dried blood and all around it, it would have put Gabby at the scene.

Of course, there was evidence putting Ingrid there, too.

On the morning Gabby stormed out high and manic, Ingrid had let her get a head start. After 15 minutes, she'd told Drake to get into the car, and they'd headed out after her. Ingrid wasn't ready for a confrontation with Peter. She wasn't ready to stop pretending, and she raced to Russell Street to tell Peter and Gabby that. She told Drake to wait in the car in the driveway at Russell Street, and then she'd headed to the back of the lot where a pool was being built, and where Gabby was screaming at Peter at the edge of the rock pit.

"Ingrid knows! You're a cheat and an asshole. And your wife knows everything. You're not fooling anyone!"

"Gabby, get the hell out of here," the harsh words had come from Ingrid and not Peter. He was tolerating her quietly. The new Peter was fully compassionate. He wasn't even rolling his eyes at Gabby, the way he had on so many other occasions.

Gabby looked shocked by Ingrid's presence and the words directed at her. Ingrid walked toward Peter, and Gabby walked away, leaving Peter and Ingrid alone, but not before throwing Ingrid's BREATHE rock back at her in disgust. Ingrid ducked to get out of the way of the rock hurtling toward her, and it hit Peter square on the forehead.

Blood began leaking out of his head quickly. *Head wounds bleed like the dickens,* Ingrid thought in spite of herself as she watched Peter struggle with a bleeding forehead. He looked dazed from the blood and the unexpected impact, as his hand stroked his bloody head.

"Gabby, for God's sake, get out of here. Before you do any more damage."

Gabby looked shocked and sorry, but she did as she was told. "Ingrid, I was only trying to help you. I swear it. Jesus. Is he going to be all right? What the hell did I do?" Ingrid watched her stumble away and for a moment she wondered if she should really be letting Gabby leave in the condition she was in. But as Gabby continued stumbling, she gave a little wave toward Ingrid's car, where Drake was sitting, and Ingrid acknowledged that her priority really wasn't Gabby at all. Ingrid couldn't see Drake from her vantage point. Which meant he couldn't see her or Peter. She registered this simple fact as she turned back to Peter.

Peter swayed with his hand on his forehead. The blood was coming fast and furious and he pulled his hand away for a moment to study it, and discovered it covered in the stuff. He looked lost and confused. Ingrid stepped toward him, putting her hand out to him, "Peter, for God's sake, take my hand, and step away from that pit before you slip and fall. Come home. To me and your son." And in his woozy state, Peter did something then that sealed his fate. He refused to take her hand.

When asked to choose between Ingrid's hand or bleeding alone there on the edge of the rocks, he chose the latter. Ingrid gasped in shock. Her shock was not that Peter would reject *her* but that he'd reject *his own son*. It reminded her of her own father's decision, a metaphorical slap that triggered Ingrid in every way. She stepped away from Peter, dropped her hand, and let Peter choose his own fate. As she watched him stagger, and eventually, trip and fall over the edge in his dizzying pain, falling with his hands up toward her as if he might actually be reconsidering Ingrid's earlier offer, she thought angrily about her own father who had also chosen death over Ingrid.

The silence in the air that came next told her all she needed to know. She didn't want to see Peter lying at the bottom of that pit. She turned and left him there. When she got to her car, she saw Gabby pulling away like a bat out of hell. She couldn't be sure what, if anything, Gabby had stuck around to see, but she was distracted by the sudden need to get Drake home and protect him. Until she put Opal on the stand at trial, she had no idea that Gabby had called Opal and summoned her to the scene. What Ingrid assumed would be labeled an accident ended up becoming a complicated murder scene by the next morning but not before Opal would show up and track her bloody footprints all over, and pick up the bloody BREATHE rock she'd once given to Ingrid, assume Ingrid had killed Peter, and become a suspect in a murder she didn't commit.

Of course, things are not always as black and white as they appear. That's one thing Ingrid has learned over the years. She rubs the rock one last time and then hurls it into the river. Its magic is gone.

Ingrid makes a call from the river's edge. "Can you meet me for a quick cup of coffee on Route 75?" She doesn't want to meet on Main Street, or anywhere else in Riversedge. She doesn't trust the anonymity she previously enjoyed.

Carly Jenner meets her at the agreed upon location. She's dressed for trial. Ingrid realizes she is simply always on. Carly is at that point in her life and her career where she has time to be perfect. She hasn't quite turned the shade of grey she'll eventually become.

With Drake next to her coloring on the back of the coffee shop placemat, Ingrid hands the manila folder back to Carly.

"Listen, I'm not your girl. Sorry to say."

"Excuse me? I don't understand. Why are you giving this back to me?"

"Because I want you to give it to someone who knows what to do with it."

"But *you* know what to do with it."

"Yes, but I mean, someone who knows what to do with it, and who will *do that thing*. I'm not the one."

"I don't understand. I watched you. I watched you defend that woman at great peril to your own reputation and heart. I watched you put her on the stand and tell the truth even though it had to hurt. It just had to. And I watched you stand up to Judge Regan. I have never seen *anyone* stand up to Judge Regan."

"I'm sorry, Carly. I'm sorry to disappoint you. But it's not as clear as you think. I had a lot of selfish reasons for wanting to help Opal. I never imagined it would go so wrong for me, frankly, but here we are. And I agree with you that Judge Regan is a terrible judge and a terrible person, but I can't take this on, now. I'm sorry. You'll find someone else. You will. Or, you know, maybe eventually, you'll take it on yourself. I'll be rooting for you from afar, either way."

"Afar? You're leaving?"

Ingrid looks over at Drake who is looking up at her. She pats his head and smiles reassuringly. "We're going on a little adventure, aren't we buddy?" He smiles tentatively and resumes coloring.

"Carly, can I give you some advice, from one colleague to another?"

Carly nods.

Ingrid channels a lost mentor. "Be careful about how much

of yourself you lose at that new law firm. Be careful how much of yourself you lose in your next chapter altogether. The goal at the finish line is to know yourself. And as you stray further and further from that knowing, it becomes almost impossible to come back. Trust me when I tell you I know this from personal experience."

Ingrid leaves Carly with these words, the manila folder, and the fervent hope that she'll do better than Jane Stewart or Ingrid herself. She hopes Carly will turn Judge Regan in herself.

In the car, Drake breaks his silence.

"Mommy, where are we going?"

"We have another stop to make, Sweetheart. I told you this is a grand adventure."

She makes another call from the coffee shop parking lot.

CHAPTER 37

I Tried to Keep You Alive

"Memorial Veterans Home, can I help you?"

"Yes, I'm wondering if you can connect me to one of your residents."

"Ma'am, I can't give out residents' info—"

"Sure you can. I'm his next of kin. The resident's name is Roy Barton. He's my father."

There is paperwork to fill out and hard vinyl seats in the waiting room with the stuffing sneaking out. It strikes Ingrid that coming to visit her father at the Veterans Home is not unlike visiting Opal in jail.

"He'll be very comfortable here." A kind-looking nurse with deep lines around her eyes and bright red lipstick had said those words to Ingrid the last time she saw her father over 20 years earlier.

After the failed suicide attempt, he landed himself a spot on the psychiatric ward for a few weeks. She had visited him daily, sitting in silent anger with him. He was ashamed and embarrassed, he said. And she let him be those things.

I tried to keep you busy, she thought. *I tried to keep you alive.*

From the day her mother was killed, Ingrid had watched the life ooze out of Roy Barton like he was a balloon losing his helium. She hadn't known how to stop it, and there was a heavy cloak of inevitability surrounding the day he stuffed his own tailpipe.

When she found the note on the kitchen counter, she ran to the garage, realizing that she'd been doing nothing but waiting for this day for the past three years. She dragged his almost life-less body out of the car, and called 911. While she waited, she pounded hard on his chest, and breathed life into her father while also screaming at him, "How could you do this? How could you leave me?"

He survived but he was dead to her after that day.

She helped get him settled at the Veterans Home. His case-worker had lined it up. His years of service in the Army before marrying Judy qualified him for a coveted spot in a beautiful nursing home with a sliding scale payment plan. He'd get the mental health care he desperately needed, and Ingrid could go on with her life. She left no forwarding address with Memorial Home other than a post office box in a nearby town that she had stopped monitoring years ago. Her father sent birthday and Christmas cards signed with a small and sad signature. When she couldn't take seeing even the cards, she stopped paying for the post office box, hoping he'd just forget about her like she was trying to forget about him.

She told people both her parents were gone. It became true to her, as true as anything else about her past. She had no real faith that her father would be able to last long at Memorial Home.

In a way, she is saddened that he is still alive now. Saddened because he was able to find some will to live surrounded by strangers instead of his own daughter, with whom he'd spent years just waiting to leave after Judy's death.

Ingrid holds tightly to Drake's hand as they are led down the hall by a cheerful nurse with bright pink scrubs who has introduced herself as "Louise."

"Your father will be so happy to see you. He talks about you all the time." She enunciates each word like she's practicing for a declamation speech. Ingrid wonders if she should explain to this woman why she hasn't been here before. She pretends that she would take her side if she explains that her father hadn't ever wanted to be alive when he was around Ingrid. That she left because she couldn't bear it and then ended up marrying a man who couldn't wait to leave her, too.

Ingrid looks down at Drake who is walking along silently but with a brave face, and she is guided by his bravery. She stays silent, too. They arrive at the end of a long hall, and they are ushered into a brightly lit room where Roy Barton sits in the corner, flanked by a tall bookshelf and a small loveseat with a quilt thrown over the arm that Ingrid vaguely remembers seeing in her childhood home. And damn it, if Roy isn't whittling. And whistling.

He looks up at Ingrid and Drake and his face lights up in a smile that takes over his whole face causing even his eyes to shine until they fill up with tears.

"Ingrid. You came."

"I'll leave you all to visit. Roy, if you need me, just press your magic button, ok?"

Roy nods vigorously like an excited child and Louise leaves Ingrid and Drake alone with her father.

"Dad, this is your grandson, Drake."

"Hello there, Drake," Roy's movements continue to look childlike and exaggerated and Ingrid isn't sure if he's impaired or just out of practice being around children, and maybe he thinks this is how he should act around one.

Drake nods at him, and Ingrid is tempted to turn around and leave. What more could she possibly say to this man who broke her?

They stare at each other in silence for a while until he says, "I listen to your podcast."

"Of course you do," Ingrid laughs and the ice is broken somewhat. She thinks about the random comments she has noticed over the years.

I'm proud of you.

She knew her father was watching from here. Somehow, she always knew.

Ingrid decides she will stay for a little while more. She sits on the loveseat with Drake next to her and they visit and they talk very little and the few words they do speak are punctuated by long awkward silences. But somewhere deep inside of Ingrid, a vise loosens and she thinks that maybe she will go ahead and forgive her father for wanting to leave her so badly. She thinks maybe she will even forgive Peter one day for wanting the same thing. In the meantime, she'll work on helping her little boy properly grieve his father. She'll tell him that his father was a man who believed in giving people second chances, something she herself is trying hard to learn how to do.

After her visit with her father, Ingrid opens the glove box to make sure the pocketknife is still in there.

There's no statute of limitations on murder. She didn't kill him, but if anyone ever gets wise that she was there at the scene and left Peter for dead, there may be trouble. If Opal ever gets talkative, someone might try to put the pieces together. And Ingrid knows better than to hope someone will come along and help her the way she did Opal. She has seen too much corruption, too much bartering at the Law Club, too much back-alley justice. She has seen *too much.*

But she's got the pocketknife and Peter might not have believed in insurance, but Ingrid sure as hell does. She gets on the highway and heads due west, with only the vaguest plan to continue her podcast from some new and hopefully beautiful remote location. A real and true small town, perhaps.

Not an impostor of a place like Riversedge.

She glances over her shoulder at Drake. It won't be all smooth sailing for him. She knows that. He's lost a parent, and

Ingrid knows too well how that loss will continue to rear its ugly head for him again and again and again. But for now, he looks serene. He's looking out the window, smiling, and naming the sights as he sees them.

A river.

A tree.

A red car.

A mailbox.

"Yes, a mailbox, buddy." She pulls over and mails a letter. It's on plain white paper. Nothing extraordinary.

Don't worry about the stone you've been holding onto for a rainy day. I've got it. It's not what you think, but still, I'll hold onto it anyway. And, listen I also have the knife you used to kill that mouse of yours. I'll get rid of it for you. You don't have to worry about it anymore. And just so you know, I've hired some construction workers to level DIVAS and put up that parking lot you guys planned. Now it's up to you to decide what you want to do with that old property. It's yours, after all.

The codicil copy is enclosed, and Ingrid doesn't sign the letter with a signature or a mark or anything other than just some parting words. All caps.

AND BY THE WAY, OPAL, I THINK WE'RE EVEN NOW.

Acknowledgements

Well, this was certainly unexpected.

Ten years ago if you would have told me I'd be writing the ACKNOWLEDGEMENTS for my SEVENTH BOOK (SIXTH NOVEL), I'm not sure I would have believed it. But if I did, I would have felt the same way I feel today: overwhelmed with gratitude and a little awestruck.

Over a decade ago, I took what was supposed to be a one-year sabbatical from the law. On the last day at my Times Square law office, I attended a luncheon with others who were also embarking on a sabbatical. We were—all of us—headed off to different corners of the world to do various things. I was leaving to do advocacy work, help a fledgling start-up company, and write. Others were planning to travel, start new businesses, do *pro bono* work, catch their breath from a career that seemed to be devouring us all whole. There was some talk about whether we'd even come back at the end of the year. But a veteran partner toasted us at the luncheon, saying: "Oh yes. You'll be back. And here's why. The most interesting and the most talented people you're ever going to meet are right here in this building. See you in a year."

I know, right? I remember hoping he was wrong. And I have been so happy to learn that indeed, many of the most interesting people I've met have been on the other side of that law career. But boy, did I leave my legal career with some *stories.* And for those stories, I gratefully acknowledge my mentors and colleagues in the law.

A wildly exuberant thank you to my long-time publisher, Nancy Cleary of Wyatt-MacKenzie Publishing. I have enjoyed every minute of this journey with you. You have been a fierce advocate and supportive mentor since the beginning, treating my stories with care and love.

Thank you also to Blackstone Publishing for bringing the Riversedge Law Club Series to life via audio books. I'm thrilled to be a new member of the Blackstone family!

To Liza Fleissig and the team at Liza Royce Agency, thank you for your zealous representation and careful editorial help getting this manuscript ready for the world. Liza, your boundless energy and creativity inspire me always.

To Ann Garvin and my Tall Poppy Writers, I would not find this journey nearly as fun without your love and support and friendship.

Like Ingrid, I have found joy and solace in the world of podcasting, and I am so grateful to the team at Speak Studio who invited me to create a space (the I KNOW HOW THIS (BOOK) ENDS podcast) where I could talk to, and connect with fellow writers. I have been inspired by and grateful to connect with writers in all genres who have encouraged me with their stories, their risks, their reinventions.

Writing for me is deeply personal, and I have been lifted up by the support of many, many family and friends, who have continued to help me feel seen and heard through my writing. Many thanks especially to my sisters, Megan and Katie, and my mother, Kathleen Shelley, for reading early drafts of IN HER DEFENSE. To Heather Christie for her unwavering support in writing and life. To my Calamity Dames sisters: Kimberly Belle, Emily Carpenter and Kate Moretti. To Kit, hands down, you are my favorite writing partner.

To those authors who have generously helped support the launch of this book in so many ways from blurbs to cover reveal shares to newsletter shout-outs to event invitations—including Hank Phillippi Ryan, Kathleen Barber, Jenny Milchman, Hannah Mary McKinnon, Audra McElyea, Isabella Maldonado, Heather Gudenkauf, Jenny Milchman, Wendy Walker, Roz Nay, Liz Fenton, Lisa Steinke, Robyn Harding, Lisa Barr, Danielle Girard, Lindsay Cameron, Lainey Cameron, Vanessa Lillie, Jennifer Bardsley, Samantha Bailey, Jackie Friedland and so many more.

A big thank you to the Bookstagrammers and Book Bloggers who have helped amplify the signal for this book, some of whom have literally been with me since the beginning including Suzy Approved Book Reviews, Marisa G Books, Barbara Bos, Jungle Red Writers, Jaymi the OC Book Girl, and many more.

And finally, to my children, Paul, Luke and Grace. I didn't leave the law to stay home with you. I left the law to open the world up to you. You are, each of you, my favorite everything.

Book Club Discussion Guide

1. The first chapter introduces us to Ingrid DiLaurio and Opal Rowen on what seems an ordinary morning. They are two mothers interacting with young sons before school—two women connected to the same man, Peter DiLaurio, who's just been found dead. How did you feel about each woman at the start of the story? Did you feel they were two very similar suburban moms? Did you feel empathy for either, both, or neither woman? How did those feelings change (if at all) as the story progressed?

2. This is a story—among other things—about the layers and complications of female friendship. Do you find it hard to make new friends as we get older? As our kids get older? What are the things you look for in a friend? Are there any non-negotiables? What are they?

3. What do you think about the way Opal treated Christopher throughout the story? From the time they were 10th grade lab partners ... to now.

4. How do you feel about the way Opal helped Ingrid launch her podcast business?

5. Ingrid is clearly haunted by her past—by her mother's death and her father's neglect afterward. Opal is haunted by her past as well—parental neglect and the discovery of Dean's betrayal. How does each woman's past trauma affect their subsequent decisions throughout the story? Do you feel that they made poor choices that led to a continuing cycle of tragedies? Or do you feel that they had limited choices and that their circumstances led to the ensuing tragedies instead?

6. Why do you think Jane sought out Ingrid to help her in her final days?

7. If you were a member of the jury at Opal's trial, how would you have voted following closing arguments?

8. "Know Thyself," is the title of a book by Ingrid Bergman's daughter, Ingrid Rossalini—and a recurring refrain in this novel. Which characters, if any, do you think truly *knew themselves* by the conclusion?

THE RIVERSEDGE LAW CLUB SERIES
BARR NONE

Excerpt from BOOK #2

The first thing Carly Jenner thinks when she opens her eyes is that the place looks like a crime scene. The next thought—if you can call it that—is the sound of Rain's voice in her head telling her to stop doing that thing she does. More precisely, Carly hears Rain say: "Stop being a fucking lawyer for once in your life."

And because Carly knows on some level that even imaginary Rain is right, she closes her eyes, re-opens them, and tries to see everything through a fresh perspective just before conceding.

Nope. Still looks like a crime scene.

The room is littered with empty and half-empty wine bottles and stylish glass bongs that look like collectors' items rather than drug paraphernalia. The glasses are arranged in groups on every surface and they remind Carly oddly of bowling pins waiting to be knocked down. Her head is pounding and her stomach is churning, acidic and empty. The sensation reminds her vaguely that when she returned back at Rain's apartment last night after several hours at the posh Nobu, she took a trip to the bathroom to give up the last remnants of the expensed dinner while Rain took a hit from a sleek, clear tower in the middle of the living room. When Carly returned from the bathroom, Rain was caressing the glass like it was a lover and murmuring.

It's too pretty to use. Just kidding. Sort of.

Now Carly is on the couch, still in her clothes from the night before, or more accurately from the day before, having gone immediately from a long day at the law firm where she and Rain both work, to Nobu. On the wall across from where Carly is now laying, she notices a large, framed, very crooked painting that looks expensive and also like it's about to crash to the floor with even the slightest disturbance. She stays very still—afraid of being the final link in a chain of events that have led to its precarious position.

Of course, she stays still also because she can't actually move. She's secured in place by the long legs of a woman whose face is only half visible to her at the other end of the couch but as she strains to get a better look, the woman is still completely unfamiliar. Carly is relieved to note they're both clothed but the way the stranger's legs are wrapped around Carly's makes her worry they've gotten their signals crossed somehow. Carly thinks they are the only ones sleeping in the living room but her visibility is obscured by her position on the couch and restricted movement so she can't actually be sure they're truly alone. She strains to conjure up scenes from the night before, but can't remember much. Truth is, she hasn't been this hungover since law school when she used to go on long blackout style binges after finals every semester. Another Rain-ism pops in her head then:

Why is it that we lawyers always reward ourselves by punishing ourselves?

Carly lays still for a few more moments trying to shed the fogginess of drunken sleep, and as she gradually emerges, she starts to feel more and more agitated. Like there are plenty of things she's supposed to remember from the night before that she can't. Or won't.

She tries stretching her legs but they're a little numb from being locked in place for who knows how long. The sound of the room starts to come into focus and it only exacerbates the growing morning-after irritation she's feeling. Between the strange woman's snoring and the low hum of 40's music that Rain has her Alexa set to play on a loop, Carly feels like she's being waterboarded. With her hands over her ears, she lifts her head trying to survey the room, confirming that it's just her and her couch companion in the room, and she also spots her phone on a nearby coffee table. She stretches widely to grasp it and the woman shifts slightly. It's not enough to un-pin Carly, however, she can now reach her phone and so she plucks it hungrily and works the screen's icons, rotating through each one, hoping for a fix that will soothe her.

Carly finds a trickle of solace on LinkedIn. She's ecstatic to note that the article the firm shared about the pending *Torsch* case that included her quote has 27,423 likes. That's nearly the number of times she herself has read and re-read the article with pride. For a moment, the wine and weed confusion makes her worry that all 27,000+ likes are actually *hers* and she has to click on them and scroll through the first few names just to re-assure herself of the truth. She clicks on the piece itself yet again, and scrolls as she always does, to the middle.

Carly Jenner, a rising star at Barr Knoll, LLP says: "I believe history will rightfully place this case alongside some of the seminal discrimination cases of our times. The bottom line is that A-Tech asked its female em-ployees to take a 20% pay cut to work from home, while rewarding male employees with bonuses when they made the same decision. A-Tech saved substantially on overhead expenses when 75% of its workforce moved to a remote work model but the disparate treatment of their male and female employees has been nothing short of egregious. Of course, this case shines a bright spotlight on how we as a country discriminate against working women, especially caregivers, and I'm proud to be on the side of justice in this case."

Carly had finessed that statement countless times and Rain mocked her endlessly (*God, Carly, would you listen to yourself?*), but she didn't care. The firm had included it in their press statement and it found its way into the Associated Press piece which had been picked up all over the country according to the Google Alerts that pinged on her phone nightly like small badges of honor. She wonders anew—and hopefully—as she scrolls through LinkedIn, whether Marna has seen the piece yet.

After all, Carly's stepmother was the reason she'd worked so hard to land that spot at Barr Knoll, LLP and why she is gunning for partner with a ferociousness that is single-minded and intense—even for a Barr Knoll associate. Not even Rain knows the precise series of deliberate, intentional steps Carly has taken over the years to work in the preeminent law firm in New York City—hell, probably in the country.

The last milestone in that journey had been suffering through the clerkship with Judge Regan, a corrupt and disgusting pig of a trial judge in Riversedge, New York. Regan was more interested in boozy lunches with his cronies than actual jurisprudence and Carly had learned to stay out of his way when he came back to chambers each afternoon, drunk on Manhattans and power. But worse than the liquid lunches was that box of files she'd found, somewhat by accident, in her last months of the clerkship. It sickened her to discover that Judge Regan's corruption was so much darker than she'd ever imagined. It sickened her more that she'd simply put a lid on that box and turned away. By the time Carly found Judge Regan's box of secrets, he'd already written her letter of recommendation to his former law school roommate, Barr Knoll, and Carly didn't want to do anything that would jeopardize her job offer from none other than Barr Knoll himself. The firm that bore his name was the only place Carly had wanted to work since discovering the particular spell Barr Knoll had placed on her stepmother, Marna Potter, the most important woman in her life, even still.

Nursing her hangover, Carly scrolls to Marna's LinkedIn page, as is her daily morning habit. Nothing new posted, shared or liked today. No real surprise there. There hasn't been any activity on the page in years. Ever since Marna retired from the law, she's been off the grid, literally and figuratively, and Carly wonders when she'll stop checking in with her this way. When she'll stop needing her so damn much. Marna is the only mother she'll ever know, but with every passing day, her absence from the world and from Carly's life is starting to feel more and more permanent. Indeed, Carly's only real connection with Marna these days is tangentially through working with Barr Knoll, Marna's former partner. And God knows, that's an arrangement that is currently hanging on by only a thin thread that Carly is starting to suspect she should slice just before she runs far, far away.

The incessant humming noise in the room grows too loud to ignore and Carly stops being delicate with the woman whose legs are wrapped around hers. She extricates herself from the scissor hold and watches as the woman turns angrily in sleep toward the back of the couch. Carly spots a blanket thrown over a chair in the room and lays it over the woman in a silent apology—for what, she's not exactly sure—as she stumbles to Rain's kitchen to make some coffee. While the Keurig gurgles to life, Carly considers whether she should take a taxi back to her apartment to shower and change for work, or whether she should just jump in Rain's shower so she can get a jump start on the work day.

It's Saturday morning which means very little deviation from her usual work schedule. She doesn't take weekends off. Especially not now. The pretrial conference in the *Torsch* case is scheduled for a month out, and there are still documents to review and pretrial motions to finalize. Up until a few weeks ago, Rain and Carly were working together around the clock on this case, the biggest one Barr Knoll is handling right now. But lately Carly notes that Rain's attention span for this case, and life itself as evidenced by her performance last night, is waning. Carly's not sure she can count on Rain for much these days, let alone to join her at the office on a Saturday following a night like last night. She decides she'll just go home rather than trying to rouse a hungover Rain, and get into yet another fight with her.

As she stands in Rain's tiny Manhattan kitchen, waiting for the Keurig machine to finish spitting out brown nectar, Carly notices a thin red stream that leads from the kitchen floor down the hall of Rain's one-bedroom apartment. She waits for her mug to fill and then she follows the trail, slowly and curiously. As the caffeine triggers her brain awake with Pavlovian accuracy, she starts to remember small pieces of the night before.

It isn't pretty.

She'd argued with Rain and some other lawyers over sushi in the darkened alcove at Nobu, about the *Torsch* case. When one of the guys—(*what was his name? Matt? James? Something so common she'd forgotten it already*) started debating the facts of the case, she'd gotten on her soapbox as usual about A-Tech's shoddy defense to the discrimination claims—the expectation that the women would be spending more time at home caregiving than working—an expectation that A-Tech said it could prove through time logs and witness statements. Rain had gutted her with a very public dismissal that incorporated very private information:

Come on, Carly. You and I both know what it is to be mothered by someone who is truly devoted to her work. These women in the Torsch class action simply aren't. This case is falling apart, and we're not going to be on the winning side for much longer. In fact, I asked to be re-assigned to that new case that just came in. I can't keep sinking my career in Torsch just to help you fix that broken inner child of yours.

Even though she was always trying to distance herself from her mother—the very famous, arguably talented, film actress, Tabitha Wells, Rain was known for her theatrical performances now and again. But with the memory of the night before trickling into her barely caffeinated brain, Carly has to admit, last night's performance felt a little too real.

And then, as she follows the thin stream of red with her coffee mug in hand, her memory gradually coming back from the night before, she remembers something worse—yes even worse - than Rain's unkind critique of her work on the *Torsch* matter.

She remembers what she confessed to Rain.

The drying, caking red stream loops down the hall toward Rain's room. It's blood. Of course it's blood.

Oh no. Oh no. Oh no.

It isn't Rain's voice in Carly's head anymore. It's strictly her own. And as she follows the blood stream down the hall toward Rain's closed bedroom door, and sees the red bloody fingerprints all over the doorknob, she stands there frozen for a moment with the dull, humming noise of the snoring stranger on the living room couch combined with piped-in 40's music, and the throbbing aching alarm bells going off in her own head.

The amorphous agitation that has been growing in shape since the moment she opened her eyes this morning comes into sharp focus and gives itself a name.

And that name is Barr Knoll.

CPSIA information can be obtained
at www.ICGtesting.com
Printed in the USA
BVHW060609030522
635668BV00001B/8